THE
INIMITABLE
JEEVES

P.G. Wodehouse

Annotated

Bumbershoot Books
P. O. Box 7
Cedar Lake, MI 48812

www.bumbershootbooks.com

ISBN # 978-1-61104-661-8

CONTENTS

CONTENTS

THE WONDER OF WODEHOUSE

Many authors are praised for their formidable grasp of the English language, but British author P.G. Wodehouse became world renown for his commanding grasp of a subset of the English language—slang.

At the time of its publication, the words of *The Inimitable Jeeves* gave voice to the cadence of current slang. Now, Wodehouse's words paint lush pictures of the previous century; he drenches the canvas of the mind with electrifying phrases of a bygone era. His slang buzzes in the brain, it zips around, it lights up the synapses like a pinball machine.

The Inimitable Jeeves is a glowing portal through time: it transports the ears of our reading to the burgeoning, rapidly changing era of the nine-teens. Entrapments of the "old way," are still in use—valets, page-boys, country homes—yet the modern world is rushing on at breakneck speed. Slang is the vehicle that catapults Wodehouse's characters into the heart of the modern movement. These words are fast, fashionable and socially with-it; they create in the reader a desire to be "with it," too.

Wodehouse's *Jeeves* steps out of a time when being 'educated' meant having mastered the classics—everything from the Bible to Tennyson. Wodehouse's Wooster references these with genteel ease and irreverence, piling allusion upon allusion, until a reader of *Jeeves* becomes a classicist to keep up.

This is the wonder of Wodehosue. Perhaps he didn't mean to bring his reader up to any sort of standard; in fact, at the time, he was bringing 'down' the standard, on purpose, so comedy would reach the every-man. But with the passage of time, the every-man has changed, and now reading *The Inimitable Jeeves* is as much an education as comedic delight.

It is most certainly the closest we have to time travel.

WODEHOUSE AND SLANG

Pelham Grenville Wodehouse was born 1881 in Surrey, England, and died in New York in 1975. He lived a life that spanned two continents and plumbed the depths of two very different forms of language—British and American—and infused both with the candor and color of slang.

For Wodehouse, slang wasn't just the flashiest way to turn a phrase (though it dazzled), it was risk-taking, barrier-breaking—an edgy means to authentic comedy and class unification.

Wodehouse's first exposure to American slang happened

during a trip abroad to New York in 1904, during which he fell in love with the ingenuity of American wordsmithing. Afterward, slang became the fuel for his imagination and written word.

"I have to take a trip to the States every so often to brush up my vocabulary," he confided to *The Evening World* in 1922. "If I'm away a long time it gets rusty. In England, you know, slang seems to go on and on. The change from 'Cheero' to 'Cheerio' was quite an innovation for us. If we had invented 'I'll tell the world,' it would have been current for years. But, six months afterward, American inventiveness had brought 'I'll inform the universe,' and other variations. With you [Americans] slang is almost a definite language, and it must be kept up to date."

Wodehouse's preference for American humor is something he proclaimed freely to the press, but his proclamations always came with an endearing nod to his home country and a shepherding wish for Brits to enjoy American comedic delivery as much as he did.

"I think," he said to *New York Times Magazine* in 1915, "that the chief characteristic of English humor is that it is cautious. American humor takes chances. That is the principal difference. The American humorist is single-minded; he wants to be funny. The English humorist wabbles; he would like to be funny, but he is haunted by the fear of being vulgar."

Wodehouse advised throwing caution to the wind, but always landed on the universality of humor, with its ability to unite rather than divide.

"The best humor is universal; a joke is a joke. And the humorist who writes special sorts of jokes with special sorts of people in view cannot write anything that is really funny. These conditions make a joke something deliberate and studied, instead of the spontaneous expression."

His greatest hope for humor was that it could triumph over the tyranny of war.

WODEHOUSE'S HOPE FOR WWI

War can do a great many things. In Wodehouse's mind, the best thing it could do would be to bring his countrymen a more relaxed sense of humor, a humor that would be shared between the classes, and break down the dividing walls that separated them.

"I think the war is going to have a great effect on the attitude toward humor of the British people," he continued to *New York Times Magazine*, in an article entitled *War Will Restore England's Sense of Humor.*

"People will be so depressed that they will become less critical of the methods used to cheer them up."

Wodehouse was well aware that looking with hope toward the social climate shift of The Great War sounded strange, but he was an eternal optimist. In the face of the devastating reality of war, Wodehouse choose to see the good that could come from his fellow citizens banding together—and a shared sense of humor was one such good.

"It may seem paradoxical that the tragedy of war should restore England's sense of humor, but I feel sure that this will be the case. The classes are being forced to know each other better than ever before. They are discovering that they have many things in common, and one of these things is the sense of humor. This general sense of humor has been there all the while, but class distinctions have kept it from being recognized as a common possession."

WODEHOUSE AND JEEVES

P.G. Wodehouse loved American slang, yet there is something uncanny and endearing about the fact that his most famous addition to the literary world is the British duo Wooster and Jeeves. The iconic pair occupied Wodehouse's pen from the second decade of the nineteen hundreds to the 1970s, and they have occupied the minds of readers worldwide ever since.

Bertie Wooster is an unattached English gentleman, one of the "idle rich," with a penchant for a zippy turn-of-phrase and careening about clubs and country homes as his appetite for leisure and social calendar dictates.

Jeeves, Bertie's valet, is superior in intelligence and competence, and pilots Bertie and his cohorts through recurring misadventures in the late Edwardian era. (The difference between a valet and a butler is that a valet is responsible for serving an individual, and a butler is in charge of a household and managing other servants).

Jeeves' character provides the scope for what may be Wodehouse's greatest accomplishment in class meshing: Jeeves masterfully pulls the strings and saves most, if not all, days. The implied rhetorical question is, of course, "What is Bertie without Jeeves?" but it fades into Wodehouse's unspoken and resounding question:

What are we without one another—and a little humor?

Angela McPherson
April 21, 2019
Cedar Lake, Michigan

CHAPTER ONE
Jeeves Exerts the Old Cerebellum

M orning, Jeeves,' I said.

'Good morning, sir,' said Jeeves.

He put the good old cup of tea softly on the table by my bed, and I took a refreshing sip. Just right, as usual. Not too hot, not too sweet, not too weak, not too strong, not too much milk, and not a drop spilled in the saucer. A most amazing cove, Jeeves. So dashed competent in every respect. I've said it before, and I'll say it again. I mean to say, take just one small instance. Every other valet I've ever had used to barge into my room in the morning while I was still asleep, causing much misery: but Jeeves seems to know when I'm awake by a sort of telepathy. He always floats in with the cup exactly two minutes after I come to life. Makes a deuce of a lot of difference to a fellow's day.

'How's the weather, Jeeves?'

'Exceptionally clement, sir.'

'Anything in the papers?'

'Some slight friction threatening in the Balkans, sir. Otherwise, nothing.'

'I say, Jeeves, a man I met at the club last night told me to put my shirt on Privateer for the two o'clock race this afternoon. How about it?'

'I should not advocate it, sir. The stable is not sanguine.'

That was enough for me. Jeeves knows. How, I couldn't say, but he knows. There was a time when I would laugh lightly, and go ahead, and lose my little all against his advice, but not now.

'Talking of shirts,' I said, 'have those mauve ones I ordered arrived yet?'

'Yes, sir. I sent them back.'

'Sent them back?'

'Yes, sir. They would not have become you.'

Well, I must say I'd thought fairly highly of those shirtings, but I bowed to superior knowledge. Weak? I don't know. Most fellows, no doubt, are all for having their valets confine their activities to creasing trousers and what not without trying to run the home; but it's different with Jeeves. Right from the first day he came to me, I have looked on him as a sort of guide, philosopher, and friend.

'Mr Little rang up on the telephone a few moments ago, sir. I informed him that you were not yet awake.'

'Did he leave a message?'

'No, sir. He mentioned that he had a matter of importance to discuss with you, but confided no details.'

'Oh, well, I expect I shall be seeing him at the club.'

'No doubt, sir.'

I wasn't what you might call in a fever of impatience. Bingo Little is a chap I was at school with, and we see a lot of each other still. He's the nephew of old Mortimer Little, who retired from business recently with a goodish pile. (You've probably heard of Little's Liniment – It Limbers Up the Legs.) Bingo biffs about London on a pretty comfortable allowance given him by his uncle, and leads on the whole a fairly unclouded life. It wasn't likely that anything which he described as a matter of importance would turn out to be really so frightfully important. I took it that he had discovered some new brand of cigarette which he wanted me to try, or something like that, and didn't spoil my breakfast by worrying.

After breakfast I lit a cigarette and went to the open window to inspect the day. It certainly was one of the best and brightest.

'Jeeves,' I said.

'Sir?' said Jeeves. He had been clearing away the breakfast things, but at the sound of the young master's voice cheesed it courteously.

'You were absolutely right about the weather. It is a juicy morning.'

'Decidedly, sir.'

'Spring and all that.'

'Yes, sir.'

'In the spring, Jeeves, a livelier iris gleams upon the

burnished dove.'

'So I have been informed, sir.'

'Right ho! Then bring me my whangee, my yellowest shoes, and the old green Homburg. I'm going into the Park to do pastoral dances.'

I don't know if you know that sort of feeling you get on these days round about the end of April and the beginning of May, when the sky's light blue, with cotton-wool clouds, and there's a bit of a breeze blowing from the west? Kind of uplifted feeling. Romantic, if you know what I mean. I'm not much of a ladies' man, but on this particular morning it seemed to me that what I really wanted was some charming girl to buzz up and ask me to save her from assassins or something. So that it was a bit of an anti-climax when I merely ran into young Bingo Little, looking perfectly foul in a crimson satin tie decorated with horseshoes.

'Hallo, Bertie,' said Bingo.

'My God, man!' I gargled. 'The cravat! The gent's neckwear! Why? For what reason?'

'Oh, the tie?' He blushed. 'I – er – I was given it.'

He seemed embarrassed, so I dropped the subject. We toddled along a bit, and sat down on a couple of chairs by the Serpentine.

'Jeeves tells me you want to talk to me about something,' I said.

'Eh?' said Bingo, with a start. 'Oh yes, yes. Yes.'

I waited for him to unleash the topic of the day, but he

didn't seem to want to get along. Conversation languished. He stared straight ahead of him in a glassy sort of manner.

'I say, Bertie,' he said, after a pause of about an hour and a quarter.

'Hallo!'

'Do you like the name Mabel?'

'No.'

'No?'

'No.'

'You don't think there's a kind of music in the word, like the wind rustling gently through the tree-tops?'

'No.'

He seemed disappointed for a moment; then cheered up.

'Of course, you wouldn't. You always were a fat-headed worm without any soul, weren't you?'

'Just as you say. Who is she? Tell me all.'

For I realized now that poor old Bingo was going through it once again. Ever since I have known him – and we were at school together – he has been perpetually falling in love with someone, generally in the spring, which seems to act on him like magic. At school he had the finest collection of actresses' photographs of anyone of his time; and at Oxford his romantic nature was a byword.

'You'd better come along and meet her at lunch,' he said, looking at his watch.

'A ripe suggestion,' I said. 'Where are you meeting her? At the Ritz?'

'Near the Ritz.'

He was geographically accurate. About fifty yards east of the Ritz there is one of those blighted tea-and-bun shops you see dotted about all over London, and into this, if you'll believe me, young Bingo dived like a homing rabbit; and before I had time to say a word we were wedged in at a table, on the brink of a silent pool of coffee left there by an early luncher.

I'm bound to say I couldn't quite follow the development of the scenario. Bingo, while not absolutely rolling in the stuff, has always had a fair amount of the ready. Apart from what he got from his uncle, I knew that he had finished up the jumping season well on the right side of the ledger. Why, then, was he lunching the girl at this God-forsaken eatery? It couldn't be because he was hard up.

Just then the waitress arrived. Rather a pretty girl.

'Aren't we going to wait—?' I started to say to Bingo, thinking it somewhat thick that, in addition to asking a girl to lunch with him in a place like this, he should fling himself on the foodstuffs before she turned up, when I caught sight of his face, and stopped.

The man was goggling. His entire map was suffused with a rich blush. He looked like the Soul's Awakening done in pink.

'Hullo, Mabel!' he said, with a sort of gulp.

'Hallo!' said the girl.

'Mabel,' said Bingo, 'this is Bertie Wooster, a pal of mine.'

'Pleased to meet you,' she said. 'Nice morning.'

'Fine,' I said.

'You see I'm wearing the tie,' said Bingo.

'It suits you beautiful,' said the girl.

Personally, if anyone had told me that a tie like that suited me, I should have risen and struck them on the mazzard, regardless of their age and sex; but poor old Bingo simply got all flustered with gratification, and smirked in the most gruesome manner.

'Well, what's it going to be today?' asked the girl, introducing the business touch into the conversation.

Bingo studied the menu devoutly.

'I'll have a cup of cocoa, cold veal and ham pie, slice of fruit cake, and a macaroon. Same for you, Bertie?'

I gazed at the man, revolted. That he could have been a pal of mine all these years and think me capable of insulting the old tum with this sort of stuff cut me to the quick.

'Or how about a bit of hot steak-pudding, with a sparkling limado to wash it down?' said Bingo.

You know, the way love can change a fellow is really frightful to contemplate. This chappie before me, who spoke in that absolutely careless way of macaroons and limado, was the man I had seen in happier days telling the head-waiter at Claridge's exactly how he wanted the chef to prepare the sole frite au gourmet aux champignons, and saying he would jolly well sling it back if it wasn't just right. Ghastly! Ghastly!

A roll and butter and a small coffee seemed the only things on the list that hadn't been specially prepared by the nastier-minded members of the Borgia family for people they had a particular grudge against, so I chose them, and Mabel hopped it.

'Well?' said Bingo rapturously.

I took it that he wanted my opinion of the female poisoner who had just left us.

'Very nice,' I said.

He seemed dissatisfied.

'You don't think she's the most wonderful girl you ever saw?' he said wistfully.

'Oh, absolutely!' I said, to appease the blighter. 'Where did you meet her?'

'At a subscription dance at Camberwell.'

'What on earth were you doing at a subscription dance at Camberwell?'

'Your man Jeeves asked me if I would buy a couple of tickets. It was in aid of some charity or other.'

'Jeeves? I didn't know he went in for that sort of thing.'

'Well, I suppose he has to relax a bit every now and then. Anyway, he was there, swinging a dashed efficient shoe. I hadn't meant to go at first, but I turned up for a lark. Oh, Bertie, think what I might have missed!'

'What might you have missed?' I asked, the old lemon being slightly clouded.

'Mabel, you chump. If I hadn't gone I shouldn't have met Mabel.'

'Oh, ah!'

At this point Bingo fell into a species of trance, and only came out of it to wrap himself round the pie and the macaroon.

'Bertie,' he said, 'I want your advice.'

'Carry on.'

'At least, not your advice, because that wouldn't be much good to anybody. I mean, you're a pretty consummate old ass, aren't you? Not that I want to hurt your feelings, of course.'

'No, no, I see that.'

'What I wish you would do is to put the whole thing to that fellow Jeeves of yours, and see what he suggests. You've often told me that he has helped other pals of yours out of messes. From what you tell me, he's by way of being the brains of the family.'

'He's never let me down yet.'

'Then put my case to him.'

'What case?'

'My problem.'

'What problem?'

'Why, you poor fish, my uncle, of course. What do you think my uncle's going to say to all this? If I sprang it on him cold, he'd tie himself in knots on the hearthrug.'

'One of these emotional johnnies, eh?'

'Somehow or other his mind has got to be prepared to receive the news. But how?'

'Ah!'

'That's a lot of help, that "ah"! You see, I'm pretty well dependent on the old boy. If he cut off my allowance, I should be very much in the soup. So you put the whole binge to Jeeves and see if he can't scare up a happy ending somehow. Tell him my future is in his hands, and that, if the wedding bells ring out, he can rely on me, even unto half my kingdom. Well, call it ten quid. Jeeves would exert himself with ten quid on the horizon, what?'

'Undoubtedly,' I said.

I wasn't in the least surprised at Bingo wanting to lug Jeeves into his private affairs like this. It was the first thing I would have thought of doing myself if I had been in a hole of any description. As I have frequently had occasion to observe, he is a bird of the ripest intellect, full of bright ideas. If anybody could fix things for poor old Bingo, he could.

I stated the case to him that night after dinner.

'Jeeves.'

'Sir?'

'Are you busy just now?'

'No, sir.'

'I mean, not doing anything in particular?'

'No, sir. It is my practice at this hour to read some improving book; but, if you desire my services, this can easily be postponed, or, indeed, abandoned altogether.'

'Well, I want your advice. It's about Mr Little.'

'Young Mr Little, sir, or the elder Mr Little, his uncle, who lives in Pounceby Gardens?'

Jeeves seemed to know everything. Most amazing thing.

I'd been pally with Bingo practically all my life, and yet I didn't remember having heard that his uncle lived anywhere in particular.

'How did you know he lived in Pounceby Gardens?' I said.

'I am on terms of some intimacy with the elder Mr Little's cook, sir. In fact, there is an understanding.'

I'm bound to say that this gave me a bit of a start. Somehow I'd never thought of Jeeves going in for that sort of thing.

'Do you mean you're engaged?'

'It may be said to amount to that, sir.'

'Well, well!'

'She is a remarkably excellent cook, sir,' said Jeeves, as though he felt called on to give some explanation. 'What was it you wished to ask me about Mr Little?'

I sprang the details on him.

'And that's how the matter stands, Jeeves,' I said. 'I think we ought to rally round a trifle and help poor old Bingo put the thing through. Tell me about old Mr Little. What sort of a chap is he?'

'A somewhat curious character, sir. Since retiring from business he has become a great recluse, and now devotes himself almost entirely to the pleasures of the table.'

'Greedy hog, you mean?'

'I would not, perhaps, take the liberty of describing him in precisely those terms, sir. He is what is usually called a gourmet. Very particular about what he eats, and for that reason sets a high value on Miss Watson's services.'

'The cook?'

'Yes, sir.'

'Well, it looks to me as though our best plan would be to shoot young Bingo in on him after dinner one night. Melting mood, I mean to say, and all that.'

'The difficulty is, sir, that at the moment Mr Little is on a diet, owing to an attack of gout.'

'Things begin to look wobbly.'

'No, sir, I fancy that the elder Mr Little's misfortune may be turned to the younger Mr Little's advantage. I was speaking only the other day to Mr Little's valet, and he was telling me that it has become his principal duty to read to Mr Little in the evenings. If I were in your place, sir, I should send young Mr Little to read to his uncle.'

'Nephew's devotion, you mean? Old man touched by kindly action, what?'

'Partly that, sir. But I would rely more on young Mr Little's choice of literature.'

'That's no good. Jolly old Bingo has a kind face, but when it comes to literature he stops at the Sporting Times.'

'That difficulty may be overcome. I would be happy to select books for Mr Little to read. Perhaps I might explain my idea a little further?'

'I can't say I quite grasp it yet.'

'The method which I advocate is what, I believe, the advertisers call Direct Suggestion, sir, consisting as it does of driving an idea home by constant repetition. You may have had experience of the system?'

'You mean they keep on telling you that some soap or other is the best, and after a bit you come under the influence and charge round the corner and buy a cake?'

'Exactly, sir. The same method was the basis of all the most valuable propaganda during the recent war. I see no reason why it should not be adopted to bring about the desired result with regard to the subject's views on class distinctions. If young Mr Little were to read day after day to his uncle a series of narratives in which marriage with young persons of an inferior social status was held up as both feasible and admirable, I fancy it would prepare the elder Mr Little's mind for the reception of the information that his nephew wishes to marry a waitress in a tea-shop.'

'Are there any books of that sort nowadays? The only ones I ever see mentioned in the papers are about married couples who find life grey, and can't stick each other at any price.'

'Yes, sir, there are a great many, neglected by the reviewers but widely read. You have never encountered All for Love, by Rosie M. Banks?'

'No.'

'Nor A Red, Red Summer Rose, by the same author?'

'No.'

'I have an aunt, sir, who owns an almost complete set of Rosie M. Banks'. I could easily borrow as many volumes as young Mr Little might require. They make very light, attractive reading.'

'Well, it's worth trying.'

'I should certainly recommend the scheme, sir.'

'All right, then. Toddle round to your aunt's tomorrow and grab a couple of the fruitiest. We can but have a dash at it.'

'Precisely, sir.'

CHAPTER TWO
No Wedding Bells for Bingo

Bingo reported three days later that Rosie M. Banks was the goods and beyond a question the stuff to give the troops. Old Little had jibbed somewhat at first at the proposed change of literary diet, he not being much of a lad for fiction and having stuck hitherto exclusively to the heavier monthly reviews; but Bingo had got chapter one of All for Love past his guard before he knew what was happening, and after that there was nothing to it. Since then they had finished A Red, Red Summer Rose, Madcap Myrtle and Only a Factory Girl, and were half-way through The Courtship of Lord Strathmorlick.

Bingo told me all this in a husky voice over an egg beaten up in sherry. The only blot on the thing from his point of view was that it wasn't doing a bit of good to the old vocal cords, which were beginning to show signs of cracking under the strain. He had been looking his symptoms up in a medical dictionary, and he thought he had got 'clergyman's throat'. But against this you had to set the fact that he was making an undoubted hit in the right quarter, and also that after the evening's reading he always stayed on to dinner; and, from what he told me, the dinners turned out by old Little's cook had to be tasted to be believed. There were tears in the old blighter's eyes as he got on the subject of the clear soup. I suppose to a fellow who for weeks had been tackling macaroons and limado it must have been like Heaven.

Old Little wasn't able to give any practical assistance at these banquets, but Bingo said that he came to the table and had his whack of arrowroot, and sniffed the dishes, and told stories of entrées he had had in the past, and sketched out scenarios of what he was going to do to the bill of fare in the future, when the doctor put him in shape; so I suppose he enjoyed himself, too, in a way. Anyhow, things seemed to be buzzing along quite satisfactorily, and Bingo said he had got an idea which, he thought, was going to clinch the thing. He wouldn't tell me what it was, but he said it was a pippin.

'We make progress, Jeeves,' I said.

'That is very satisfactory, sir.'

'Mr Little tells me that when he came to the big scene in Only a Factory Girl, his uncle gulped like a stricken bull-pup.'

'Indeed, sir?'

'Where Lord Claude takes the girl in his arms, you know, and says—'

'I am familiar with the passage, sir. It is distinctly moving. It was a great favourite of my aunt's.'

'I think we're on the right track.'

'It would seem so, sir.'

'In fact, this looks like being another of your successes. I've always said, and I always shall say, that for sheer brains, Jeeves, you stand alone. All the other great thinkers of the age are simply in the crowd, watching you go by.'

'Thank you very much, sir. I endeavour to give satisfaction.'

About a week after this, Bingo blew in with the news that his uncle's gout had ceased to trouble him, and that on the morrow he would be back at the old stand working away with knife and fork as before.

'And, by the way,' said Bingo, 'he wants you to lunch with him tomorrow.'

'Me? Why me? He doesn't know I exist.'

'Oh, yes, he does. I've told him about you.'

'What have you told him?'

'Oh, various things. Anyhow, he wants to meet you. And take my tip, laddie – you go! I should think lunch tomorrow would be something special.'

I don't know why it was, but even then it struck me that there was something dashed odd – almost sinister, if you know what I mean – about young Bingo's manner. The old egg had the air of one who has something up his sleeve.

'There is more in this than meets the eye,' I said. 'Why should your uncle ask a fellow to lunch whom he's never seen?'

'My dear old fathead, haven't I just said that I've been

P.G. Wodehouse

telling him all about you – that you're my best pal – at school together, and all that sort of thing?'

'But even then – and another thing. Why are you so dashed keen on my going?'

Bingo hesitated for a moment.

'Well, I told you I'd got an idea. This is it. I want you to spring the news on him. I haven't the nerve myself.'

'What! I'm hanged if I do!'

'And you call yourself a pal of mine!'

'Yes, I know; but there are limits.'

'Bertie,' said Bingo reproachfully, 'I saved your life once.'

'When?'

'Didn't I? It must have been some other fellow, then. Well, anyway, we were boys together and all that. You can't let me down.'

'Oh, all right,' I said. 'But, when you say you haven't nerve enough for any dashed thing in the world, you misjudge yourself. A fellow who—'

'Cheerio!' said young Bingo. 'One-thirty tomorrow. Don't be late.'

I'm bound to say that the more I contemplated the binge, the less I liked it. It was all very well for Bingo to say that I was slated for a magnificent lunch; but what good is the best possible lunch to a fellow if he is slung out into the street on his ear during the soup course? However, the word of a Wooster is his bond and all that sort of rot, so at one-thirty next day I tottered up the steps of No. 16, Pounceby Gardens, and punched the bell. And half a minute later I was up in the drawing-room, shaking hands with the fattest man I have ever seen in my life.

The motto of the Little family was evidently 'variety'. Young Bingo is long and thin and hasn't had a superfluous ounce on him since we first met; but the uncle restored the average and a bit over. The hand which grasped mine wrapped it round and enfolded it till I began to wonder if I'd ever get it out without excavating machinery.

'Mr Wooster, I am gratified – I am proud – I am honoured.'

It seemed to me that young Bingo must have boosted me to some purpose.

'Oh, ah!' I said.

He stepped back a bit, still hanging on to the good right hand.

'You are very young to have accomplished so much!'

I couldn't follow the train of thought. The family, especially my Aunt Agatha, who has savaged me incessantly from childhood up, have always rather made a point of the fact that mine is a wasted life, and that, since I won the prize at my first school for the best collection of wild flowers made during the summer holidays, I haven't done a dam' thing to land me on the nation's scroll of fame. I was wondering if he couldn't have got me mixed up with someone else, when the telephone-bell rang outside in the hall, and the maid came in to say that I was wanted. I buzzed down, and found it was young Bingo.

'Hallo!' said young Bingo. 'So you've got there? Good man! I knew I could rely on you. I say, old crumpet, did my uncle seem pleased to see you?'

'Absolutely all over me. I can't make it out.'

'Oh, that's all right. I just rang up to explain. The fact is, old man, I know you won't mind, but I told him that you were the author of those books I've been reading to him.'

'What!'

'Yes, I said that "Rosie M. Banks" was your pen-name, and you didn't want it generally known, because you were a modest, retiring sort of chap. He'll listen to you now. Absolutely hang on your words. A brightish idea, what? I doubt if Jeeves in person could have thought up a better one than that. Well, pitch it strong, old lad, and keep steadily before you the fact that I must have my allowance raised. I can't possibly marry on what I've got now. If this film is to end with the slow fade-out on the embrace, at least double is indicated. Well, that's that. Cheerio!'

And he rang off. At that moment the gong sounded, and the genial host came tumbling downstairs like the delivery of a ton of coals.

I always look back to that lunch with a sort of aching regret. It was the lunch of a lifetime, and I wasn't in a fit state to appreciate it. Subconsciously, if you know what I mean, I could see it was pretty special, but I had got the wind up to such a frightful extent over the ghastly situation in which young Bingo had landed me that its deeper meaning never really penetrated. Most of the time I might have been eating sawdust for all the good it did me.

Old Little struck the literary note right from the start.

'My nephew has probably told you that I have been making a close study of your books of late?' he began.

'Yes. He did mention it. How – er – how did you like the bally things?'

He gazed reverently at me.

'Mr Wooster, I am not ashamed to say that the tears came into my eyes as I listened to them. It amazes me that a man as young as you can have been able to plumb human nature so surely to its depths; to play with so unerring a hand on the quivering heart-strings of your reader; to write novels so true, so human, so moving, so vital!'

'Oh, it's just a knack,' I said.

The good old persp. was bedewing my forehead by this time in a pretty lavish manner. I don't know when I've been so rattled.

'Do you find the room a trifle warm?'

'Oh, no, no, rather not. Just right.'

'Then it's the pepper. If my cook has a fault – which I am not prepared to admit – it is that she is inclined to stress the pepper a trifle in her made dishes. By the way, do you like her cooking?'

I was so relieved that we had got off the subject of my literary output that I shouted approval in a ringing baritone.

'I am delighted to hear it, Mr Wooster. I may be prejudiced, but to my mind that woman is a genius.'

'Absolutely!' I said.

'She has been with me seven years, and in all that time I have not known her guilty of a single lapse from the highest standard. Except once, in the winter of 1917, when a purist might have condemned a certain mayonnaise of hers as lacking in creaminess. But one must make allowances. There had been several air-raids about that time, and no doubt the poor woman was shaken. But nothing is perfect in this world, Mr Wooster, and I have had my cross to bear. For seven years I have lived in constant apprehension lest some evilly-disposed person might lure her from my employment. To my certain knowledge she has received offers, lucrative offers, to accept service elsewhere. You may judge of my dismay, Mr Wooster, when only this morning the bolt fell. She gave notice!'

'Good Lord!'

'Your consternation does credit, if I may say so, to the heart of the author of A Red, Red Summer Rose. But I am thankful to say the worst has not happened. The matter has been adjusted. Jane is not leaving me.'

'Good egg!'

'Good egg, indeed – though the expression is not familiar to me. I do not remember having come across it in your books. And speaking of your books, may I say that what has impressed me about them even more than the moving poignancy of the actual narrative, is your philosophy of life. If there were more men like you, Mr Wooster, London would be a better place.'

This was dead opposite to my Aunt Agatha's philosophy of life, she having always rather given me to understand that it is the presence in it of chappies like me that makes London more or less of a plague spot; but I let it go.

'Let me tell you, Mr Wooster, that I appreciate your splendid defiance of the outworn fetishes of a purblind social system. I appreciate it! You are big enough to see that rank is but the guinea stamp and that, in the magnificent words of Lord Bletchmore in Only a Factory Girl, "Be her origin ne'er so humble, a good woman is the equal of the finest lady on earth!" '

'I say! Do you think that?'

'I do, Mr Wooster. I am ashamed to say that there was a time when I was like other men, a slave to the idiotic convention which we call Class Distinction. But, since I read your books—'

I might have known it. Jeeves had done it again.

'You think it's all right for a chappie in what you might call a certain social position to marry a girl of what you might describe as the lower classes?'

'Most assuredly I do, Mr Wooster.'

I took a deep breath, and slipped him the good news.

'Young Bingo – your nephew, you know – wants to marry a waitress,' I said.

'I honour him for it,' said old Little.

'You don't object?'

'On the contrary.'

I took another deep breath and shifted to the sordid side of the business.

'I hope you won't think I'm butting in, don't you know,' I said, 'but – er – well, how about it?'

'I fear I do not quite follow you.'

'Well, I mean to say, his allowance and all that. The money you're good enough to give him. He was rather hoping that you might see your way to jerking up the total a bit.'

Old Little shook his head regretfully.

'I fear that can hardly be managed. You see, a man in my position is compelled to save every penny. I will gladly continue my nephew's existing allowance, but beyond that I cannot go. It would not be fair to my wife.'

'What! But you're not married?'

'Not yet. But I propose to enter upon that holy state almost immediately. The lady who for years has cooked so well for me honoured me by accepting my hand this very morning.' A cold gleam of triumph came into his eye. 'Now let 'em try to get her away from me!' he muttered, defiantly.

'Young Mr Little has been trying frequently during the afternoon to reach you on the telephone, sir,' said Jeeves that night, when I got home.

'I'll bet he has,' I said. I had sent poor old Bingo an outline of the situation by messenger-boy shortly after lunch.

'He seemed a trifle agitated.'

'I don't wonder, Jeeves,' I said, 'so brace up and bite the bullet. I'm afraid I've bad news for you. That scheme of yours – reading those books to old Mr Little and all that – has blown out a fuse.'

'They did not soften him?'

'They did. That's the whole bally trouble. Jeeves, I'm sorry to say that fiancée of yours – Miss Watson, you know – the cook, you know – well, the long and the short of it is that she's chosen riches instead of honest worth, if you know what I mean.'

'Sir?'

'She's handed you the mitten and gone and got engaged to old Mr Little!'

'Indeed, sir?'

'You don't seem much upset.'

'The fact is, sir, I had anticipated some such outcome.'

I stared at him. 'Then what on earth did you suggest the scheme for?'

'To tell you the truth, sir, I was not wholly averse from a severance of my relations with Miss Watson. In fact, I greatly desired it. I respect Miss Watson exceedingly, but I have seen for a long time that we were not suited. Now, the other young person with whom I have an understanding—'

'Great Scott, Jeeves! There isn't another?'

'Yes, sir.'

'How long has this been going on?'

'For some weeks, sir. I was greatly attracted by her when I

27

first met her at a subscription dance at Camberwell.'

'My sainted aunt! Not—'

Jeeves inclined his head gravely.

'Yes, sir. By an odd coincidence it is the same young person that young Mr Little—I have placed the cigarettes on the small table. Good night, sir.'

CHAPTER THREE
Aunt Agatha Speaks Her Mind

I suppose in the case of a chappie of really fine fibre and all that sort of thing, a certain amount of gloom and anguish would have followed this dishing of young Bingo's matrimonial plans. I mean, if mine had been a noble nature, I would have been all broken up. But, what with one thing and another, I can't let it weigh on me very heavily. The fact that less than a week after he had had the bad news I came on young Bingo dancing like an untamed gazelle at Ciro's helped me to bear up.

A resilient bird, Bingo. He may be down, but he is never out. While these little love-affairs of his are actually on, nobody could be more earnest and blighted; but once the fuse has blown out and the girl has handed him his hat and begged him as a favour never to let her see him again, up he bobs as merry and bright as ever. If I've seen it happen once, I've seen it happen a dozen times.

So I didn't worry about Bingo. Or about anything else,

as a matter of fact. What with one thing and another, I can't remember ever having been chirpier than at about this period in my career. Everything seemed to be going right. On three separate occasions horses on which I'd invested a sizeable amount won by lengths instead of sitting down to rest in the middle of the race, as horses usually do when I've got money on them.

Added to this, the weather continued topping to a degree; my new socks were admitted on all sides to be just the kind that mother makes; and to round it all off, my Aunt Agatha had gone to France and wouldn't be on hand to snooter me for at least another six weeks. And, if you knew my Aunt Agatha, you'd agree that that alone was happiness enough for anyone.

It suddenly struck me so forcibly, one morning while I was having my bath, that I hadn't a worry on earth that I began to sing like a bally nightingale as I sploshed the sponge about. It seemed to me that everything was absolutely for the best in the best of all possible worlds.

But have you ever noticed a rummy thing about life? I mean the way something always comes along to give it you in the neck at the very moment when you're feeling most braced about things in general. No sooner had I dried the old limbs and shoved on the suiting and toddled into the sitting-room than the blow fell. There was a letter from Aunt Agatha on the mantelpiece.

'Oh gosh!' I said when I'd read it.

'Sir?' said Jeeves. He was fooling about in the background

on some job or other.

'It's from my Aunt Agatha, Jeeves. Mrs Gregson, you know.'

'Yes, sir?'

'Ah, you wouldn't speak in that light, careless tone if you knew what was in it,' I said with a hollow, mirthless laugh. 'The curse has come upon us, Jeeves. She wants me to go and join her at – what's the name of the dashed place? – at Roville-sur-mer. Oh, hang it all!'

'I had better be packing, sir?'

'I suppose so.'

To people who don't know my Aunt Agatha I find it extraordinarily difficult to explain why it is that she has always put the wind up me to such a frightful extent. I mean, I'm not dependent on her financially or anything like that. It's simply personality, I've come to the conclusion. You see, all through my childhood and when I was a kid at school she was always able to turn me inside out with a single glance, and I haven't come out from under the 'fluence yet. We run to height a bit in our family, and there's about five-foot-nine of Aunt Agatha, topped off with a beaky nose, an eagle eye, and a lot of grey hair, and the general effect is pretty formidable. Anyway, it never even occurred to me for a moment to give her the miss-in-baulk on this occasion. If she said I must go to Roville, it was all over except buying the tickets.

'What's the idea, Jeeves? I wonder why she wants me.'

'I could not say, sir.'

Well, it was no good talking about it. The only gleam of consolation, the only bit of blue among the clouds, was the fact that at Roville I should at last be able to wear the rather fruity cummerbund I had bought six months ago and had never had the nerve to put on. One of those silk contrivances, you know, which you tie round your waist instead of a waistcoat, something on the order of a sash only more substantial. I had never been able to muster up the courage to put it on so far, for I knew that there would be trouble with Jeeves when I did, it being a pretty brightish scarlet. Still, at a place like Roville, presumably dripping with the gaiety and joie de vivre of France, it seemed to me that something might be done.

Roville, which I reached early in the morning after a beastly choppy crossing and a jerky night in the train, is a fairly nifty spot where a chappie without encumbrances in the shape of aunts might spend a somewhat genial week or so. It is like all these French places, mainly sands and hotels and casinos. The hotel which had had the bad luck to draw Aunt Agatha's custom was the Splendide, and by the time I got there there wasn't a member of the staff who didn't seem to be feeling it deeply. I sympathized with them. I've had experience of Aunt Agatha at hotels before. Of course, the real rough work was all over when I arrived, but I could tell by the way everyone grovelled before her that she had started by having her first room changed because it hadn't a southern exposure and her next because it had a creaking wardrobe and that she had said her say on the subject of the cooking, the waiting, the chambermaiding and everything else, with perfect freedom and candour. She had got the whole gang nicely under control by now. The manager, a whiskered cove who looked like a bandit, simply tied himself into knots whenever she looked at him.

All this triumph had produced a sort of grim geniality in her, and she was almost motherly when we met.

'I am so glad you were able to come, Bertie,' she said. 'The air will do you so much good. Far better for you than spending your time in stuffy London night clubs.'

'Oh, ah,' I said.

'You will meet some pleasant people, too. I want to introduce you to a Miss Hemmingway and her brother, who have become great friends of mine. I am sure you will like Miss Hemmingway. A nice, quiet girl, so different from so many of the bold girls one meets in London nowadays. Her brother is curate at Chiplye-in-the-Glen in Dorsetshire. He tells me they are connected with the Kent Hemmingways. A very good family. She is a charming girl.'

I had a grim foreboding of an awful doom. All this boosting was so unlike Aunt Agatha, who normally is one of the most celebrated right-and-left-hand knockers in London society. I felt a clammy suspicion. And, by Jove, I was right.

'Aline Hemmingway,' said Aunt Agatha, 'is just the girl I should like to see you marry, Bertie. You ought to be thinking of getting married. Marriage might make something of you.

And I could not wish you a better wife than dear Aline. She would be such a good influence in your life.'

'Here, I say!' I chipped in at this juncture, chilled to the marrow.

'Bertie!' said Aunt Agatha, dropping the motherly manner for a bit and giving me the cold eye.

'Yes, but I say . . .'

'It is young men like you, Bertie, who make the person with the future of the race at heart despair. Cursed with too much money, you fritter away in idle selfishness a life which might have been made useful, helpful and profitable. You do nothing but waste your time on frivolous pleasures. You are simply an antisocial animal, a drone. Bertie, it is imperative that you marry.'

'But, dash it all . . .'

'Yes! You should be breeding children to . . .'

'No, really, I say, please!' I said, blushing richly. Aunt Agatha belongs to two or three of these women's clubs, and she keeps forgetting she isn't in the smoking-room.

'Bertie,' she resumed, and would no doubt have hauled up her slacks at some length, had we not been interrupted. 'Ah here they are!' she said. 'Aline, dear!'

And I perceived a girl and a chappie bearing down on me, smiling in a pleased sort of manner.

'I want you to meet my nephew, Bertie Wooster,' said Aunt Agatha. 'He has just arrived. Such a surprise! I had no notion that he intended coming to Roville.'

I gave the couple the wary up-and-down, feeling rather like a cat in the middle of a lot of hounds. Sort of trapped feeling, if you know what I mean. An inner voice was whispering that Bertram was up against it.

The brother was a small round cove with a face rather like a sheep. He wore pince-nez, his expression was benevolent, and he had on one of those collars which button at the back.

'Welcome to Roville, Mr Wooster,' he said.

'Oh, Sidney!' said the girl. 'Doesn't Mr Wooster remind you of Canon Blenkinsop, who came to Chipley to preach last Easter?'

'My dear! The resemblance is most striking!'

They peered at me for a while as if I were something in a glass case, and I goggled back and had a good look at the girl. There's no doubt about it, she was different from what Aunt Agatha had called the bold girls one meets in London nowadays. No bobbed hair and gaspers about her! I don't know when I've met anybody who looked so – respectable is the only word. She had on a kind of plain dress, and her hair was plain, and her face was sort of mild and saint-like. I don't pretend to be a Sherlock Holmes or anything of that order, but the moment I looked at her I said to myself, 'The girl plays the organ in a village church!'

Well, we gazed at one another for a bit, and there was a certain amount of chit-chat, and then I tore myself away. But before I went I had been booked up to take brother and girl for a nice drive that afternoon. And the thought of it depressed me to such an extent that I felt there was only one thing to be done. I went straight back to my room, dug out the cummerbund, and draped it round the old tum. I turned round and Jeeves shied like a startled mustang.

'I beg your pardon, sir,' he said in a sort of hushed voice. 'You are surely not proposing to appear in public in that thing?'

'The cummerbund?' I said in a careless, debonair way, passing it off. 'Oh, rather!'

'I should not advise it, sir, really I shouldn't.'

'Why not?'

'The effect, sir, is loud in the extreme.'

I tackled the blighter squarely. I mean to say, nobody knows better than I do that Jeeves is a master mind and all that, but, dash it, a fellow must call his soul his own. You can't be a serf to your valet. Besides, I was feeling pretty low and the cummerbund was the only thing which could cheer me up.

'You know, the trouble with you, Jeeves,' I said, 'is that you're too – what's the word I want? – too bally insular. You can't realize that you aren't in Piccadilly all the time. In a place like this a bit of colour and touch of the poetic is expected of you. Why, I've just seen a fellow downstairs in a morning suit of yellow velvet.'

'Nevertheless, sir—'

'Jeeves,' I said firmly, 'my mind is made up. I am feeling a little low-spirited and need cheering. Besides, what's wrong with it? This cummerbund seems to me to be called for. I consider that it has rather a Spanish effect. A touch of the hidalgo. Sort of Vicente y Blasco What's-his-name stuff. The jolly old hidalgo off to the bull fight.'

'Very good, sir,' said Jeeves coldly.

Dashed upsetting, this sort of thing. If there's one thing that gives me the pip, it's unpleasantness in the home; and I could see that relations were going to be fairly strained for a while. And, coming on top of Aunt Agatha's bombshell about the Hemmingway girl, I don't mind confessing it made me feel more or less as though nobody loved me.

The drive that afternoon was about as mouldy as I had expected. The curate chappie prattled on of this and that; the girl admired the view; and I got a headache early in the proceedings which started at the sole of my feet and got worse all the way up. I tottered back to my room to dress for dinner, feeling like a toad under the harrow. If it hadn't been for that cummerbund business earlier in the day I could have sobbed on Jeeves's neck and poured out all my troubles to him. Even as it was, I couldn't keep the thing entirely to myself.

'I say, Jeeves,' I said.

'Sir?'

'Mix me a stiffish brandy and soda.'

'Yes, sir.'

'Stiffish, Jeeves. Not too much soda, but splash the brandy about a bit.'

'Very good, sir.'

After imbibing, I felt a shade better.

'Jeeves,' I said.

'Sir?'

'I rather fancy I'm in the soup, Jeeves.'

'Indeed, sir?'

I eyed the man narrowly. Dashed aloof his manner was. Still brooding over the cummerbund.

'Yes. Right up to the hocks,' I said, suppressing the pride of the Woosters and trying to induce him to be a bit matier. 'Have you seen a girl popping about here with a parson brother?'

'Miss Hemmingway, sir? Yes, sir.'

'Aunt Agatha wants me to marry her.'

'Indeed, sir?'

'Well, what about it?'

'Sir?'

'I mean, have you anything to suggest?'

'No, sir.'

The blighter's manner was so cold and unchummy that I bit the bullet and had a dash at being airy.

'Oh, well, tra-la-la!' I said.

'Precisely, sir,' said Jeeves.

And that was, so to speak, that.

CHAPTER FOUR
Pearls Mean Tears

I remember – it must have been when I was at school because I don't go in for that sort of thing very largely nowadays – reading a poem or something about something or other in which there was a line which went, if I've got it rightly, 'Shades of the prison house begin to close upon the growing boy'. Well, what I'm driving at is that during the next two weeks that's exactly how it was with me. I mean to say, I could hear the wedding bells chiming faintly in the distance and getting louder and louder every day, and how the deuce to slide out of it was more than I could think. Jeeves, no doubt, could have dug up a dozen brainy schemes in a couple of minutes, but he was still aloof and chilly and I couldn't bring myself to ask him point-blank. I mean, he could see easily enough that the young master was in a bad way and, if that wasn't enough to make him overlook the fact that I was still gleaming brightly about the waistband, well, what it amounted to was that the old feudal spirit was dead in the blighter's bosom and there was nothing to be done about it.

It really was rummy the way the Hemmingway family had taken to me. I wouldn't have said off-hand that there was anything particularly fascinating about me – in fact, most people look on me as rather an ass; but there was no getting away from the fact that I went like a breeze with this girl and her brother. They didn't seem happy if they were away from me. I couldn't move a step, dash it, without one of them popping out from somewhere and freezing on. In fact, I'd got into the habit now of retiring to my room when I wanted to take it easy for a bit. I had managed to get a rather decent suite on the third floor, looking down on to the promenade.

I had gone to earth in my suite one evening and for the first time that day was feeling that life wasn't so bad after all. Right through the day from lunch time I'd had the Hemmingway girl on my hands, Aunt Agatha having shooed us off together immediately after the midday meal. The result was, as I looked down on the lighted promenade and saw all the people popping happily about on their way to dinner and the Casino and what not, a kind of wistful feeling came over me. I couldn't help thinking how dashed happy I could have contrived to be in this place if only Aunt Agatha and the other blisters had been elsewhere.

I heaved a sigh, and at that moment there was a knock at the door.

'Someone at the door, Jeeves,' I said.

'Yes, sir.'

He opened the door, and in popped Aline Hemmingway and her brother. The last person I had expected. I really had thought that I could be alone for a minute in my own room.

'Oh, hallo!' I said.

'Oh, Mr Wooster!' said the girl in a gasping sort of way. 'I don't know how to begin.'

Then I noticed that she appeared considerably rattled, and as for the brother, he looked like a sheep with a secret sorrow.

This made me sit up and take notice. I had supposed that this was just a social call, but apparently something had happened to give them a jolt. Though I couldn't see why they should come to me about it.

'Is anything up?' I said.

'Poor Sidney – it was my fault – I ought never to have let him go there alone,' said the girl. Dashed agitated.

At this point the brother, who after shedding a floppy overcoat and parking his hat on a chair had been standing by wrapped in the silence, gave a little cough, like a sheep caught in the mist on a mountain top.

'The fact is Mr Wooster,' he said, 'a sad, a most deplorable thing has occurred. This afternoon, while you were so kindly escorting my sist-ah, I found the time hang a little heavy upon my hands and I was tempted to – ah – gamble at the Casino.'

I looked at the man in a kindlier spirit than I had been able to up to date. This evidence that he had sporting blood in his veins made him seem more human, I'm bound to say. If only I'd known earlier that he went in for that sort of thing, I felt that we might have had a better time together.

'Oh!' I said. 'Did you click?'

He sighed heavily.

'If you mean was I successful, I must answer in the negative. I rashly persisted in the view that the colour red, having appeared no fewer than seven times in succession, must inevitably at no distant date give place to black. I was in error. I lost my little all, Mr Wooster.'

'Tough luck,' I said.

'I left the Casino,' proceeded the chappie, 'and returned to the hotel. There I encountered one of my parishioners, a Colonel Musgrave, who chanced to be holiday-making over here. I – er – induced him to cash me a cheque for one hundred pounds on my little account in my London bank.'

'Well, that was all to the good, what?' I said, hoping to induce the poor fish to look on the bright side. 'I mean, bit of luck finding someone to slip it into first crack out of the box.'

'On the contrary, Mr Wooster, it did but make matters worse. I burn with shame as I make the confession, but I immediately went back to the Casino and lost the entire sum – this time under the mistaken supposition that the colour black was, as I believe the expression is, due for a run.'

'I say!' I said. 'You are having a night out!'

'And,' concluded the chappie, 'the most lamentable feature of the whole affair is that I have no funds in the bank to meet the cheque when presented.'

I'm free to confess that, though I realized by this time that all this was leading up to a touch and that my ear was shortly going to be bitten in no uncertain manner, my heart warmed to the poor prune. Indeed, I gazed at him with no little interest and admiration. Never before had I encountered a curate so genuinely all to the mustard. Little as he might look like one of the lads of the village, he certainly appeared to be the real tabasco, and I wished he had shown me this side of his character before.

'Colonel Musgrave,' he went on, gulping somewhat, 'is not a man who would be likely to overlook the matter. He is a hard man. He will expose me to my vic-ah. My vic-ah is a hard man. In short, Mr Wooster, if Colonel Musgrave presents that cheque I shall be ruined. And he leaves for England tonight.'

The girl, who had been standing by biting her handkerchief and gurgling at intervals while the brother got the above off his chest, now started in once more.

'Mr Wooster,' she cried, 'won't you, won't you help us? Oh, do say you will! We must have the money to get back the cheque from Colonel Musgrave before nine o'clock – he leaves on the nine-twenty. I was at my wits' end what to do when I remembered how kind you had always been. Mr Wooster, will you lend Sidney the money and take these as security?' And before I knew what she was doing she had dived into her bag, produced a case, and opened it. 'My pearls,' she said. 'I don't know what they are worth – they were a present from my poor father—'

'Now, alas, no more—' chipped in the brother.

'But I know they must be worth ever so much more than the amount we want.'

Dashed embarrassing. Made me feel like a pawnbroker. More than a touch of popping the watch about the whole business.

'No, I say, really,' I protested. 'There's no need of any security, you know, or any rot of that kind. Only too glad to let you have the money. I've got it on me, as a matter of fact. Rather luckily drew some this morning.'

And I fished it out and pushed it across. The brother shook his head.

'Mr Wooster,' he said, 'we appreciate your generosity, your beautiful, heartening confidence in us, but we cannot permit this.'

'What Sidney means,' said the girl, 'is that you really don't know anything about us when you come to think of it. You mustn't risk lending all this money without any security at all to two people who, after all, are almost strangers. If I hadn't thought that you would be quite business-like about this I would never have dared to come to you.'

'The idea of – er – pledging the pearls at the local Mont de Pieté was, you will readily understand, repugnant to us,' said the brother.

'If you will just give me a receipt, as a matter of form—'

'Oh, right-o!'

I wrote out the receipt and handed it over, feeling more or less of an ass.

'Here you are,' I said.

The girl took the piece of paper, shoved it in her bag, grabbed the money and slipped it to brother Sidney, and then, before I knew what was happening, she had darted at me, kissed me, and legged it from the room.

I'm bound to say the thing rattled me. So dashed sudden and unexpected. I mean, a girl like that. Always been quiet and demure and what not – by no means the sort of female you'd have expected to go about the place kissing fellows. Through a sort of mist I could see that Jeeves had appeared from the background and was helping the brother on with his coat; and I remember wondering idly how the dickens a man could bring himself to wear a coat like that, it being more like a sack than anything else. Then the brother came up to me and grasped my hand.

'I cannot thank you sufficiently, Mr Wooster!'

'Oh, not at all.'

'You have saved my good name. Good name in man or woman, dear my lord,' he said, massaging the fin with some fervour, 'is the immediate jewel of their souls. Who steals my purse steals trash. 'Twas mine, 'tis his, and has been slave to thousands. But he that filches my good name robs me of that which enriches not him and makes me poor indeed. I thank you from the bottom of my heart. Good night, Mr Wooster.'

'Good night, old thing,' I said.

I blinked at Jeeves as the door shut. 'Rather a sad affair

Jeeves,' I said.

'Yes, sir.'

'Lucky I happened to have all that money handy.'

'Well – er – yes, sir.'

'You speak as though you didn't think much of it.'

'It is not my place to criticize your actions, sir, but I will venture to say that I think you behaved a little rashly.'

'What, lending that money?'

'Yes, sir. These fashionable French watering places are notoriously infested by dishonest characters.'

This was a bit too thick.

'Now look here, Jeeves,' I said. 'I can stand a lot but when it comes to your casting asp-whatever-the-word-is on a bird in Holy Orders—'

'Perhaps I am over-suspicious, sir. But I have seen a great deal of these resorts. When I was in the employment of Lord Frederick Ranelagh, shortly before I entered your service, his lordship was very neatly swindled by a criminal known, I believe, by the soubriquet of Soapy Sid, who scraped acquaintance with us in Monte Carlo with the assistance of a female accomplice. I have never forgotten the circumstances.'

'I don't want to butt in on your reminiscences, Jeeves,' I said, coldly, 'but you're talking through your hat. How can there have been anything fishy about this business? They've left me the pearls, haven't they? Very well, then, think before you speak. You had better be tooling down to the desk now and having these things shoved in the hotel safe.' I picked up the case and opened it. 'Oh Great Scott!'

The bally thing was empty!

'Oh, my Lord!' I said, staring. 'Don't tell me there's been dirty work at the crossroads after all!'

'Precisely, sir. It was in exactly the same manner that Lord Frederick was swindled on the occasion to which I have alluded. While his female accomplice was gratefully embracing his lordship, Soapy Sid substituted a duplicate case for the one containing the pearls and went off with the jewels, the money and the receipt. On the strength of the receipt he subsequently demanded from his lordship the return of the pearls, and his lordship, not being able to produce them, was obliged to pay a heavy sum in compensation. It is a simple but effective ruse.'

I felt as if the bottom had dropped out of things with a jerk.

'Soapy Sid? Sid! Sidney! Brother Sidney! Why, by Jove, Jeeves, do you think that parson was Soapy Sid?'

'Yes, sir.'

'But it seems extraordinary. Why, his collar buttoned at the back – I mean, he would have deceived a bishop. Do you really think he was Soapy Sid?'

'Yes, sir. I recognized him directly he came into the room.'

I stared at the blighter.

'You recognized him?'

'Yes, sir.'

'Then, dash it all,' I said, deeply moved. 'I think you might have told me.'

'I thought it would save disturbance and unpleasantness if

I merely extracted the case from the man's pocket as I assisted him with his coat, sir. Here it is.'

He laid another case on the table beside the dud one, and, by Jove, you couldn't tell them apart. I opened it, and there were the good old pearls, as merry and bright as dammit, smiling up at me. I gazed feebly at the man. I was feeling a bit overwrought.

'Jeeves,' I said. 'You're an absolute genius!'

'Yes, sir.'

Relief was surging over me in great chunks by now. Thanks to Jeeves I was not going to be called on to cough up several thousand quid.

'It looks to me as though you have saved the old home. I mean, even a chappie endowed with the immortal rind of dear old Sid is hardly likely to have the nerve to come back and retrieve these little chaps.'

'I should imagine not, sir.'

'Well, then—Oh, I say, you don't think they are just paste or anything like that?'

'No, sir. These are genuine pearls and extremely valuable.'

'Well, then, dash it, I'm on velvet. Absolutely reclining on the good old plush! I may be down a hundred quid but I'm up a jolly good string of pearls. Am I right or wrong?'

'Hardly that, sir. I think that you will have to restore the pearls.'

'What! To Sid? Not while I have my physique!'

'No, sir. To their rightful owner.'

'But who is their rightful owner?'

'Mrs Gregson, sir.'

'What! How do you know?'

'It was all over the hotel an hour ago that Mrs Gregson's pearls had been abstracted. I was speaking to Mrs Gregson's maid shortly before you came in and she informed me that the manager of the hotel is now in Mrs Gregson's suite.'

'And having a devil of a time, what?'

'So I should be disposed to imagine, sir.'

The situation was beginning to unfold before me.

'I'll go and give them back to her, eh? It'll put me one up, what?'

'Precisely, sir. And, if I may make the suggestion, I think it might be judicious to stress the fact that they were stolen by—'

'Great Scott! By the dashed girl she was hounding me on to marry, by Jove!'

'Exactly, sir.'

'Jeeves,' I said, 'this is going to be the biggest score off my jolly old relative that has ever occurred in the world's history.'

'It is not unlikely, sir.'

'Keep her quiet for a bit, what? Make her stop snootering me for a while?'

'It should have that effect, sir.'

'Golly!' I said, bounding for the door.

Long before I reached Aunt Agatha's lair I could tell that the hunt was up. Divers chappies in hotel uniform and not a few chambermaids of sorts were hanging about in the corridor and through the panels I could hear a mixed assortment of voices, with Aunt Agatha's topping the lot. I knocked but no one took any notice, so I trickled in. Among those present I noticed a chambermaid in hysterics, Aunt Agatha with her hair bristling and the whiskered cove who looked like a bandit, the hotel manager fellow.

'Oh, hallo!' I said. 'Hallo-allo-allo!'

Aunt Agatha shooshed me away. No welcoming smile for Bertram.

'Don't bother me now, Bertie,' she snapped, looking at me as if I were more or less the last straw.

'Something up?'

'Yes, yes, yes! I've lost my pearls.'

'Pearls? Pearls? Pearls?' I said. 'No, really? Dashed annoying. Where did you see them last?'

'What does it matter where I saw them last? They have been stolen.'

Here Wilfred the Whisker King, who seemed to have been taking a rest between rounds, stepped into the ring again and began to talk rapidly in French. Cut to the quick he seemed. The chambermaid whooped in the corner.

'Sure you've looked everywhere?' I said.

'Of course I've looked everywhere.'

'Well, you know, I've often lost a collar stud and—'

'Do try not to be so maddening, Bertie! I have enough to bear without your imbecilities. Oh, be quiet! Be quiet!' she shouted in the sort of voice used by sergeant-majors and those who call the cattle home across the Sands of Dee. And such was the magnetism of her forceful personality that Wilfred subsided as if he had run into a wall. The chambermaid continued to go strong.

'I say,' I said, 'I think there's something the matter with this girl. Isn't she crying or something? You may not have spotted it, but I'm rather quick at noticing things.'

'She stole my pearls! I am convinced of it.'

This started the whisker specialist off again, and in about a couple of minutes Aunt Agatha had reached the frozen grande-dame stage and was putting the last of the bandits through it in the voice she usually reserves for snubbing waiters in restaurants.

'I tell you, my good man, for the hundredth time—'

'I say,' I said, 'don't want to interrupt you and all that sort of thing, but these aren't the little chaps by any chance, are they?'

I pulled the pearls out of my pocket and held them up.

'These look like pearls, what?'

I don't know when I've had a more juicy moment. It was one of those occasions about which I shall prattle to my grandchildren – if I ever have any, which at the moment of going to press seems more or less of a hundred-to-one shot. Aunt Agatha simply deflated before my eyes. It reminded me of when I once saw some chappies letting the gas out of a balloon.

'Where – where – where—' she gurgled.

'I got them from your friend, Miss Hemmingway.'

Even now she didn't get it.

'From Miss Hemmingway. Miss Hemmingway! But – but how did they come into her possession?'

'How?' I said. 'Because she jolly well stole them. Pinched them! Swiped them! Because that's how she makes her living, dash it – palling up to unsuspicious people in hotels and sneaking their jewellery. I don't know what her alias is, but her bally brother, the chap whose collar buttons at the back, is known in criminal circles as Soapy Sid.'

She blinked.

'Miss Hemmingway a thief ! I – I—' She stopped and looked feebly at me. 'But how did you manage to recover the pearls, Bertie dear?'

'Never mind,' I said crisply. 'I have my methods.' I dug out my entire stock of manly courage, breathed a short prayer and let her have it right in the thorax.

'I must say, Aunt Agatha, dash it all,' I said severely, 'I think you have been infernally careless. There's a printed notice in every bedroom in this place saying that there's a safe in the manager's office, where jewellery and valuables ought to be placed, and you absolutely disregarded it. And what's the result? The first thief who came along simply walked into your room and pinched your pearls. And instead of admitting that it was all your fault, you started biting this poor man here in the gizzard. You have been very, very unjust to this poor man.'

'Yes, yes,' moaned the poor man.

'And this unfortunate girl, what about her? Where does she get off? You've accused her of stealing the things on absolutely no evidence. I think she would be jolly well advised to bring an action for – for whatever it is and soak you for substantial damages.'

'Mais oui, mais ouis, c'est trop fort! ' shouted the Bandit Chief, backing me up like a good 'un. And the chambermaid looked up inquiringly, as if the sun was breaking through the clouds.

'I shall recompense her,' said Aunt Agatha feebly.

'If you take my tip you jolly well will, and that eftsoons or right speedily. She's got a cast-iron case, and if I were her I wouldn't take a penny under twenty quid. But what gives me the pip most is the way you've unjustly abused this poor man here and tried to give his hotel a bad name—'

'Yes, by damn! It's too bad!' cried the whiskered marvel. 'You careless old woman! You give my hotel bad names, would you or wasn't it? Tomorrow you leave my hotel, by great Scotland!'

And more to the same effect, all good, ripe stuff. And presently, having said his say, he withdrew, taking the chambermaid with him, the latter with a crisp tenner clutched in a vice-like grip. I suppose she and the bandit split it outside. A French hotel manager wouldn't be likely to let real money wander away from him without counting himself in on the division.

I turned to Aunt Agatha, whose demeanour was now

rather like that of one who, picking daisies on the railway, has just caught the down express in the small of the back.

'I don't want to rub it in, Aunt Agatha,' I said coldly, 'but I should just like to point out before I go that the girl who stole your pearls is the girl you've been hounding me on to marry ever since I got here. Good heavens! Do you realize that if you had brought the thing off I should probably have had children who would have sneaked my watch while I was dandling them on my knee? I'm not a complaining sort of chap as a rule, but I must say that another time I do think you might be more careful how you go about egging me on to marry females.'

I gave her one look, turned on my heel and left the room.

'Ten o'clock, a clear night, and all's well, Jeeves,' I said, breezing back into the good old suite.

'I am gratified to hear it, sir.'

'If twenty quid would be any use to you, Jeeves—'

'I am much obliged, sir.'

There was a pause. And then – well, it was a wrench, but I did it. I unstripped the cummerbund and handed it over.

'Do you wish me to press this, sir?'

I gave the thing one last, longing look. It had been very dear to me.

'No,' I said, 'take it away; give it to the deserving poor – I shall never wear it again.'

'Thank you very much, sir,' said Jeeves.'

CHAPTER FIVE
The Pride of the Woosters is Wounded

I f there's one thing I like, it's a quiet life. I'm not one of those fellows who get all restless and depressed if things aren't happening to them all the time. You can't make it too placid for me. Give me regular meals, a good show with decent music every now and then, and one or two pals to totter round with, and I ask no more.

That is why the jar, when it came, was such a particularly nasty jar. I mean, I'd returned from Roville with a sort of feeling that from now on nothing could occur to upset me. Aunt Agatha, I imagined, would require at least a year to recover from the Hemmingway affair: and apart from Aunt Agatha there isn't anybody who really does much in the way of harrying me. It seemed to me that the skies were blue, so to speak, and no clouds in sight.

I little thought . . . Well, look here, what happened was this, and I ask you if it wasn't enough to rattle anybody.

Once a year Jeeves takes a couple of weeks' vacation and

biffs off to the sea or somewhere to restore his tissues. Pretty rotten for me, of course, while he's away. But it has to be stuck, so I stick it; and I must admit that he usually manages to get hold of a fairly decent fellow to look after me in his absence.

Well, the time had come round again, and Jeeves was in the kitchen giving the understudy a few tips about his duties. I happened to want a stamp or something, and I toddled down the passage to ask him for it. The silly ass had left the kitchen door open, and I hadn't gone two steps when his voice caught me squarely in the eardrum.

'You will find Mr Wooster,' he was saying to the substitute chappie, 'an exceedingly pleasant and amiable young gentleman, but not intelligent. By no means intelligent. Mentally he is negligible – quite negligible.'

Well, I mean to say, what!

I suppose, strictly speaking, I ought to have charged in and ticked the blighter off properly in no uncertain voice. But I doubt whether it's humanly possible to tick Jeeves off. Personally, I didn't even have a dash at it. I merely called for my hat and stick in a marked manner and legged it. But the memory rankled, if you know what I mean. We Woosters do not lightly forget. At least, we do – some things – appointments, and people's birthdays, and letters to post, and all that – but not an absolute bally insult like the above. I brooded like the dickens.

I was still brooding when I dropped in at the oyster-bar at Buck's for a quick bracer. I needed a bracer rather particularly at the moment, because I was on my way to lunch with Aunt Agatha. A pretty frightful ordeal, believe me or believe me not, even though I took it that after what had happened at Roville she would be in a fairly subdued and amiable mood. I had just had one quick and another rather slower, and was feeling about as cheerio as was possible under the circs, when a muffled voice hailed me from the north-east, and, turning round, I saw young Bingo Little propped up in a corner, wrapping himself round a sizeable chunk of bread and cheese.

'Hallo-allo-allo!' I said. 'Haven't seen you for ages. You've not been in here lately. have you?'

'No. I've been living out in the country.'

'Eh?' I said, for Bingo's loathing for the country was well known. 'Whereabouts?'

'Down in Hampshire, at a place called Ditteredge.'

'No, really? I know some people who've got a house there. The Glossops. Have you met them?'

'Why, that's where I'm staying!' said young Bingo. 'I'm tutoring the Glossop kid.'

'What for?' I said. I couldn't seem to see young Bingo as a tutor. Though, of course, he did get a degree of sorts at Oxford, and I suppose you can always fool some of the people some of the time.

'What for? For money, of course! An absolute sitter came unstitched in the second race at Haydock Park,' said young Bingo, with some bitterness, 'and I dropped my entire month's allowance. I hadn't the nerve to touch my uncle for any more so it was a case of buzzing round to the agents and getting a job. I've been down there three weeks.'

'I haven't met the Glossop kid.'

'Don't!' advised Bingo, briefly.

'The only one of the family I really know is the girl.' I had hardly spoken these words when the most extraordinary change came over young Bingo's face. His eyes bulged, his cheeks flushed, and his Adam's apple hopped about like one of those india-rubber balls on the top of the fountain in a shooting-gallery.

'Oh, Bertie!' he said, in a strangled sort of voice.

I looked at the poor fish anxiously. I knew that he was always falling in love with someone, but it didn't seem possible that even he could have fallen in love with Honoria Glossop. To me the girl was simply nothing more nor less than a pot of poison. One of those dashed large, brainy, strenuous, dynamic girls you see so many of these days. She had been at Girton, where, in addition to enlarging her brain to the most frightful extent, she had gone in for every kind of sport and developed the physique of a middleweight catch-as-catch-can wrestler. I'm not sure she didn't box for the Varsity while she was up. The effect she had on me whenever she appeared was to make me want to slide into a cellar and lie low till they blew the All-Clear.

Yet here was young Bingo obviously all for her. There was no mistaking it. The love-light was in the blighter's eyes.

'I worship her, Bertie! I worship the very ground she treads on!' continued the patient, in a loud, penetrating voice. Fred Thompson and one or two fellows had come in, and McGarry, the chappie behind the bar, was listening with his ears flapping. But there's no reticence about Bingo. He always reminds me of the hero of a musical comedy who takes the centre of the stage, gathers the boys round him in a circle, and tells them all about his love at the top of his voice.

'Have you told her?'

'No. I haven't the nerve. But we walk together in the garden most evenings, and it sometimes seems to me that there is a look in her eyes.'

'I know that look. Like a sergeant-major.'

'Nothing of the kind! Like a tender goddess.'

'Half a second, old thing,' I said. 'Are you sure we're talking about the same girl? The one I mean is Honoria. Perhaps there's a younger sister or something I've not heard of?'

'Her name is Honoria,' bawled Bingo reverently.

'And she strikes you as a tender goddess?'

'She does.'

'God bless you!' I said.

'She walks in beauty like the night of cloudless climes and starry skies; and all that's best of dark and bright meet in her aspect and her eyes. Another bit of bread and cheese,' he said to the lad behind the bar.

'You're keeping your strength up,' I said.

'This is my lunch. I've got to meet Oswald at Waterloo at one-fifteen, to catch the train back. I brought him up to town to see the dentist.'

'Oswald? Is that the kid?'

'Yes. Pestilential to a degree.'

'Pestilential! That reminds me, I'm lunching with my Aunt Agatha. I'll have to pop off now, or I'll be late.'

I hadn't seen Aunt Agatha since that little affair of the pearls; and, while I didn't anticipate any great pleasure from gnawing a bone in her society, I must say that there was one topic of conversation I felt pretty confident she wouldn't touch on, and that was the subject of my matrimonial future. I mean, when a woman's made a bloomer like the one Aunt Agatha made at Roville, you'd naturally think that a decent shame would keep her off it for, at any rate, a month or two.

But women beat me. I mean to say, as regards nerve. You'll hardly credit it, but she actually started in on me with the fish. Absolutely with the fish, I give you my solemn word. We'd hardly exchanged a word about the weather, when she let me have it without a blush.

'Bertie,' she said, 'I've been thinking again about you and how necessary it is that you should get married. I quite admit that I was dreadfully mistaken in my opinion of that terrible, hypocritical girl at Roville, but this time there is no danger of an error. By great good luck I have found the very wife for you, a girl whom I have only recently met, but whose family is above suspicion. She has plenty of money, too, though that does not matter in your case. The great point is that she is strong, self-reliant and sensible, and will counterbalance the deficiencies and weaknesses of your character. She has met you; and, while there is naturally much in you of which she disapproves, she does not dislike you. I know this, for I have sounded her – guardedly, of course – and I am sure that you have only to make the first advances—'

'Who is it?' I would have said it long before, but the shock had made me swallow a bit of roll the wrong way, and I had only just finished turning purple and trying to get a bit of air back into the old windpipe. 'Who is it?'

'Sir Roderick Glossop's daughter, Honoria.'

'No, no!' I cried, paling beneath the tan.

'Don't be silly, Bertie. She is just the wife for you.'

'Yes, but look here—'

'She will mould you.'

'But I don't want to be moulded.'

Aunt Agatha gave me the kind of look she used to give me when I was a kid and had been found in the jam cupboard.

'Bertie! I hope you are not going to be troublesome.'

'Well, but I mean—'

'Lady Glossop has very kindly invited you to Ditteredge Hall for a few days. I told her you would be delighted to come down tomorrow.'

'I'm sorry, but I've got a dashed important engagement tomorrow.'

'What engagement?'

'Well – er—'

'You have no engagement. And, even if you had, you must put it off. I shall be very seriously annoyed, Bertie, if you do not go to Ditteredge Hall tomorrow.'

'Oh, right-o!' I said.

It wasn't two minutes after I had parted from Aunt Agatha before the old fighting spirit of the Woosters reasserted itself. Ghastly as the peril was which loomed before me, I was conscious of a rummy sort of exhilaration. It was a tight corner, but the tighter the corner, I felt, the more juicily should I score off Jeeves when I got myself out of it without a bit of help from him. Ordinarily, of course, I should have consulted him and trusted to him to solve the difficulty; but after what I had heard him saying in the kitchen, I was dashed if I was going to demean myself. When I got home I addressed the man with light abandon.

'Jeeves,' I said, 'I'm in a bit of a difficulty.'

'I'm sorry to hear that, sir.'

'Yes, quite a bad hole. In fact, you might say on the brink of a precipice, and faced by an awful doom.'

'If I could be of any assistance, sir—'

'Oh, no. No, no. Thanks very much, but no, no. I won't trouble you. I've no doubt I shall be able to get out of it by myself.'

'Very good, sir.'

So that was that. I'm bound to say I'd have welcomed a bit more curiosity from the fellow, but that is Jeeves all over.

Cloaks his emotions, if you know what I mean.

Honoria was away when I got to Ditteredge on the following afternoon. Her mother told me that she was staying with some people named Braythwayt in the neighbourhood, and would be back next day, bringing the daughter of the house with her for a visit. She said I would find Oswald out in the grounds, and such is a mother's love that she spoke as if that were a bit of a boost for the grounds and an inducement to go there.

Rather decent, the grounds at Ditteredge. A couple of terraces, a bit of lawn with a cedar on it, a bit of shrubbery, and finally a small but goodish lake with a stone bridge running across it. Directly I'd worked my way round the shrubbery I spotted young Bingo leaning against the bridge smoking a cigarette. Sitting on the stonework, fishing, was a species of kid whom I took to be Oswald the Plague-Spot.

Bingo was both surprised and delighted to see me, and introduced me to the kid. If the latter was surprised and delighted too, he concealed it like a diplomat. He just looked at me, raised his eyebrows slightly, and went on fishing. He was one of those supercilious striplings who give you the impression that you went to the wrong school and that your clothes don't fit.

'This is Oswald,' said Bingo.

'What,' I replied cordially, 'could be sweeter? How are you?'

'Oh, all right,' said the kid.

'Nice place, this.'

'Oh, all right,' said the kid.

'Having a good time fishing?'

'Oh, all right,' said the kid.

Young Bingo led me off to commune apart.

'Doesn't jolly old Oswald's incessant flow of prattle make your head ache sometimes?' I asked.

Bingo sighed.

'It's a hard job.'

'What's a hard job?'

'Loving him.'

'Do you love him?' I asked, surprised. I shouldn't have thought it could be done.

'I try to,' said young Bingo, 'for Her sake. She's coming back tomorrow, Bertie.'

'So I heard.'

'She is coming, my love, my own—'

'Absolutely,' I said. 'But touching on young Oswald once more. Do you have to be with him all day? How do you manage to stick it?'

'Oh, he doesn't give much trouble. When we aren't working he sits on that bridge all the time, trying to catch tiddlers.'

'Why don't you shove him in?'

'Shove him in?'

'It seems to me distinctly the thing to do,' I said, regarding the stripling's back with a good deal of dislike. 'It would wake him up a bit, and make him take an interest in things.'

Bingo shook his head a bit wistfully.

'Your proposition attracts me,' he said, 'but I'm afraid it can't be done. You see, She would never forgive me. She is devoted to the little brute.'

'Great Scott!' I cried. 'I've got it!' I don't know if you know that feeling when you get an inspiration, and tingle all down your spine from the soft collar as now worn to the very soles of the old Waukeesis? Jeeves, I suppose, feels that way more or less all the time, but it isn't often it comes to me. But now all Nature seemed to be shouting at me, 'You've clicked!' and I grabbed young Bingo by the arm in a way that must have made him feel as if a horse had bitten him. His finely-chiselled features were twisted with agony and what not, and he asked me what the dickens I thought I was playing at.

'Bingo,' I said, 'what would Jeeves have done?'

'How do you mean, what would Jeeves have done?'

'I mean what would he have advised in a case like yours? I mean you wanting to make a hit with Honoria Glossop and all that. Why, take it from me, laddie, he would have shoved you behind that clump of bushes over there; he would have got me to lure Honoria on to the bridge somehow; then, at the proper time, he would have told me to give the kid a pretty hefty jab in the small of the back, so as to shoot him into the water; and then you would have dived in and hauled him out. How about it?'

'You didn't think that out by yourself, Bertie?' said young

Bingo, in a hushed sort of voice.

'Yes, I did. Jeeves isn't the only fellow with ideas.'

'But it's absolutely wonderful.'

'Just a suggestion.'

'The only objection I can see is that it would be so dashed awkward for you. I mean to say, suppose the kid turned round and said you had shoved him in, that would make you frightfully unpopular with Her.'

'I don't mind risking that.'

The man was deeply moved.

'Bertie, this is noble.'

'No, no.'

He clasped my hand silently, then chuckled like the last drop of water going down the waste-pipe in a bath.

'Now what?' I said.

'I was only thinking,' said young Bingo, 'how fearfully wet Oswald will get. Oh, happy day!'

CHAPTER SIX
The Hero's Reward

I don't know if you've noticed it, but it's rummy how nothing in this world ever seems to be absolutely perfect. The drawback to this otherwise singularly fruity binge was, of course, the fact that Jeeves wouldn't be on the spot to watch me in action. Still, apart from that there wasn't a flaw. The beauty of the thing was, you see, that nothing could possibly go wrong. You know how it is, as a rule, when you want to get Chappie A on Spot B at exactly the same moment when Chappie C is on Spot D. There's always a chance of a hitch. Take the case of a general, I mean to say, who's planning out a big movement. He tells one regiment to capture the hill with the windmill on it at the exact moment when another regiment is taking the bridgehead or something down in the valley; and everything gets all messed up. And then, when they're chatting the thing over in camp that night, the colonel of the first regiment says, 'Oh, sorry! Did you say the hill with the windmill? I thought you said the one with the flock of sheep.' And there you are! But in this case, nothing like that could happen, because Oswald and Bingo would be on the spot right along, so that all I had to worry about was getting Honoria there in due season. And I managed that all right, first shot, by asking her if she would come for a stroll in the grounds with me, as I had something particular to say to her.

She had arrived shortly after lunch in the car with the Braythwayt girl. I was introduced to the latter, a tallish girl with blue eyes and fair hair. I rather took to her – she was so unlike Honoria – and, if I had been able to spare the time, I shouldn't have minded talking to her for a bit. But business was business – I had fixed it up with Bingo to be behind the bushes at three sharp, so I got hold of Honoria and steered her out through the grounds in the direction of the lake.

'You've very quiet, Mr Wooster,' she said.

Made me jump a bit. I was concentrating pretty tensely at the moment. We had just come in sight of the lake, and I was casting a keen eye over the ground to see that everything was in order. Everything appeared to be as arranged. The kid Oswald was hunched up on the bridge; and, as Bingo wasn't visible, I took it that he had got into position. My watch made it two minutes after the hour.

'Eh?' I said. 'Oh, ah, yes. I was just thinking.'

'You said you had something important to say to me.'

'Absolutely!' I had decided to open the proceedings by sort of paving the way for young Bingo. I mean to say, without actually mentioning his name, I wanted to prepare the girl's mind for the fact that, surprising as it might seem, there was someone who had long loved her from afar and all that sort of rot. 'It's like this,' I said. 'It may sound rummy and all that, but there's somebody who's frightfully in love with you and so forth – a friend of mine, you know.'

'Oh, a friend of yours?'

'Yes.'

She gave a kind of a laugh.

'Well, why doesn't he tell me so?'

'Well, you see, that's the sort of chap he is. Kind of shrinking, diffident kind of fellow. Hasn't got the nerve. Thinks you so much above him, don't you know. Looks on you as a sort of goddess. Worships the ground you tread on, but can't whack up the ginger to tell you so.'

'This is very interesting.'

'Yes. He's not a bad chap, you know, in his way. Rather an ass, perhaps, but well-meaning. Well, that's the posish. You might just bear it in mind, what?'

'How funny you are!'

She chucked back her head and laughed with considerable vim. She had a penetrating sort of laugh. Rather like a train going into a tunnel. It didn't sound over-musical to me, and on the kid Oswald it appeared to jar not a little. He gazed at us with a good deal of dislike.

'I wish the dickens you wouldn't make that row,' he said. 'Scaring all the fish away.'

It broke the spell a bit. Honoria changed the subject.

'I do wish Oswald wouldn't sit on the bridge like that,' she said. 'I'm sure it isn't safe. He might easily fall in.'

'I'll go and tell him,' I said.

I suppose the distance between the kid and me at this juncture was about five yards, but I got the impression that it was nearer a hundred. And, as I started to toddle across the intervening space, I had a rummy feeling that I'd done this very thing before. Then I remembered. Years ago, at a country-house party, I had been roped in to play the part of a butler in some amateur theatricals in aid of some ghastly charity or other; and I had had to open the proceedings by walking across the empty stage from left upper entrance and shoving a tray on a table down right. They had impressed it on me at rehearsals that I mustn't take the course at a quick heel-and-toe, like a chappie finishing strongly in a walking-race; and the result was that I kept the brakes on to such an extent that it seemed to me as if I was never going to get to the bally table at all. The stage seemed to stretch out in front of me like a trackless desert, and there was a kind of breathless hush as if all Nature had paused to concentrate its attention on me personally. Well, I felt just like that now. I had a kind of dry gulping in my throat, and the more I walked the farther away the kid seemed to get, till suddenly I found myself standing just behind him without quite knowing how I'd got there.

'Hallo!' I said, with a sickly sort of grin – wasted on the kid, because he didn't bother to turn round and look at me. He merely wiggled his left ear in a rather peevish manner. I don't know when I've met anybody in whose life I appeared to mean so little.

'Hallo!' I said. 'Fishing?'

I laid my hand in a sort of elder-brotherly way on his shoulder.

'Here, look out!' said the kid, wobbling on his foundations.

It was one of those things that want doing quickly or not at all. I shut my eyes and pushed. Something seemed to give. There was a scrambling sound, a kind of yelp, a scream in the offing, and a splash. And so the long day wore on, so to speak.

I opened my eyes. The kid was just coming to the surface.

'Help!' I shouted, cocking an eye on the bush from which young Bingo was scheduled to emerge.

Nothing happened. Young Bingo didn't emerge to the slightest extent whatever.

'I say! Help!' I shouted again.

I don't want to bore you with reminiscences of my theatrical career, but I must just touch once more on that appearance of mine as the butler. The scheme on that occasion had been that when I put the tray on the table the heroine would come on and say a few words to get me off. Well, on the night the misguided female forgot to stand by, and it was a full minute before the search-party located her and shot her on to the stage. And all that time I had to stand there, waiting. A rotten sensation, believe me, and this was just the same, only worse. I understood what these writer-chappies mean when they talk about time standing still.

Meanwhile, the kid Oswald was presumably being cut off in his prime, and it began to seem to me that some sort of steps ought to be taken about it. What I had seen of the lad hadn't particularly endeared him to me, but it was undoubtedly a bit thick to let him pass away. I don't know when I have seen anything more grubby and unpleasant than the lake as viewed from the bridge; but the thing apparently had to be done. I chucked off my coat and vaulted over.

It seems rummy that water should be so much wetter when you go into it with your clothes on than when you're just bathing, but take it from me that it is. I was only under about three seconds, I suppose, but I came up feeling like the bodies you read of in the paper which 'had evidently been in the water several days'. I felt clammy and bloated.

At this point the scenario struck another snag. I had assumed that directly I came to the surface I should get hold of the kid and steer him courageously to shore. But he hadn't waited to be steered. When I had finished getting the water out of my eyes and had time to look round, I saw him about ten yards away, going strongly and using, I think, the Australian crawl. The spectacle took all the heart out of me. I mean to say, the whole essence of a rescue, if you know what I mean, is that the party of the second part shall keep fairly still and in one spot. If he starts swimming off on his own account and can obviously give you at least forty yards in the hundred, where are you? The whole thing falls through. It didn't seem to me that there was much to be done except get ashore, so I got ashore. By the time I had landed, the kid was half-way to the house. Look at it from whatever angle you like, the thing was a wash-out.

I was interrupted in my meditations by a noise like the Scotch express going under a bridge. It was Honoria Glossop laughing. She was standing at my elbow, looking at me in a rummy manner.

'Oh, Bertie, you are funny!' she said. And even in that moment there seemed to me something sinister in the words. She had never called me anything except 'Mr Wooster' before. 'How wet you are!'

'Yes, I am wet.'

'You had better hurry into the house and change.'

'Yes.'

I wrung a gallon or two of water out of my clothes.

'You are funny!' she said again. 'First proposing in that extraordinary roundabout way, and then pushing poor little Oswald into the lake so as to impress me by saving him.'

I managed to get the water out of my throat sufficiently to try to correct this fearful impression.

'No, no!'

'He said you pushed him in, and I saw you do it. Oh, I'm not angry, Bertie. I think it was too sweet of you. But I'm quite sure it's time that I took you in hand. You certainly want someone to look after you. You've been seeing too many moving-pictures. I suppose the next thing you would have done would have been to set the house on fire so as to rescue me.' She looked at me in a proprietary sort of way. 'I think,' she said, 'I shall be able to make something of you, Bertie. It is true yours has been a wasted life up to the present, but you are still young, and there is a lot of good in you.'

'No, really there isn't.'

'Oh, yes, there is. It simply wants bringing out. Now you run straight up to the house and change your wet clothes, or you will catch cold.'

And, if you know what I mean, there was a sort of motherly note in her voice which seemed to tell me, even more than her actual words, that I was for it.

As I was coming downstairs after changing, I ran into young Bingo, looking festive to a degree.

'Bertie!' he said. 'Just the man I wanted to see. Bertie, a wonderful thing has happened.'

'You blighter!' I cried. 'What became of you? Do you know—?'

'Oh, you mean about being in those bushes? I hadn't time to tell you about that. It's all off.'

'All off?'

'Bertie, I was actually starting to hide in those bushes when the most extraordinary thing happened. Walking across the lawn I saw the most radiant, the most beautiful girl in the world. There is none like her, none. Bertie, do you believe in love at first sight? You do believe in love at first sight, don't you, Bertie, old man? Directly I saw her she seemed to draw me like a magnet. I seemed to forget everything. We two were alone in a world of music and sunshine. I joined her. I got into conversation. She is a Miss Braythwayt, Bertie – Daphne Braythwayt. Directly our eyes met, I realized that what I had imagined to be my love for Honoria Glossop had been a mere passing whim. Bertie, you do believe in love at first sight, don't you? She is so wonderful, so sympathetic. Like a tender goddess—'

At this point I left the blighter.

Two days later I got a letter from Jeeves.

'. . . The weather,' it ended, 'continues fine. I have had one exceedingly enjoyable bathe.'

I gave one of those hollow, mirthless laughs, and went downstairs to join Honoria. I had an appointment with her in the drawing-room. She was going to read Ruskin to me.

CHAPTER SEVEN
Introducing Claude and Eustace

The blow fell precisely at one forty-five (summer time). Spenser, Aunt Agatha's butler, was offering me the fried potatoes at the moment, and such was my emotion that I lofted six of them on to the sideboard with the spoon. Shaken to the core, if you know what I mean.

Mark you, I was in a pretty enfeebled condition already. I had been engaged to Honoria Glossop nearly two weeks, and during all that time not a day had passed without her putting in some heavy work in the direction of what Aunt Agatha had called 'moulding' me. I had read solid literature till my eyes bubbled; we had legged it together through miles of picture-galleries; and I had been compelled to undergo classical concerts to an extent you would hardly believe. All in all, therefore, I was in no fit state to receive shocks, especially shocks like this. Honoria had lugged me round to lunch at Aunt Agatha's, and I had just been saying to myself, 'Death, where is thy jolly old sting?' when she hove the bomb.

'Bertie,' she said, suddenly, as if she had just remembered it, 'what is the name of that man of yours – your valet?'

'Eh? Oh, Jeeves.'

'I think he's a bad influence for you,' said Honoria. 'When we are married, you must get rid of Jeeves.'

It was at this point that I jerked the spoon and sent six of the best and crispest sailing on to the sideboard, with Spenser gambolling after them like a dignified old retriever.

'Get rid of Jeeves!' I gasped.

'Yes. I don't like him.'

'I don't like him,' said Aunt Agatha.

'But I can't. I mean – why, I couldn't carry on for a day without Jeeves.'

'You will have to,' said Honoria. 'I don't like him at all.'

'I don't like him at all,' said Aunt Agatha. 'I never did.'

Ghastly, what? I'd always had an idea that marriage was a bit of a wash-out, but I'd never dreamed that it demanded such frightful sacrifices from a fellow. I passed the rest of the meal in a sort of stupor.

The scheme had been, if I remember, that after lunch I should go off and caddy for Honoria on a shopping tour down Regent Street; but when she got up and started collecting me and the rest of her things, Aunt Agatha stopped her.

'You run along, dear,' she said. 'I want to say a few words to Bertie.'

So Honoria legged it, and Aunt Agatha drew up her chair and started in.

'Bertie,' she said, 'dear Honoria does not know it, but a little difficulty has arisen about your marriage.'

'By Jove! not really?' I said, hope starting to dawn.

'Oh, it's nothing at all, of course. It is only a little exasperating. The fact is, Sir Roderick is being rather troublesome.'

'Thinks I'm not a good bet? Wants to scratch the fixture? Well, perhaps he's right.'

'Pray do not be so absurd, Bertie. It is nothing so serious as that. But the nature of Sir Roderick's profession unfortunately makes him – over-cautious.'

I didn't get it.

'Over-cautious?'

'Yes. I suppose it is inevitable. A nerve specialist with his extensive practice can hardly help taking a rather warped view of humanity.'

I got what she was driving at now. Sir Roderick Glossop, Honoria's father, is always called a nerve specialist, because it sounds better, but everybody knows that he's really a sort of janitor to the looney-bin. I mean to say, when your uncle the Duke begins to feel the strain a bit and you find him in the blue drawing-room sticking straws in his hair, old Glossop is the first person you send for. He toddles round, gives the patient the once-over, talks about over-excited nervous systems, and recommends complete rest and seclusion and all that sort of thing. Practically every posh family in the country has called him in at one time or another, and I suppose that, being in that position – I mean constantly having to sit on people's heads while their nearest and dearest phone to the asylum to send round the wagon – does tend to make a chappie take what you might call a warped view of humanity.

'You mean he thinks I may be a looney, and he doesn't want a looney son-in-law?' I said.

Aunt Agatha seemed rather peeved than otherwise at my beady intelligence.

'Of course, he does not think anything so ridiculous. I told you he was simply exceedingly cautious. He wants to satisfy himself that you are perfectly normal.' Here she paused, for Spenser had come in with the coffee. When he had gone, she went on: 'He appears to have got hold of some extraordinary story about your having pushed his son Oswald into the lake at Ditteredge Hall. Incredible, of course. Even you would hardly do a thing like that.'

'Well, I did sort of lean against him, you know, and he shot off the bridge.'

'Oswald definitely accuses you of having pushed him into the water. That has disturbed Sir Roderick, and unfortunately it has caused him to make inquiries, and he has heard about your poor Uncle Henry.'

She eyed me with a good deal of solemnity, and I took a grave sip of coffee. We were peeping into the family cupboard and having a look at the good old skeleton. My late Uncle Henry, you see, was by way of being the blot on the Wooster escutcheon. An extremely decent chappie personally, and one who had always endeared himself to me by tipping me with considerable lavishness when I was at school; but there's no doubt he did at times do rather rummy things, notably keeping eleven pet rabbits in his bedroom; and I suppose a purist might have considered him more or less off his onion. In fact, to be perfectly frank, he wound up his career, happy to the last and completely surrounded by rabbits, in some sort of a home.

'It is very absurd, of course,' continued Aunt Agatha. 'If any of the family had inherited poor Henry's eccentricity – and it was nothing more – it would have been Claude and Eustace, and there could not be two brighter boys.'

Claude and Eustace were twins, and had been kids at school with me in my last summer term. Casting my mind back, it seemed to me that 'bright' just about described them. The whole of that term, as I remembered it, had been spent in getting them out of a series of frightful rows.

'Look how well they are doing at Oxford. Your Aunt Emily had a letter from Claude only the other day saying that they hoped to be elected shortly to a very important college club, called The Seekers.'

'Seekers?' I couldn't recall any club of the name in my time at Oxford. 'What do they seek?'

'Claude did not say. Truth or knowledge, I should imagine. It is evidently a very desirable club to belong to, for Claude added that Lord Rainsby, the Earl of Datchet's son, was one of his fellow-candidates. However, we are wandering from the point, which is that Sir Roderick wants to have a quiet talk with you quite alone. Now I rely on you, Bertie, to be – I won't say intelligent, but at least sensible. Don't giggle nervously; try to keep that horrible glassy expression out of your eyes: don't yawn or fidget; and remember that Sir Roderick is the president of the West London branch of the anti-gambling league, so please do not talk about horse-racing. He will lunch with you at your flat tomorrow at one-thirty. Please remember that he drinks no wine, strongly disapproves of smoking, and can only eat the simplest food, owing to an impaired digestion. Do not offer him coffee, for he considers it the root of half the nerve-trouble in the world.'

'I should think a dog-biscuit and a glass of water would about meet the case, what?'

'Bertie!'

'Oh, all right. Merely persiflage.'

'Now it is precisely that sort of idiotic remark that would be calculated to arouse Sir Roderick's worst suspicions. Do please try to refrain from any misguided flippancy when you are with him. He is a very serious-minded man. . . . Are you going? Well, please remember all I have said. I rely on you, and, if anything goes wrong, I shall never forgive you.'

'Right-o!' I said.

And so home, with a jolly day to look forward to.

I breakfasted pretty late next morning and went for a stroll afterwards. It seemed to me that anything I could do to clear the old lemon ought to be done, and a bit of fresh air generally relieves that rather foggy feeling that comes over a fellow early in the day. I had taken a stroll in the park, and got back as far as Hyde Park Corner, when some blighter sloshed me between the shoulder-blades. It was young Eustace, my cousin. He was arm-in-arm with two other fellows, the one on the outside being my cousin Claude and the one in the middle a pink-faced chappie with light hair and an apologetic sort of look.

'Bertie, old egg!' said young Eustace affably.

'Hallo!' I said, not frightfully chirpily.

'Fancy running into you, the one man in London who can support us in the style we are accustomed to! By the way, you've never met old Dog-Face, have you? Dog-Face, this is my cousin Bertie. Lord Rainsby – Mr Wooster. We've just been round to your flat, Bertie. Bitterly disappointed that you were out, but were hospitably entertained by old Jeeves. That man's a corker, Bertie. Stick to him.'

'What are you doing in London?' I asked.

'Oh, buzzing round. We're just up for the day. Flying visit, strictly unofficial. We oil back on the three-ten. And now, touching that lunch you very decently volunteered to stand us, which shall it be? Ritz? Savoy? Carlton? Or, if you're a member of Ciro's or the Embassy, that would do just as well.'

'I can't give you lunch. I've got an engagement myself. And, by Jove,' I said, taking a look at my watch, 'I'm late.' I hailed a taxi. 'Sorry.'

'As man to man, then,' said Eustace, 'lend us a fiver.'

I hadn't time to stop and argue. I unbelted the fiver and hopped into the cab. It was twenty to two when I got to the flat. I bounded into the sitting-room, but it was empty.

Jeeves shimmied in.

'Sir Roderick has not yet arrived, sir.'

'Good egg!' I said. 'I thought I should find him smashing up the furniture.' My experience is that the less you want a fellow, the more punctual he's bound to be, and I had had a vision of the old lad pacing the rug in my sitting-room, saying 'He cometh not!' and generally hotting up. 'Is everything in order?'

'I fancy you will find the arrangements quite satisfactory, sir.'

'What are you giving us?'

'Cold consommé, a cutlet, and a savoury, sir. With lemonsquash, iced.'

'Well, I don't see how that can hurt him. Don't go getting carried away by the excitement of the thing and start bringing in coffee.'

'No, sir.'

'And don't let your eyes get glassy, because, if you do, you're apt to find yourself in a padded cell before you know where you are.'

'Very good, sir.'

There was a ring at the bell.

'Stand by, Jeeves,' I said. 'We're off!'

CHAPTER EIGHT
Sir Roderick Comes to Lunch

I had met Sir Roderick Glossop before, of course, but only when I was with Honoria; and there is something about Honoria which makes almost anybody you meet in the same room seem sort of under-sized and trivial by comparison. I had never realized till this moment what an extraordinarily formidable old bird he was. He had a pair of shaggy eyebrows which gave his eyes a piercing look which was not at all the sort of thing a fellow wanted to encounter on an empty stomach. He was fairly tall and fairly broad, and he had the most enormous head, with practically no hair on it, which made it seem bigger and much more like the dome of St Paul's. I suppose he must have taken about a nine or something in hats. Shows what a rotten thing it is to let your brain develop too much.

'What ho! What ho! What ho!' I said, trying to strike the genial note, and then had a sudden feeling that that was just the sort of thing I had been warned not to say. Dashed difficult it is to start things going properly on an occasion like this. A fellow living in a London flat is so handicapped. I mean to say, if I had been the young squire greeting the visitor in the country, I could have said, 'Welcome to Meadowsweet Hall!' or something zippy like that. It sounds silly to say 'Welcome to Number 6A, Crichton Mansions, Berkeley Street, W.'

'I am afraid I am a little late,' he said, as we sat down. 'I was detained at my club by Lord Alastair Hungerford, the Duke of Ramfurline's son. His Grace, he informed me, had exhibited a renewal of the symptoms which have been causing the family so much concern. I could not leave him immediately. Hence my unpunctuality, which I trust has not discommoded you.'

'Oh, not at all. So the Duke is off his rocker, what?'

'The expression which you use is not precisely the one I should have employed myself with reference to the head of perhaps the noblest family in England, but there is no doubt that cerebral excitement does, as you suggest, exist in no small degree.' He sighed as well as he could with his mouth full of cutlet. 'A profession like mine is a great strain, a great strain.'

'Must be.'

'Sometimes I am appalled at what I see around me.' He stopped suddenly and sort of stiffened. 'Do you keep a cat, Mr Wooster?'

'Eh? What? Cat? No, no cat.'

'I was conscious of a distinct impression that I had heard a cat mewing either in the room or very near to where we are sitting.'

'Probably a taxi or something in the street.'

'I fear I do not follow you.'

'I mean to say, taxis squawk, you know. Rather like cats in a sort of way.'

'I had not observed the resemblance,' he said, rather coldly.

'Have some lemon-squash,' I said. The conversation seemed to be getting rather difficult.

'Thank you. Half a glassful, if I may.' The hell-brew appeared to buck him up, for he resumed in a slightly more pally manner. 'I have a particular dislike for cats. But I was saying— Oh, yes. Sometimes I am positively appalled at what I see around me. It is not only the cases which come under my professional notice, painful as many of those are. It is what I see as I go about London. Sometimes it seems to me that the whole world is mentally unbalanced. This very morning, for example, a most singular and distressing occurrence took place as I was driving from my house to the club. The day being clement, I had instructed my chauffeur to open my landaulette, and I was leaning back, deriving no little pleasure from the sunshine, when our progress was arrested in the middle of the thoroughfare by one of those blocks in the traffic which are inevitable in so congested a system as that of London.'

I suppose I had been letting my mind wander a bit, for when he stopped and took a sip of lemon-squash I had a feeling that I was listening to a lecture and was expected to say something.

'Hear, hear!' I said.

'I beg your pardon?'

'Nothing, nothing. You were saying—'

'The vehicles proceeding in the opposite direction had also been temporarily arrested, but after a moment they were permitted to proceed. I had fallen into a meditation, when suddenly the most extraordinary thing took place. My hat was snatched abruptly from my head! And as I looked back I perceived it being waved in a kind of feverish triumph from the interior of a taxicab, which, even as I looked, disappeared through a gap in the traffic and was lost to sight.'

I didn't laugh, but I distinctly heard a couple of my floating ribs part from their moorings under the strain.

'Must have been meant for a practical joke,' I said. 'What?'

This suggestion didn't seem to please the old boy.

'I trust,' he said, 'I am not deficient in an appreciation of the humorous, but I confess that I am at a loss to detect anything akin to pleasantry in the outrage. The action was beyond all question that of a mentally unbalanced subject. These mental lesions may express themselves in almost any form. The Duke of Ramfurline, to whom I had occasion to allude just now, is under the impression – this is in the strictest confidence – that he is a canary: and his seizure today, which so perturbed Lord Alastair, was due to the fact that a careless footman had neglected to bring him his morning lump of sugar. Cases are common, again, of men waylaying women and cutting off portions of their hair. It is from a branch of this latter form of mania that I should be disposed to imagine that my assailant was suffering. I can only trust that he will be placed under proper control before he – Mr Wooster, there is a cat close at hand! It is not in the street! The mewing appears to come from the adjoining room.'

This time I had to admit there was no doubt about it. There was a distinct sound of mewing coming from the next room. I punched the bell for Jeeves, who drifted in and stood waiting with an air of respectful devotion.

'Sir?'

'Oh, Jeeves,' I said. 'Cats! What about it? Are there any cats in the flat?'

'Only the three in your bedroom, sir.'

'What!'

'Cats in his bedroom!' I heard Sir Roderick whisper in a kind of stricken way, and his eyes hit me amidships like a couple of bullets.

'What do you mean,' I said, 'only the three in my bedroom?'

'The black one, the tabby and the small lemon-coloured animal, sir.'

'What on earth—?'

I charged round the table in the direction of the door Unfortunately, Sir Roderick had just decided to edge in that direction himself, with the result that we collided in the doorway with a good deal of force, and staggered out into the hall together. He came smartly out of the clinch and grabbed an umbrella from the rack.

'Stand back!' he shouted, waving it overhead. 'Stand back, sir! I am armed!'

It seemed to me that the moment had come to be soothing.

'Awfully sorry I barged into you,' I said. 'Wouldn't have had it happen for worlds. I was just dashing out to have a look into things.'

He appeared a trifle reassured, and lowered the umbrella. But just then the most frightful shindy started in the bedroom. It sounded as though all the cats in London, assisted by delegates from outlying suburbs, had got together to settle their differences once for all. A sort of augmented orchestra of cats.

'This noise is unendurable,' yelled Sir Roderick. 'I cannot hear myself speak.'

'I fancy, sir,' said Jeeves respectfully, 'that the animals may have become somewhat exhilarated as the result of having discovered the fish under Mr Wooster's bed.'

The old boy tottered.

'Fish! Did I hear you rightly?'

'Sir?'

'Did you say that there was a fish under Mr Wooster's bed?'

'Yes, sir.'

Sir Roderick gave a low moan, and reached for his hat and stick.

'You aren't going?' I said.

'Mr Wooster, I am going! I prefer to spend my leisure time

in less eccentric society.'

'But I say. Here, I must come with you. I'm sure the whole business can be explained. Jeeves, my hat.'

Jeeves rallied round. I took the hat from him and shoved it on my head.

'Good heavens!'

Beastly shock it was! The bally thing had absolutely engulfed me, if you know what I mean. Even as I was putting it on I got a sort of impression that it was a trifle roomy; and no sooner had I let it go than it settled down over my ears like a kind of extinguisher.

'I say! This isn't my hat!'

'It is my hat!' said Sir Roderick in about the coldest, nastiest voice I'd ever heard. 'The hat which was stolen from me this morning as I drove in my car.'

'But—'

I suppose Napoleon or somebody like that would have been equal to the situation, but I'm bound to say it was too much for me. I just stood there goggling in a sort of coma, while the old boy lifted the hat off me and turned to Jeeves.

'I should be glad, my man,' he said, 'if you would accompany me a few yards down the street. I wish to ask you some questions.'

'Very good, sir.'

'Here, but, I say—!' I began, but he left me standing. He stalked out, followed by Jeeves. And at that moment the row in the bedroom started again, louder than ever.

I was about fed up with the whole thing. I mean, cats in your bedroom – a bit thick, what? I didn't know how the dickens they had got in, but I was jolly well resolved that they weren't going to stay picnicking there any longer. I flung open the door. I got a momentary flash of about a hundred and fifteen cats of all sizes and colours scrapping in the middle of the room, and then they all shot past me with a rush and out of the front door; and all that was left of the mob-scene was the head of a whacking big fish, lying on the carpet and staring up at me in a rather austere sort of way, as if it wanted a written explanation and apology.

There was something about the thing's expression that absolutely chilled me, and I withdrew on tiptoe and shut the door. And, as I did so, I bumped into someone.

'Oh, sorry!' he said.

I spun round. It was the pink-faced chappie, Lord Something or other, the fellow I had met with Claude and Eustace.

'I say,' he said apologetically, 'awfully sorry to bother you, but those weren't my cats I met just now legging it downstairs, were they? They looked like my cats.'

'They came out of my bedroom.'

'Then they were my cats!' he said sadly. 'Oh, dash it!'

'Did you put cats in my bedroom?'

'Your man, what's-his-name, did. He rather decently said I could keep them there till my train went. I'd just come to fetch them. And now they've gone! Oh, well, it can't be helped,

I suppose. I'll take the hat and the fish, anyway.'

I was beginning to dislike this chappie.

'Did you put that bally fish there, too?'

'No, that was Eustace's. The hat was Claude's.'

I sank limply into a chair.

'I say, you couldn't explain this, could you?' I said. The chappie gazed at me in mild surprise.

'Why, don't you know all about it? I say!' He blushed profusely. 'Why, if you don't know about it, I shouldn't wonder if the whole thing didn't seem rummy to you.'

'Rummy is the word.'

'It was for The Seekers, you know?'

'The Seekers?'

'Rather a blood club, you know, up at Oxford, which your cousins and I are rather keen on getting into. You have to pinch something, you know, to get elected. Some sort of a souvenir, you know. A policeman's helmet, you know, or a door-knocker or something, you know. The room's decorated with the things at the annual dinner, and everybody makes speeches and all that sort of thing. Rather jolly! Well, we wanted rather to make a sort of special effort and do the thing in style, if you understand, so we came up to London to see if we couldn't pick up something here that would be a bit out of the ordinary. And we had the most amazing luck right from the start. Your cousin Claude managed to collect a quite decent top-hat out of a passing car and your cousin Eustace got away with a really goodish salmon or something from Harrods, and

I snaffled three excellent cats all in the first hour. We were fearfully braced, I can tell you. And then the difficulty was to know where to park the things till our train went. You look so beastly conspicuous, you know, tooling about London with a fish and a lot of cats. And then Eustace remembered you, and we all came on here in a cab. You were out, but your man said it would be all right. When we met you, you were in such a hurry that we hadn't time to explain. Well, I think I'll be taking the hat, if you don't mind.'

'It's gone.'

'Gone?'

'The fellow you pinched it from happened to be the man who was lunching here. He took it away with him.'

'Oh, I say! Poor old Claude will be upset. Well, how about the goodish salmon or something?'

'Would you care to view the remains?' He seemed all broken up when he saw the wreckage.

'I doubt if the committee would accept that,' he said sadly. 'There isn't a frightful lot of it left, what?'

'The cats ate the rest.'

He sighed deeply.

'No cats, no fish, no hat. We've had all our trouble for nothing. I do call that hard! And on top of that – I say, I hate to ask you, but you couldn't lend me a tenner, could you?'

'A tenner? What for?'

'Well, the fact is, I've got to pop round and bail Claude and Eustace out. They've been arrested.'

'Arrested!'

'Yes. You see, what with the excitement of collaring the hat and the salmon or something, added to the fact that we had rather a festive lunch, they got a bit above themselves, poor chaps, and tried to pinch a motor-lorry. Silly, of course, because I don't see how they could have got the thing to Oxford and shown it to the committee. Still, there wasn't any reasoning with them, and when the driver started making a fuss, there was a bit of a mix-up, and Claude and Eustace are more or less languishing in Vine Street police-station till I pop round and bail them out. So if you could manage a tenner – Oh, thanks, that's fearfully good of you. It would have been too bad to leave them there, what? I mean, they're both such frightfully good chaps, you know. Everybody likes them up at the Varsity. They're fearfully popular.'

'I bet they are!' I said.

When Jeeves came back, I was waiting for him on the mat. I wanted speech with the blighter.

'Well?' I said.

'Sir Roderick asked me a number of questions, sir, respecting your habits and mode of life, to which I replied guardedly.'

'I don't care about that. What I want to know is why you didn't explain the whole thing to him right at the start? A word from you would have put everything clear.'

'Yes, sir.'

'Now he's gone off thinking me a looney.'

'I should not be surprised, from his conversation with me, sir, if some such idea had not entered his head.'

I was just starting in to speak, when the telephone bell rang. Jeeves answered it.

'No, madam, Mr Wooster is not in. No, madam, I do not know when he will return. No, madam, he left no message. Yes, madam, I will inform him.' He put back the receiver. 'Mrs Gregson, sir.'

Aunt Agatha! I had been expecting it. Ever since the luncheon-party had blown out a fuse, her shadow had been hanging over me, so to speak.

'Does she know? Already?'

'I gather that Sir Roderick has been speaking to her on the telephone, sir, and—'

'No wedding bells for me, what?'

Jeeves coughed.

'Mrs Gregson did not actually confide in me, sir, but I fancy that some such thing may have occurred. She seemed decidedly agitated, sir.'

It's a rummy thing, but I'd been so snootered by the old boy and the cats and the fish and the hat and the pink-faced chappie and all the rest of it that the bright side simply hadn't occurred to me till now. By Jove, it was like a bally weight rolling off my chest! I gave a yelp of pure relief.

'Jeeves!' I said, 'I believe you worked the whole thing!'

'Sir?'

'I believe you had the jolly old situation in hand right from the start.'

'Well, sir, Spenser, Mrs Gregson's butler, who inadvertently chanced to overhear something of your conversation when you were lunching at the house, did mention certain of the details to me; and I confess that, though it may be a liberty to say so, I entertained hopes that something might occur to prevent the match. I doubt if the young lady was entirely suitable to you, sir.'

'And she would have shot you out on your ear five minutes after the ceremony.'

'Yes, sir. Spenser informed me that she had expressed some such intention. Mrs Gregson wishes you to call upon her immediately, sir.'

'She does, eh? What do you advise, Jeeves?'

'I think a trip abroad might prove enjoyable, sir.'

I shook my head. 'She'd come after me.'

'Not if you went far enough afield, sir. There are excellent boats leaving every Wednesday and Saturday for New York.'

'Jeeves,' I said, 'you are right, as always. Book the tickets.'

CHAPTER NINE
A Letter of Introduction

You know, the longer I live, the more clearly I see that half the trouble in this bally world is caused by the light-hearted and thoughtless way in which chappies dash off letters of introduction and hand them to other chappies to deliver to chappies of the third part. It's one of those things that make you wish you were living in the Stone Age. What I mean to say is, if a fellow in those days wanted to give anyone a letter of introduction, he had to spend a month or so carving it on a large-sized boulder, and the chances were that the other chappie got so sick of lugging the thing round in the hot sun that he dropped it after the first mile. But nowadays it's so easy to write letters of introduction that everybody does it without a second thought, with the result that some perfectly harmless cove like myself gets in the soup.

Mark you, all the above is what you might call the result of my riper experience. I don't mind admitting that in the first flush of the thing, so to speak, when Jeeves told me – this would be about three weeks after I'd landed in America – that a blighter called Cyril Bassington-Bassington had arrived and I found that he had brought a letter of introduction to me from Aunt Agatha . . . where was I? Oh, yes . . . I don't mind admitting, I was saying, that just at first I was rather bucked. You see, after the painful events which had resulted in my leaving England I hadn't expected to get any sort of letter from Aunt Agatha which would pass the censor, so to speak. And it was a pleasant surprise to open this one and find it almost civil. Chilly, perhaps, in parts, but on the whole quite tolerably polite. I looked on the thing as a hopeful sign. Sort of olive branch, you know. Or do I mean orange blossom? What I'm getting at is that the fact that Aunt Agatha was writing to me without calling me names seemed, more or less, like a step in the direction of peace.

And I was all for peace, and that right speedily. I'm not saying a word against New York, mind you. I liked the place, and was having quite a ripe time there. But the fact remains that a fellow who's been used to London all his life does get a trifle homesick on a foreign strand, and I wanted to pop back to the cosy old flat in Berkeley Street – which could only be done when Aunt Agatha had simmered down and got over the Glossop episode. I know that London is a biggish city, but, believe me, it isn't half big enough for any fellow to live in with Aunt Agatha when she's after him with the old hatchet. And so I'm bound to say I looked on this chump Bassington-Bassington, when he arrived, more or less as a Dove of Peace, and was all for him.

He would seem from contemporary accounts to have blown in one morning at seven forty-five, that being the ghastly sort of hour they shoot you off the liner in New York. He was given the respectful raspberry by Jeeves, and told to try again about three hours later, when there would be a sporting chance of my having sprung from my bed with a glad cry to welcome another day and all that sort of thing. Which was rather decent of Jeeves, by the way, for it so happened that there was a slight estrangement, a touch of coldness, a bit of a row in other words, between us at the moment because of some rather priceless purple socks which I was wearing against his wishes: and a lesser man might easily have snatched at the chance of getting back at me a bit by loosing Cyril into my bedchamber at a moment when I couldn't have stood a two-minutes' conversation with my dearest pal. For until I have had my early cup of tea and have brooded on life for a bit absolutely undisturbed, I'm not much of a lad for the merry chit-chat.

So Jeeves very sportingly shot Cyril out into the crisp morning air, and didn't let me know of his existence till he brought his card in with the Bohea.

'And what might all this be, Jeeves?' I said, giving the thing the glassy gaze.

'The gentleman has arrived from England, I understand, sir. He called to see you earlier in the day.'

'Good Lord, Jeeves! You don't mean to say the day starts

earlier than this?'

'He desired me to say he would return later, sir.'

'I've never heard of him. Have you ever head of him, Jeeves?'

'I am familiar with the name Bassington-Bassington, sir. There are three branches of the Bassington-Bassington family – the Shropshire Bassington-Bassingtons, the Hampshire Bassington-Bassingtons, and the Kent Bassington-Bassingtons.'

'England seems pretty well stocked up with Bassington-Bassingtons.'

'Tolerably so, sir.'

'No chance of a sudden shortage, I mean, what?'

'Presumably not, sir.'

'And what sort of a specimen is this one?'

'I could not say, sir, on such short acquaintance.'

'Will you give me a sporting two to one, Jeeves, judging from what you have seen of him, that this chappie is not a blighter or an excrescence?'

'No, sir. I should not care to venture such liberal odds.'

'I knew it. Well, the only thing that remains to be discovered is what kind of a blighter he is.'

'Time will tell, sir. The gentleman brought a letter for you, sir.'

'Oh, he did, did he?' I said, and grasped the communication. And then I recognized the handwriting. 'I say, Jeeves, this is from my Aunt Agatha!'

'Indeed, sir?'

'Don't dismiss it in that light way. Don't you see what this means? She says she wants me to look after this excrescence while he's in New York. By Jove, Jeeves, if I only fawn on him a bit, so that he sends back a favourable report to headquarters, I may yet be able to get back to England in time for Goodwood. Now is certainly the time for all good men to come to the aid of the party, Jeeves. We must rally round and cosset this cove in no uncertain manner.'

'Yes, sir.'

'He isn't going to stay in New York long,' I said, taking another look at the letter. 'He's headed for Washington. Going to give the nibs there the once-over, apparently, before taking a whirl at the Diplomatic Service. I should say that we can win this lad's esteem and affection with a lunch and a couple of dinners, what?'

'I fancy that should be entirely adequate, sir.'

'This is the jolliest thing that's happened since we left England. It looks to me as if the sun were breaking through the clouds.'

'Very possibly, sir.'

He started to put out my things, and there was an awkward sort of silence.

'Not those socks, Jeeves,' I said, gulping a bit but having a dash at the careless, off-hand tone. 'Give me the purple ones.'

'I beg your pardon, sir?'

'Those jolly purple ones.'

'Very good, sir.'

He lugged them out of the drawer as if he were a vegetarian fishing a caterpillar out of the salad. You could see he was feeling deeply. Deuced painful and all that, this sort of thing, but a chappie has got to assert himself every now and then. Absolutely.

I was looking for Cyril to show up again any time after breakfast, but he didn't appear: so towards one o'clock I trickled out to the Lambs Club, where I had an appointment to feed the Wooster face with a cove of the name of Caffyn I'd got pally with since my arrival – George Caffyn, a fellow who wrote plays and what not. I'd made a lot of friends during my stay in New York, the city being crammed with bonhomous lads who one and all extended a welcoming hand to the stranger in their midst.

Caffyn was a bit late, but bobbed up finally, saying that he had been kept at a rehearsal of his new musical comedy, Ask Dad; and we started in. We had just reached the coffee, when the waiter came up and said that Jeeves wanted to see me.

Jeeves was in the waiting-room. He gave the socks one pained look as I came in, then averted his eyes.

'Mr Bassington-Bassington has just telephoned, sir.'

'Oh?'

'Yes, sir.'

'Where is he?'

'In prison, sir.'

I reeled against the wallpaper. A nice thing to happen to Aunt Agatha's nominee on his first morning under my wing, I did not think!

'In prison!'

'Yes, sir. He said on the telephone that he had been arrested and would be glad if you could step round and bail him out.'

'Arrested! What for?'

'He did not favour me with his confidence in that respect, sir.'

'This is a bit thick, Jeeves.'

'Precisely, sir.'

I collected old George, who very decently volunteered to stagger along with me, and we hopped into a taxi. We sat around at the police-station for a bit on a wooden bench in a sort of anteroom, and presently a policeman appeared, leading in Cyril.

'Hallo! Hallo! Hallo!' I said. 'What?'

My experience is that a fellow never really looks his best just after he's come out of a cell. When I was up at Oxford, I used to have a regular job bailing out a pal of mine who never failed to get pinched every Boat-Race night, and he always looked like something that had been dug up by the roots. Cyril was in pretty much the same sort of shape. He had a black eye and a torn collar, and altogether was nothing to write home about – especially if one was writing to Aunt Agatha. He was a thin, tall chappie with a lot of light hair and pale-blue goggly eyes which made him look like one of the rarer kinds of fish.

'I got your message,' I said.

'Oh, are you Bertie Wooster?'

'Absolutely. And this is my pal George Caffyn. Writes plays and what not, don't you know.'

We all shook hands, and the policeman, having retrieved a piece of chewing-gum from the underside of a chair, where he had parked it against a rainy day, went off into a corner and began to contemplate the infinite.

'This is a rotten country,' said Cyril.

'Oh, I don't know, you know, don't you know!' I said.

'We do our best,' said George.

'Old George is an American,' I explained. 'Writes plays, don't you know, and what not.'

'Of course, I didn't invent the country,' said George. 'That was Columbus. But I shall be delighted to consider any improvements you may suggest and lay them before the proper authorities.'

'Well, why don't the policemen in New York dress properly?'

George took a look at the chewing officer across the room.

'I don't see anything missing,' he said.

'I mean to say, why don't they wear helmets like they do in London? Why do they look like postmen? It isn't fair on a fellow. Makes it dashed confusing. I was simply standing on the pavement, looking at things, when a fellow who looked like a postman prodded me in the ribs with a club. I didn't see why I should have postmen prodding me. Why the dickens should a fellow come three thousand miles to be prodded by postmen?'

'The point is well taken,' said George. 'What did you do?'

'I gave him a shove, you know. I've got a frightfully hasty temper, you know. All the Bassington-Bassingtons have got frightfully hasty tempers, don't you know! And then he biffed me in the eye and lugged me off to this beastly place.'

'I'll fix it, old son,' I said. And I hauled out the bank-roll and went off to open negotiations, leaving Cyril to talk to George. I don't mind admitting that I was a bit perturbed. There were furrows in the old brow, and I had a kind of foreboding feeling. As long as this chump stayed in New York, I was responsible for him: and he didn't give me the impression of being the species of cove a reasonable chappie would care to be responsible for for more than about three minutes.

I mused with a considerable amount of tensity over Cyril that night, when I had got home and Jeeves had brought me the final whisky. I couldn't help feeling that this first visit of his to America was going to be one of those times that try men's souls and what not. I hauled out Aunt Agatha's letter of introduction and re-read it, and there was no getting away from the fact that she undoubtedly appeared to be somewhat wrapped up in this blighter and to consider it my mission in life to shield him from harm while on the premises. I was deuced thankful that he had taken such a liking for George Caffyn, old George being a steady sort of cove. After I had got him out of his dungeon-cell, he and George had gone off together, as chummy as brothers, to watch the afternoon rehearsal of Ask Dad. There was some talk, I gathered, of their dining together. I felt pretty easy in my mind while George had his eye on him.

I had got about as far as this in my meditations, when Jeeves came in with a telegram. At least, it wasn't a telegram: it was a cable – from Aunt Agatha, and this is what it said:

Has Cyril Bassington-Bassington called yet? On no account introduce him into theatrical circles. Vitally important. Letter follows.

I read it a couple of times.

'This is rummy, Jeeves!'

'Yes, sir?'

'Very rummy and dashed disturbing!'

'Will there be anything further tonight, sir?'

Of course, if he was going to be as bally unsympathetic as that there was nothing to be done. My idea had been to show him the cable and ask his advice. But if he was letting those purple socks rankle to that extent, the good old noblesse oblige of the Woosters couldn't lower itself to the extent of pleading with the man. Absolutely not. So I gave it a miss.

'Nothing more, thanks.'

'Good night, sir.'

'Good night.'

He floated away, and I sat down to think the thing over.

I had been directing the best efforts of the old bean to the problem for a matter of half an hour, when there was a ring at the bell. I went to the door, and there was Cyril, looking pretty festive.

'I'll come in for a bit if I may,' he said. 'Got something rather priceless to tell you.'

He curveted past me into the sitting-room, and when I got there after shutting the front door I found him reading Aunt Agatha's cable and giggling in a rummy sort of manner. 'Oughtn't to have looked at this, I suppose. Caught sight of my name and read it without thinking. I say, Wooster, old friend of my youth, this is rather funny. Do you mind if I have a drink? Thanks awfully and all that sort of rot. Yes, it's rather funny, considering what I came to tell you. Jolly old Caffyn has given me a small part in that musical comedy of his, Ask Dad. Only a bit, you know, but quite tolerably ripe. I'm feeling frightfully braced, don't you know!'

He drank his drink, and went on. He didn't seem to notice that I wasn't jumping about the room, yapping with joy.

'You know, I've always wanted to go on the stage, you know,' he said. 'But my jolly old guv'nor wouldn't stick it at any price. Put the old Waukeesi down with a bang, and turned bright purple whenever the subject was mentioned. That's the real reason why I came over here, if you want to know. I knew there wasn't a chance of my being able to work this stage wheeze in London without somebody getting on to it and tipping off the guv'nor, so I rather brainily sprang the scheme of popping over to Washington to broaden my mind. There's nobody to interfere on this side, you see, so I can go right ahead!'

I tried to reason with the poor chump.

'But your guv'nor will have to know some time.'

'That'll be all right. I shall be the jolly old star by then, and he won't have a leg to stand on.'

'It seems to me he'll have one leg to stand on while he kicks me with the other.'

'Why, where do you come in? What have you got to do with it?'

'I introduced you to George Caffyn.'

'So you did, old top, so you did. I'd quite forgotten. I ought to have thanked you before. Well, so long. There's an early rehearsal of Ask Dad tomorrow morning, and I must be toddling. Rummy the thing should be called Ask Dad, when that's just what I'm not going to do. See what I mean, what, what? Well, pip-pip!'

'Toodle-oo!' I said sadly, and the blighter scudded off. I dived for the phone and called up George Caffyn.

'I say, George, what's all this about Cyril Bassington-Bassington?'

'What about him?'

'He tells me you've given him a part in your show.'

'Oh, yes. Just a few lines.'

'But I've just had fifty-seven cables from home telling me on no account to let him go on the stage.'

'I'm sorry. But Cyril is just the type I need for that part. He's simply got to be himself.'

'It's pretty tough on me, George, old man. My Aunt Agatha sent this blighter over with a letter of introduction to me, and she will hold me responsible.'

'She'll cut you out of her will?'

'It isn't a question of money. But – of course, you've never met my Aunt Agatha, so it's rather hard to explain. But she's a sort of human vampire-bat, and she'll make things most fearfully unpleasant for me when I go back to England. She's the kind of woman who comes and rags you before breakfast, don't you know.'

'Well, don't go back to England, then. Stick here and become President.'

'But, George, old top—!'

'Good night!'

'But, I say, George, old man!'

'You didn't get my last remark. It was "Good night!" You Idle Rich may not need any sleep, but I've got to be bright and fresh in the morning. God bless you!'

I felt as if I hadn't a friend in the world. I was so jolly well worked up that I went and banged on Jeeves's door. It wasn't a thing I'd have cared to do as a rule, but it seemed to me that now was the time for all good men to come to the aid of the party, so to speak, and that it was up to Jeeves to rally round the young master, even if it broke up his beauty-sleep.

Jeeves emerged in a brown dressing-gown.

'Sir?'

'Deuced sorry to wake you up, Jeeves, and what not, but all sorts of dashed disturbing things have been happening.'

'I was not asleep. It is my practice, on retiring, to read a few pages of some instructive book.'

'That's good! What I mean to say is, if you've just finished exercising the old bean, it's probably in mid-season form for tackling problems. Jeeves, Mr Bassington-Bassington is going on the stage!'

'Indeed, sir?'

'Ah! The thing doesn't hit you! You don't get it properly! Here's the point. All his family are most fearfully dead against his going on the stage. There's going to be no end of trouble if he isn't headed off. And, what's worse, my Aunt Agatha will blame me, you see.'

'I see, sir.'

'Well, can't you think of some way of stopping him?'

'Not, I confess, at the moment, sir.'

'Well, have a stab at it.'

'I will give the matter my best consideration, sir. Will there be anything further tonight?'

'I hope not! I've had all I can stand already.'

'Very good, sir.'

He popped off.

CHAPTER TEN
Startling Dressiness of a Lift Attendant

The part which old George had written for the chump
Cyril took up about two pages of typescript; but it
might have been Hamlet, the way that poor, misguided
pinhead worked himself to the bone over it. I suppose, if I
heard him read his lines once I did it a dozen times in the first
couple of days. He seemed to think that my only feeling about
the whole affair was one of enthusiastic admiration, and that
he could rely on my support and sympathy. What with trying
to imagine how Aunt Agatha was going to take this thing, and
being woken up out of the dreamless in the small hours every
other night to give my opinion of some new bit of business
which Cyril had invented, I became more or less the good old
shadow. And all the time Jeeves remained still pretty cold and
distant about the purple socks. It's this sort of thing that ages a
chappie, don't you know, and makes his youthful joie-de-vivre
go a bit groggy at the knees.

In the middle of it Aunt Agatha's letter arrived. It took her about six pages to do justice to Cyril's father's feelings in regard to his going on the stage and about six more to give me a kind of sketch of what she would say, think, and do if I didn't keep him clear of injurious influences while he was in America. The letter came by the afternoon mail, and left me with a pretty firm conviction that it wasn't a thing I ought to keep to myself. I didn't even wait to ring the bell: I whizzed for the kitchen, bleating for Jeeves, and butted into the middle of a regular tea-party of sorts. Seated at the table were a depressed-looking cove who might have been a valet or something, and a boy in a Norfolk suit. The valet-chappie was drinking a whisky and soda, and the boy was being tolerably rough with some jam and cake.

'Oh, I say, Jeeves!' I said. 'Sorry to interrupt the feast of reason and flow of soul and so forth, but—'

At this juncture the small boy's eye hit me like a bullet and stopped me in my tracks. It was one of those cold, clammy, accusing sort of eyes – the kind that makes you reach up to see if your tie is straight: and he looked at me as if I were some sort of unnecessary product which Cuthbert the Cat had brought in after a ramble among the local ash-cans. He was a stoutish infant with a lot of freckles and a good deal of jam on his face.

'Hallo! Hallo! Hallo!' I said. 'What?' There didn't seem much else to say.

The stripling stared at me in a nasty sort of way through the jam. He may have loved me at first sight, but the impression he gave me was that he didn't think a lot of me and wasn't betting much that I would improve a great deal on acquaintance. I had a kind of feeling that I was about as popular with him as a cold Welsh rarebit.

'What's your name?' he asked.

'My name? Oh, Wooster, don't you know, and what not.'

'My pop's richer than you are!'

That seemed to be all about me. The child, having said his say, started in on the jam again. I turned to Jeeves: 'I say, Jeeves, can you spare a moment? I want to show you something.'

'Very good, sir.' We toddled into the sitting-room.

'Who is your little friend, Sidney the Sunbeam, Jeeves?'

'The young gentleman, sir?'

'It's a loose way of describing him, but I know what you mean.'

'I trust I was not taking a liberty in entertaining him, sir?'

'Not a bit. If that's your idea of a large afternoon, go ahead.'

'I happened to meet the young gentleman taking a walk with his father's valet, sir, whom I used to know somewhat intimately in London, and I ventured to invite them both to join me here.'

'Well, never mind about him, Jeeves. Read this letter.'

He gave it the up-and-down.

'Very disturbing, sir!' was all he could find to say.

'What are we going to do about it?'

'Time may provide a solution, sir.'

'On the other hand, it mayn't, what?'

'Extremely true, sir.'

We'd got as far as this, when there was a ring at the door. Jeeves shimmered off, and Cyril blew in, full of good cheer and blitheringness.

'I say, Wooster, old thing,' he said, 'I want your advice. You know this jolly old part of mine. How ought I to dress it? What I mean is, the first act scene is laid in an hotel of sorts, at about three in the afternoon. What ought I to wear, do you think?'

I wasn't feeling fit for a discussion of gent's suitings.

'You'd better consult Jeeves,' I said.

'A hot and by no means unripe idea! Where is he?'

'Gone back to the kitchen, I suppose.'

'I'll smite the good old bell, shall I? Yes. No?'

'Right-o!'

Jeeves poured silently in.

'Oh, I say, Jeeves,' began Cyril, 'I just wanted to have a syllable or two with you. It's this way— Hallo, who's this?'

I then perceived that the stout stripling had trickled into the room after Jeeves. He was standing near the door looking at Cyril as if his worst fears had been realized. There was a bit of a silence. The child remained there, drinking Cyril in for about half a minute; then he gave his verdict:

'Fish-face!'

'Eh? What?' said Cyril.

The child, who had evidently been taught at his mother's knee to speak the truth, made his meaning a trifle clearer.

'You've a face like a fish!'

He spoke as if Cyril was more to be pitied than censured, which I am bound to say I thought rather decent and broadminded of him. I don't mind admitting that, whenever I looked at Cyril's face, I always had a feeling that he couldn't have got that way without its being mostly his own fault. I found myself warming to this child. Absolutely, don't you know. I liked his conversation.

It seemed to take Cyril a moment or two really to grasp the thing, and then you could hear the blood of the Bassington-Bassingtons begin to sizzle.

'Well, I'm dashed!' he said. 'I'm dashed if I'm not!'

'I wouldn't have a face like that,' proceeded the child, with a good deal of earnestness, 'not if you gave me a million dollars.' He thought for a moment, then corrected himself. 'Two million dollars!' he added.

Just what occurred then I couldn't exactly say, but the next few minutes were a bit exciting. I take it that Cyril must have made a dive for the infant. Anyway, the air seemed pretty well congested with arms and legs and things. Something bumped into the Wooster waistcoat just around the third button, and I collapsed on to the settee and rather lost interest in things for the moment. When I had unscrambled myself, I found that Jeeves and the child had retired and Cyril was standing in the middle of the room snorting a bit.

'Who's that frightful little brute, Wooster?'

'I don't know. I never saw him before today.'

'I gave him a couple of tolerably juicy buffets before he

legged it. I say, Wooster, that kid said a dashed odd thing. He yelled out something about Jeeves promising him a dollar if he called me – er – what he said.'

It sounded pretty unlikely to me.

'What would Jeeves do that for?'

'It struck me as rummy, too.'

'Where would be the sense of it?'

'That's what I can't see.'

'I mean to say, it's nothing to Jeeves what sort of a face you have!'

'No!' said Cyril. He spoke a little coldly, I fancied. I don't know why. 'Well, I'll be popping. Toodle-oo!'

'Pip-pip!'

It must have been about a week after this rummy little episode that George Caffyn called me up and asked me if I would care to go and see a run-through of his show. Ask Dad, it seemed, was to open out of town in Schenectady on the following Monday, and this was to be a sort of preliminary dress-rehearsal. A preliminary dress-rehearsal, old George explained, was the same as a regular dress-rehearsal inasmuch as it was apt to look like nothing on earth and last into the small hours, but more exciting because they wouldn't be timing the piece and consequently all the blighters who on these occasions let their angry passions rise would have plenty of scope for interruptions, with the result that a pleasant time would be had by all.

The thing was billed to start at eight o'clock, so I rolled up at ten-fifteen, so as not to have too long to wait before they began. The dress-parade was still going on. George was on the stage, talking to a cove in shirt-sleeves and an absolutely round chappie with big spectacles and a practically hairless dome. I had seen George with the latter merchant once or twice at the club, and I knew that he was Blumenfield, the manager. I waved to George, and slid into a seat at the back of the house, so as to be out of the way when the fighting started. Presently George hopped down off the stage and came and joined me, and fairly soon after that the curtain went down. The chappie at the piano whacked out a well-meant bar or two, and the curtain went up again.

I can't quite recall what the plot of Ask Dad was about, but I do know that it seemed able to jog along all right without much help from Cyril. I was rather puzzled at first. What I mean is, through brooding on Cyril and hearing him in his part and listening to his views on what ought and what ought not to be done, I suppose I had got a sort of impression rooted in the old bean that he was pretty well the backbone of the show, and that the rest of the company didn't do much except go on and fill in when he happened to be off the stage. I sat there for nearly half an hour, waiting for him to make his entrance, until I suddenly discovered he had been on from the start. He was, in fact, the rummy-looking plug-ugly who was now leaning against a potted palm a couple of feet from the O.P. side, trying to appear intelligent while the heroine sang a song about Love being like something which for the moment has slipped my memory. After the second refrain he began to dance in company with a dozen other equally weird birds. A painful spectacle for one who could see a vision of Aunt Agatha reaching for the hatchet and old Bassington-Bassington senior putting on his strongest pair of hob-nailed boots. Absolutely!

The dance had just finished, and Cyril and his pals had shuffled off into the wings when a voice spoke from the darkness on my right.

'Pop!'

Old Blumenfield clapped his hands, and the hero, who had just been about to get the next line off his diaphragm, cheesed it. I peered into the shadows. Who should it be but Jeeves's little playmate with the freckles! He was now strolling down the aisle with his hands in his pockets as if the place belonged to him. An air of respectful attention seemed to pervade the building.

'Pop,' said the stripling, 'that number's no good.' Old Blumenfield beamed over his shoulder.

'Don't you like it, darling?'

'It gives me a pain.'

'You're dead right.'

'You want something zippy there. Something with a bit of jazz to it!'

'Quite right, my boy. I'll make a note of it. All right. Go on!'

I turned to George, who was muttering to himself in rather an overwrought way.

'I say, George, old man, who the dickens is that kid?'

Old George groaned a bit hollowly, as if things were a trifle thick.

'I didn't know he had crawled in! It's Blumenfield's son. Now we're going to have a Hades of a time!'

'Does he always run things like this?'

'Always!'

'But why does old Blumenfield listen to him?'

'Nobody seems to know. It may be pure fatherly love, or he may regard him as a mascot. My own idea is that he thinks the kid has exactly the amount of intelligence of the average member of the audience, and that what makes a hit with him will please the general public. While, conversely, what he doesn't like will be too rotten for anyone. The kid is a pest, a wart, and a pot of poison, and should be strangled!'

The rehearsal went on. The hero got off his line. There was a slight outburst of frightfulness between the stage-manager and a Voice named Bill that came from somewhere near the roof, the subject under discussion being where the devil Bill's 'ambers' were at that particular juncture. Then things went on again until the moment arrived for Cyril's big scene.

I was still a trifle hazy about the plot, but I had got on to the fact that Cyril was some sort of an English peer who had come over to America doubtless for the best reasons. So far he had only had two lines to say. One was 'Oh, I say!' and the other was 'Yes, by Jove!'; but I seemed to recollect, from hearing him read his part, that pretty soon he was due rather to spread himself. I sat back in my chair and waited for him to bob up.

He bobbed up about five minutes later. Things had got a bit stormy by that time. The Voice and the stage-director had had another of their love-feasts – this time something to do with why Bill's 'blues' weren't on the job or something. And, almost as soon as that was over, there was a bit of unpleasantness because a flower-pot fell off a window-ledge and nearly brained the hero. The atmosphere was consequently more or less hotted up when Cyril, who had been hanging about at the back of the stage, breezed down centre and toed the mark for his most substantial chunk of entertainment. The heroine had been saying something – I forget what – and all the chorus, with Cyril at their head, had begun to surge round her in the restless sort of way those chappies always do when there's a number coming along.

Cyril's first line was, 'Oh, I say, you know, you mustn't say that, really!' and it seemed to me he passed it over the larynx with a goodish deal of vim and je-ne-sais-quoi. But, by Jove, before the heroine had time for the come-back, our little friend with the freckles had risen to lodge a protest.

'Pop!'

'Yes, darling?'

'That one's no good.'

'Which one, darling?'

'The one with a face like a fish.'

'But they all have faces like fish, darling.'

The child seemed to see the justice of this objection. He

became more definite.

'The ugly one.'

'Which ugly one? That one?' said old Blumenfield, pointing to Cyril.

'Yep! He's rotten!'

'I thought so myself.'

'He's a pill!'

'You're dead right, my boy. I've noticed it for some time.' Cyril had been gaping a bit while these few remarks were in progress. He now shot down to the footlights. Even from where I was sitting, I could see that these harsh words had hit the old Bassington-Bassington family pride a frightful wallop. He started to get pink in the ears, and then in the nose, and then in the cheeks, till in about a quarter of a minute he looked pretty much like an explosion in a tomato cannery on a sunset evening.

'What the deuce do you mean?'

'What the deuce do you mean?' shouted old Blumenfield. 'Don't yell at me across the footlights!'

'I've a dashed good mind to come down and spank that little brute!'

'What!'

'A dashed good mind!'

Old Blumenfield swelled like a pumped-up tyre. He got rounder than ever.

'See here, mister – I don't know your darn name—!'

'My name's Bassington-Bassington, and the jolly old

Bassington-Bassingtons – I mean the Bassington-Bassingtons aren't accustomed—'

Old Blumenfield told him in a few brief words pretty much what he thought of the Bassington-Bassingtons and what they weren't accustomed to. The whole strength of the company rallied round to enjoy his remarks. You could see them jutting out from the wings and protruding from behind trees.

'You got to work good for my pop!' said the stout child, waggling his head reprovingly at Cyril.

'I don't want any bally cheek from you!' said Cyril, gurgling a bit.

'What's that?' barked old Blumenfield. 'Do you understand that this boy is my son?'

'Yes, I do,' said Cyril. 'And you both have my sympathy!'

'You're fired!' bellowed old Blumenfield, swelling a good bit more. 'Get out of my theatre!'

About half past ten next morning, just after I had finished lubricating the good old interior with a soothing cup of Oolong, Jeeves filtered into my bedroom, and said that Cyril was waiting to see me in the sitting-room.

'How does he look, Jeeves?'

'Sir?'

'What does Mr Bassington-Bassington look like?'

'It is hardly my place, sir, to criticize the facial peculiarities of your friends.'

'I don't mean that. I mean, does he appear peeved and

what not?'

'Not noticeably, sir. His manner is tranquil.'

'That's rum!'

'Sir?'

'Nothing. Show him in, will you?'

I'm bound to say I had expected to see Cyril showing a few more traces of last night's battle. I was looking for a bit of the overwrought soul and the quivering ganglions, if you know what I mean. He seemed pretty ordinary and quite fairly cheerful.

'Hallo, Wooster, old thing!'

'Cheero!'

'I just looked in to say good-bye.'

'Good-bye?'

'Yes. I'm off to Washington in an hour.' He sat down on the bed. 'You know, Wooster, old top,' he went on, 'I've been thinking it all over, and really it doesn't seem quite fair to the jolly old guv'nor, my going on the stage and so forth. What do you think?'

'I see what you mean.'

'I mean to say, he sent me over here to broaden my jolly old mind and words to that effect, don't you know, and I can't help thinking it would be a bit of a jar for the old boy if I gave him the bird and went on the stage instead. I don't know if you understand me, but what I mean to say is, it's a sort of question of conscience.'

'Can you leave the show without upsetting everything?'

'Oh, that's all right. I've explained everything to old Blumenfield, and he quite sees my position. Of course, he's sorry to lose me – said he didn't see how he could fill my place and all that sort of thing – but, after all, even if it does land him in a bit of a hole, I think I'm right in resigning my part, don't you?'

'Oh, absolutely.'

'I thought you'd agree with me. Well, I ought to be shifting. Awfully glad to have seen something of you, and all that sort of rot. Pip-pip!'

'Toodle-oo!'

He sallied forth, having told all those bally lies with the clear, blue, pop-eyed gaze of a young child. I rang for Jeeves. You know, ever since last night I had been exercising the old bean to some extent, and a good deal of light had dawned upon me.

'Jeeves!'

'Sir?'

'Did you put that pie-faced infant up to bally-ragging Mr Bassington-Bassington?'

'Sir?'

'Oh, you know what I mean. Did you tell him to get Mr Bassington-Bassington sacked from the Ask Dad company?'

'I would not take such a liberty, sir.' He started to put out my clothes. 'It is possible that young Master Blumenfield may have gathered from casual remarks of mine that I did not consider the stage altogether a suitable sphere for Mr

Bassington-Bassington.'

'I say, Jeeves, you know, you're a bit of a marvel.'

'I endeavour to give satisfaction, sir.'

'And I'm frightfully obliged, if you know what I mean. Aunt Agatha would have had sixteen or seventeen fits if you hadn't headed him off.'

'I fancy there might have been some little friction and unpleasantness, sir. I am laying out the blue suit with the thin red stripe, sir. I fancy the effect will be pleasing.'

It's a rummy thing, but I had finished breakfast and gone out and got as far as the lift before I remembered what it was that I had meant to do to reward Jeeves for his really sporting behaviour in this matter of the chump Cyril. It cut me to the heart to do it, but I had decided to give him his way and let those purple socks pass out of my life. After all, there are times when a cove must make sacrifices. I was just going to nip back and break the glad news to him, when the lift came up, so I thought I would leave it till I got home.

The coloured chappie in charge of the lift looked at me, as I hopped in, with a good deal of quiet devotion and what not.

'I wish to thank yo', suh,' he said, 'for yo' kindness.'

'Eh? What?'

'Misto' Jeeves done give me them purple socks, as you told him. Thank yo' very much, suh!'

I looked down. The blighter was a blaze of mauve from the ankle-bone southward. I don't know when I've seen anything so dressy.

'Oh, ah! Not at all! Right-o! Glad you like them!' I said.

Well, I mean to say, what? Absolutely!

CHAPTER ELEVEN
Comrade Bingo

The thing really started in the Park – at the Marble Arch end – where weird birds of every description collect on Sunday afternoons and stand on soap-boxes and make speeches. It isn't often you'll find me there, but it so happened that on the Sabbath after my return to the good old Metrop. I had a call to pay in Manchester Square, and, taking a stroll round in that direction so as not to arrive too early, I found myself right in the middle of it.

Now that the Empire isn't the place it was, I always think the Park on a Sunday is the centre of London, if you know what I mean. I mean to say, that's the spot that makes the returned exile really sure he's back again. After what you might call my enforced sojourn in New York I'm bound to say that I stood there fairly lapping it all up. It did me good to listen to the lads giving tongue and realize that all had ended happily and Bertram was home again.

On the edge of the mob farthest away from me a gang of

top-hatted chappies were starting an open-air missionary service; nearer at hand an atheist was letting himself go with a good deal of vim, though handicapped a bit by having no roof to his mouth; while in front of me there stood a little group of serious thinkers with a banner labelled 'Heralds of the Red Dawn'; and as I came up, one of the heralds, a bearded egg in a slouch hat and a tweed suit, was slipping it into the Idle Rich with such breadth and vigour that I paused for a moment to get an earful. While I was standing there somebody spoke to me.

'Mr Wooster, surely?'

Stout chappie. Couldn't place him for a second. Then I got him. Bingo Little's uncle, the one I had lunch with at the time when young Bingo was in love with that waitress at the Piccadilly bun-shop. No wonder I hadn't recognized him at first. When I had seen him last he had been a rather sloppy old gentleman – coming down to lunch, I remember, in carpet slippers and a velvet smoking-jacket; whereas now dapper simply wasn't the word. He absolutely gleamed in the sunlight in a silk hat, morning coat, lavender spats and sponge-bag trousers, as now worn. Dressy to a degree.

'Oh, hallo!' I said. 'Going strong?'

'I am in excellent health, I thank you. And you?'

'In the pink. Just been over to America.'

'Ah! Collecting local colour for one of your delightful romances?'

'Eh?' I had to think a bit before I got on to what he meant.

'Oh, no,' I said. 'Just felt I needed a change. Seen anything of Bingo lately?' I asked quickly, being desirous of heading the old thing off what you might call the literary side of my life.

'Bingo?'

'Your nephew.'

'Oh, Richard? No, not very recently. Since my marriage a little coolness seems to have sprung up.'

'Sorry to hear that. So you've married since I saw you, what? Mrs Little all right?'

'My wife is happily robust. But – er – not Mrs Little. Since we last met a gracious Sovereign has been pleased to bestow on me a signal mark of his favour in the shape of – ah – a peerage. On the publication of the last Honours List I became Lord Bittlesham.'

'By Jove! Really? I say, heartiest congratulations. That's the stuff to give the troops, what? Lord Bittlesham?' I said. 'Why, you're the owner of Ocean Breeze.'

'Yes. Marriage has enlarged my horizon in many directions. My wife is interested in horse-racing, and I now maintain a small stable. I understand that Ocean Breeze is fancied, as I am told the expression is, for a race which will take place at the end of the month at Goodwood, the Duke of Richmond's seat in Sussex.'

'The Goodwood Cup. Rather! I've got my chemise on it for one.'

'Indeed? Well, I trust the animal will justify your confidence. I know little of these matters myself, but my wife tells me that it is regarded in knowledgeable circles as what I believe is termed a snip.'

At this moment I suddenly noticed that the audience was gazing in our direction with a good deal of interest, and I saw that the bearded chappie was pointing at us.

'Yes, look at them! Drink them in!' he was yelling, his voice rising above the perpetual-motion fellow's and beating the missionary service all to nothing. 'There you see two typical members of the class which has down-trodden the poor for centuries. Idlers! Non-producers! Look at the tall thin one with the face like a motor-mascot. Has he ever done an honest day's work in his life? No! A prowler, a trifler, and a blood-sucker! And I bet he still owes his tailor for those trousers!'

He seemed to me to be verging on the personal, and I didn't think a lot of it. Old Bittlesham, on the other hand, was pleased and amused.

'A great gift of expression these fellows have,' he chuckled. 'Very trenchant.'

'And the fat one!' proceeded the chappie. 'Don't miss him. Do you know who that is? That's Lord Bittlesham! One of the worst. What has he ever done except eat four square meals a day? His god is his belly, and he sacrifices burnt-offerings to it. If you opened that man now you would find enough lunch to support ten working-class families for a week.'

'You know, that's rather well put,' I said, but the old boy didn't seem to see it. He had turned a brightish magenta and was bubbling like a kettle on the boil.

'Come away, Mr Wooster,' he said. 'I am the last man to oppose the right of free speech, but I refuse to listen to this vulgar abuse any longer.'

We legged it with quiet dignity, the chappie pursuing us with his foul innuendoes to the last. Dashed embarrassing.

Next day I looked in at the club, and found young Bingo in the smoking-room.

'Hallo, Bingo,' I said, toddling over to his corner full of bonhomie, for I was glad to see the chump. 'How's the boy?'

'Jogging along.'

'I saw your uncle yesterday.'

Young Bingo unleashed a grin that split his face in half.

'I know you did, you trifler. Well, sit down, old thing, and suck a bit of blood. How's the prowling these days?'

'Good Lord! You weren't there!'

'Yes, I was.'

'I didn't see you.'

'Yes, you did. But perhaps you didn't recognize me in the shrubbery.'

'The shrubbery?'

'The beard, my boy. Worth every penny I paid for it. Defies detection. Of course, it's a nuisance having people shouting "Beaver!" at you all the time, but one's got to put up with that.'

I goggled at him.

'I don't understand.'

'It's a long story. Have a martini or a small gore-and-soda, and I'll tell you all about it. Before we start, give me your honest opinion. Isn't she the most wonderful girl you ever saw in your puff?'

He had produced a photograph from somewhere, like a conjurer taking a rabbit out of a hat, and was waving it in front of me. It appeared to be a female of sorts, all eyes and teeth.

'Oh, Great Scott!' I said. 'Don't tell me you're in love again.'

He seemed aggrieved.

'What do you mean – again?'

'Well, to my certain knowledge you've been in love with at least half a dozen girls since the spring, and it's only July now. There was that waitress and Honoria Glossop and—'

'Oh, tush! Not to say pish! Those girls? Mere passing fancies. This is the real thing.'

'Where did you meet her?'

'On top of a bus. Her name is Charlotte Corday Rowbotham.'

'My God!'

'It's not her fault, poor child. Her father had her christened that because he's all for the Revolution, and it seems that the original Charlotte Corday used to go about stabbing oppressors in their baths, which entitles her to consideration and respect. You must meet old Rowbotham, Bertie. A delightful chap. Wants to massacre the bourgeoisie, sack Park Lane and disembowel the hereditary aristocracy. Well, nothing could be fairer than that, what? But about Charlotte.

We were on top of the bus, and it started to rain. I offered her my umbrella, and we chatted of this and that. I fell in love and got her address, and a couple of days later I bought the beard and toddled round and met the family.'

'But why the beard?'

'Well, she had told me all about her father on the bus, and I saw that to get any footing at all in the home I should have to join these Red Dawn blighters; and naturally, if I was to make speeches in the Park, where at any moment I might run into a dozen people I knew, something in the nature of a disguise was indicated. So I bought the beard, and, by Jove, old boy, I've become dashed attached to the thing. When I take it off to come in here, for instance, I feel absolutely nude. It's done me a lot of good with old Rowbotham. He thinks I'm a Bolshevist of sorts who has to go about disguised because of the police. You really must meet old Rowbotham, Bertie. I tell you what, are you doing anything tomorrow afternoon?'

'Nothing special. Why?'

'Good! Then you can have us all to tea at your flat. I had promised to take the crowd to Lyons' Popular Café after a meeting we're holding down in Lambeth, but I can save money this way; and, believe me, laddie, nowadays, as far as I'm concerned, a penny saved is a penny earned. My uncle told you he'd got married?'

'Yes. And he said there was a coolness between you.'

'Coolness? I'm down to zero. Ever since he married he's been launching out in every direction and economizing on me. I suppose that peerage cost the old devil the deuce of a sum. Even baronetcies have gone up frightfully nowadays, I'm told. And he's started a racing-stable. By the way, put your last collar stud on Ocean Breeze for the Goodwood Cup. It's a cert.'

'I'm going to.'

'It can't lose. I mean to win enough on it to marry Charlotte with. You're going to Goodwood, of course?'

'Rather!'

'So are we. We're holding a meeting on Cup day just outside the paddock.'

'But, I say, aren't you taking frightful risks? Your uncle's sure to be at Goodwood. Suppose he spots you? He'll be fed to the gills if he finds out that you're the fellow who ragged him in the Park.'

'How the deuce is he to find out? Use your intelligence, you prowling inhaler of red corpuscles. If he didn't spot me yesterday, why should he spot me at Goodwood? Well, thanks for your cordial invitation for tomorrow, old thing. We shall be delighted to accept. Do us well, laddie, and blessings shall reward you. By the way, I may have misled you by using the word "tea". None of your wafer slices of bread-and-butter. We're good trenchermen, we of the Revolution. What we shall require will be something on the order of scrambled eggs, muffins, jam, ham, cake and sardines. Expect us at five sharp.'

'But, I say, I'm not quite sure—'

'Yes, you are. Silly ass, don't you see that this is going

to do you a bit of good when the Revolution breaks loose? When you see old Rowbotham sprinting up Piccadilly with a dripping knife in each hand, you'll be jolly thankful to be able to remind him that he once ate your tea and shrimps. There will be four of us: Charlotte, self, the old man, and Comrade Butt. I suppose he will insist on coming along.'

'Who the devil's Comrade Butt?'

'Did you notice a fellow standing on my left in our little troupe yesterday? Small, shrivelled chap. Looks like a haddock with lung-trouble. That's Butt. My rival, dash him. He's sort of semi-engaged to Charlotte at the moment. Till I came along he was the blue-eyed boy. He's got a voice like a foghorn, and old Rowbotham thinks a lot of him. But, hang it, if I can't thoroughly encompass this Butt and cut him out and put him where he belongs among the discards – well, I'm not the man I was, that's all. He may have a big voice, but he hasn't my gift of expression. Thank heaven I was once cox of my college boat. Well, I must be pushing now. I say, you don't know how I could raise fifty quid somehow, do you?'

'Why don't you work?'

'Work?' said young Bingo, surprised. 'What, me? No, I shall have to think of some way. I must put at least fifty on Ocean Breeze. Well, see you tomorrow. God bless you, old sport, and don't forget the muffins.'

I don't know why, ever since I first knew him at school, I should have felt a rummy feeling of responsibility for young

Bingo. I mean to say, he's not my son (thank goodness) or my brother or anything like that. He's got absolutely no claim on me at all, and yet a large-sized chunk of my existence seems to be spent in fussing over him like a bally old hen and hauling him out of the soup. I suppose it must be some rare beauty in my nature or something. At any rate, this latest affair of his worried me. He seemed to be doing his best to marry into a family of pronounced loonies, and how the deuce he thought he was going to support even a mentally afflicted wife on nothing a year beat me. Old Bittlesham was bound to knock off his allowance if he did anything of the sort and, with a fellow like young Bingo, if you knocked off his allowance, you might just as well hit him on the head with an axe and make a clean job of it.

'Jeeves,' I said, when I got home, 'I'm worried.'

'Sir?'

'About Mr Little. I won't tell you about it now, because he's bringing some friends of his to tea tomorrow, and then you will be able to judge for yourself. I want you to observe closely, Jeeves, and form your decision.'

'Very good, sir.'

'And about the tea. Get in some muffins.'

'Yes, sir.'

'And some jam, ham, cake, scrambled eggs, and five or six wagonloads of sardines.'

'Sardines, sir?' said Jeeves, with a shudder.

'Sardines.'

There was an awkward pause.

'Don't blame me, Jeeves,' I said. 'It isn't my fault.'

'No, sir.'

'Well, that's that.'

'Yes, sir.'

I could see the man was brooding tensely.

I've found, as a general rule in life, that the things you think are going to be the scaliest nearly always turn out not so bad after all; but it wasn't that way with Bingo's tea-party. From the moment he invited himself I felt that the thing was going to be blue round the edges, and it was. And I think the most gruesome part of the whole affair was the fact that, for the first time since I'd known him, I saw Jeeves come very near to being rattled. I suppose there's a chink in everyone's armour, and young Bingo found Jeeves's right at the drop of the flag when he breezed in with six inches or so of brown beard hanging on to his chin. I had forgotten to warn Jeeves about the beard, and it came on him absolutely out of a blue sky. I saw the man's jaw drop, and he clutched at the table for support. I don't blame him, mind you. Few people have ever looked fouler than young Bingo in the fungus. Jeeves paled a little; then the weakness passed and he was himself again. But I could see that he had been shaken.

Young Bingo was too busy introducing the mob to take much notice. They were a very C3 collection. Comrade Butt looked like one of the things that come out of dead trees after the rain; moth-eaten was the word I should have used to describe old Rowbotham; and as for Charlotte, she seemed to take me straight into another and a dreadful world. It wasn't that she was exactly bad-looking. In fact, if she had knocked off starchy foods and done Swedish exercises for a bit, she might have been quite tolerable. But there was too much of her. Billowy curves. Well-nourished, perhaps, expresses it best. And, while she may have had a heart of gold, the thing you noticed about her first was that she had a tooth of gold. I know that young Bingo, when in form, could fall in love with practically anything of the other sex; but this time I couldn't see any excuse for him at all.

'My friend, Mr Wooster,' said Bingo, completing the ceremonial.

Old Rowbotham looked at me and then he looked round the room, and I could see he wasn't particularly braced. There's nothing of absolutely Oriental luxury about the old flat, but I have managed to make myself fairly comfortable, and I suppose the surroundings jarred him a bit.

'Mr Wooster?' said old Rowbotham. 'May I say Comrade Wooster?'

'I beg your pardon?'

'Are you of the movement?'

'Well – er—'

'Do you yearn for the Revolution?'

'Well, I don't know that I exactly yearn. I mean to say, as far as I can make out, the whole hub of the scheme seems to be to massacre coves like me; and I don't mind owning I'm not frightfully keen on the idea.'

'But I'm talking him round,' said Bingo. 'I'm wrestling with him. A few more treatments ought to do the trick.'

Old Rowbotham looked at me a bit doubtfully.

'Comrade Little has great eloquence,' he admitted.

'I think he talks something wonderful,' said the girl, and young Bingo shot a glance of such succulent devotion at her that I reeled in my tracks. It seemed to depress Comrade Butt a good deal too. He scowled at the carpet and said something about dancing on volcanoes.

'Tea is served, sir,' said Jeeves.

'Tea, pa!' said Charlotte, starting at the word like the old war-horse who hears the bugle; and we got down to it.

Funny how one changes as the years roll on. At school, I remember, I would cheerfully have sold my soul for scrambled eggs and sardines at five in the afternoon; but somehow, since reaching man's estate, I had rather dropped out of the habit; and I'm bound to admit I was appalled to a goodish extent at the way the sons and daughter of the Revolution shoved their heads down and went for the foodstuffs. Even Comrade Butt cast off his gloom for a space and immersed his whole being in scrambled eggs, only coming to the surface at intervals to grab another cup of tea. Presently the hot water gave out, and I turned to Jeeves.

'More hot water.'

'Very good, sir.'

'Hey! what's this? What's this?' Old Rowbotham had

lowered his cup and was eyeing us sternly. He tapped Jeeves on the shoulder. 'No servility, my lad; no servility!'

'I beg your pardon, sir?'

'Don't call me "sir". Call me Comrade. Do you know what you are, my lad? You're an obsolete relic of an exploded feudal system.'

'Very good, sir.'

'If there's one thing that makes my blood boil in my veins—'

'Have another sardine,' chipped in young Bingo – the first sensible thing he'd done since I had known him. Old Rowbotham took three and dropped the subject, and Jeeves drifted away. I could see by the look of his back what he felt.

At last, just as I was beginning to feel that it was going on for ever, the thing finished. I woke up to find the party getting ready to leave.

Sardines and about three quarts of tea had mellowed old Rowbotham. There was quite a genial look in his eye as he shook my hand.

'I must thank you for your hospitality, Comrade Wooster,' he said.

'Oh, not at all! Only too glad—'

'Hospitality?' snorted the man Butt, going off in my ear like a depth-charge. He was scowling in a morose sort of manner at young Bingo and the girl, who were giggling together by the window. 'I wonder the food didn't turn to ashes in our mouths! Eggs! Muffins! Sardines! All wrung from the bleeding lips of the starving poor!'

'Oh, I say! What a beastly idea!'

'I will send you some literature on the subject of the Cause,' said old Rowbotham. 'And soon, I hope, we shall see you at one of our little meetings.'

Jeeves came in to clear away, and found me sitting among the ruins. It was all very well for Comrade Butt to knock the food, but he had pretty well finished the ham; and if you had shoved the remainder of the jam into the bleeding lips of the starving poor it would hardly have made them sticky.

'Well, Jeeves,' I said, 'how about it?'

'I would prefer to express no opinion, sir.'

'Jeeves, Mr Little is in love with that female.'

'So I gathered, sir. She was slapping him in the passage.'

I clutched my brow.

'Slapping him?'

'Yes, sir. Roguishly.'

'Great Scott! I didn't know it had got as far as that. How did Comrade Butt seem to be taking it? Or perhaps he didn't see?'

'Yes, sir, he observed the entire proceedings. He struck me as extremely jealous.'

'I don't blame him. Jeeves, what are we to do?'

'I could not say, sir.'

'It's a bit thick.'

'Very much so, sir.'

And that was all the consolation I got from Jeeves.

CHAPTER TWELVE
Bingo Has a Bad Goodwood

I had promised to meet young Bingo next day, to tell him what I thought of his infernal Charlotte, and I was mooching slowly up St James's Street, trying to think how the dickens I could explain to him, without hurting his feelings, that I considered her one of the world's foulest, when who should come toddling out of the Devonshire Club but old Bittlesham and Bingo himself. I hurried on and overtook them.

'What-ho!' I said.

The result of this simple greeting was a bit of a shock. Old Bittlesham quivered from head to foot like a poleaxed blancmange. His eyes were popping and his face had gone sort of greenish.

'Mr Wooster!' He seemed to recover somewhat, as if I wasn't the worst thing that could have happened to him. 'You gave me a severe start.'

'Oh, sorry!'

'My uncle,' said young Bingo in a hushed, bedside sort of voice, 'isn't feeling quite himself this morning. He's had a threatening letter.'

'I go in fear of my life,' said old Bittlesham.

'Threatening letter?'

'Written,' said old Bittlesham, 'in an uneducated hand and couched in terms of uncompromising menaces. Mr Wooster, do you recall a sinister, bearded man who assailed me in no measured terms in Hyde Park last Sunday?'

I jumped, and shot a look at young Bingo. The only expression on his face was one of grave, kindly concern.

'Why – ah – yes,' I said. 'Bearded man. Chap with a beard.'

'Could you identify him, if necessary?'

'Well, I – er – how do you mean?'

'The fact is, Bertie,' said Bingo, 'we think this man with the beard is at the bottom of all this business. I happened to be walking late last night through Pounceby Gardens, where Uncle Mortimer lives, and as I was passing the house a fellow came hurrying down the steps in a furtive sort of way. Probably he had just been shoving the letter in at the front door. I noticed that he had a beard. I didn't think any more of it, however, until this morning, when Uncle Mortimer showed me the letter he had received and told me about the chap in the Park. I'm going to make inquiries.'

'The police should be informed,' said Lord Bittlesham.

'No,' said young Bingo firmly, 'not at this stage of the proceedings. It would hamper me. Don't you worry, uncle; I think I can track this fellow down. You leave it all to me. I'll pop you into a taxi now, and go and talk it over with Bertie.'

'You're a good boy, Richard,' said old Bittlesham, and we put him in a passing cab and pushed off. I turned and looked young Bingo squarely in the eyeball.

'Did you send that letter?' I said.

'Rather! You ought to have seen it, Bertie! One of the best gent's ordinary threatening letters I ever wrote.'

'But where's the sense of it?'

'Bertie, my lad,' said Bingo, taking me earnestly by the coat-sleeve, 'I had an excellent reason. Posterity may say of me what it will, but one thing it can never say – that I have not a good solid business head. Look here!' He waved a bit of paper in front of my eyes.

'Great Scott!' It was a cheque – an absolute, dashed cheque for fifty of the best, signed Bittlesham, and made out to the order of R. Little.

'What's that for?'

'Expenses,' said Bingo, pouching it. 'You don't suppose an investigation like this can be carried on for nothing, do you! I now proceed to the bank and startle them into a fit with it. Later I edge round to my bookie and put the entire sum on Ocean Breeze. What you want in situations of this kind, Bertie, is tact. If I had gone to my uncle and asked him for fifty quid, would I have got it? No! But by exercising tact— Oh! by the way, what do you think of Charlotte?'

'Well – er—'

Young Bingo massaged my sleeve affectionately.

'I know, old man, I know. Don't try to find words. She bowled you over, eh? Left you speechless, what? I know! That's the effect she has on everybody. Well, I leave you here, laddie. Oh, before we part – Butt! What of Butt? Nature's worst blunder, don't you think?'

'I must say I've seen cheerier souls.'

'I think I've got him licked, Bertie. Charlotte is coming to the Zoo with me this afternoon. Alone. And later on to the pictures. That looks like the beginning of the end, what? Well, toodleoo, friend of my youth. If you've nothing better to do this morning, you might take a stroll along Bond Street and be picking out a wedding present.'

I lost sight of Bingo after that. I left messages a couple of times at the club, asking him to ring me up, but they didn't have any effect. I took it that he was too busy to respond. The Sons of the Red Dawn also passed out of my life, though Jeeves told me he had met Comrade Butt one evening and had a brief chat with him. He reported Butt as gloomier than ever. In the competition for the bulging Charlotte, Butt had apparently gone right back in the betting.

'Mr Little would appear to have eclipsed him entirely, sir,' said Jeeves.

'Bad news, Jeeves; bad news!'

'Yes, sir.'

'I suppose what it amounts to, Jeeves, is that, when young Bingo really takes his coat off and starts in, there is no power of God or man that can prevent him making a chump of himself.'

'It would seem so, sir,' said Jeeves.

Then Goodwood came along, and I dug out the best suit and popped down.

I never know, when I'm telling a story, whether to cut the thing down to plain facts or whether to drool on and shove in a lot of atmosphere, and all that. I mean, many a cove would no doubt edge into the final spasm of this narrative with a long description of Goodwood, featuring the blue sky, the rolling prospect, the joyous crowds of pickpockets, and the parties of the second part who were having their pockets picked, and – in a word, what not. But better give it a miss, I think. Even if I wanted to go into details about the bally meeting I don't think I'd have the heart to. The thing's too recent. The anguish hasn't had time to pass. You see, what happened was that Ocean Breeze (curse him!) finished absolutely nowhere for the Cup. Believe me, nowhere.

These are the times that try men's souls. It's never pleasant to be caught in the machinery when a favourite comes unstitched, and in the case of this particular dashed animal, one had come to look on the running of the race as a pure formality, a sort of quaint, old-world ceremony to be gone through before one sauntered up to the bookie and collected. I had wandered out of the paddock to try and forget, when I bumped into old Bittlesham: and he looked so rattled and purple, and his eyes were standing out of his head at such an angle, that I simply pushed my hand out and shook his in silence.

'Me, too,' I said. 'Me, too. How much did you drop?'

'Drop?'

'On Ocean Breeze.'

'I did not bet on Ocean Breeze.'

'What! You owned the favourite for the Cup, and didn't back it!'

'I never bet on horse-racing. It is against my principles. I am told that the animal failed to win the contest.'

'Failed to win! Why, he was so far behind that he nearly came in first in the next race.'

'Tut!' said old Bittlesham.

'Tut is right,' I agreed. Then the rumminess of the thing struck me. 'But if you haven't dropped a parcel over the race,' I said, 'why are you looking so rattled?'

'That fellow is here!'

'What fellow?'

'That bearded man.'

It will show you to what an extent the iron had entered into my soul when I say that this was the first time I had given a thought to young Bingo. I suddenly remembered now that he had told me he would be at Goodwood.

'He is making an inflammatory speech at this very moment, specifically directed at me. Come! Where that crowd is.' He lugged me along and, by using his weight scientifically, got us into the front rank. 'Look! Listen!'

Young Bingo was certainly tearing off some ripe stuff. Inspired by the agony of having put his little all on a stumer that hadn't finished in the first six, he was fairly letting himself go on the subject of the blackness of the hearts of plutocratic owners who allowed a trusting public to imagine a horse was the real goods when it couldn't trot the length of its stable without getting its legs crossed and sitting down to rest. He then went on to draw what I'm bound to say was a most moving picture of a working man's home, due to this dishonesty. He showed us the working man, all optimism and simple trust, believing every word he read in the papers about Ocean Breeze's form; depriving his wife and children of food in order to back the brute; going without beer so as to be able to cram an extra bob on; robbing the baby's money-box with a hatpin on the eve of the race; and finally getting let down with a thud. Dashed impressive it was. I could see old Rowbotham nodding his head gently, while poor old Butt glowered at the speaker with ill-concealed jealousy. The audience ate it.

'But what does Lord Bittlesham care,' shouted Bingo, 'if the poor working man loses his hard-earned savings? I tell you, friends and comrades, you may talk, and you may argue, and you may cheer, and you may pass resolutions, but what you need is Action! Action! The world won't be a fit place for honest men to live in till the blood of Lord Bittlesham and his kind flows down the gutters of Park Lane!'

Roars of approval from the populace, most of whom, I suppose, had had their little bit on blighted Ocean Breeze, and were feeling it deeply. Old Bittlesham bounded over to a large, sad policeman who was watching the proceedings, and appeared to be urging him to rally round. The policeman pulled at his moustache, and smiled gently, but that was as far as he seemed inclined to go; and old Bittlesham came back to me, puffing not a little.

'It's monstrous! The man definitely threatens my personal safety, and that policeman declines to interfere. Said it was just talk! Talk! It's monstrous!'

'Absolutely,' I said, but I can't say it seemed to cheer him up much.

Comrade Butt had taken the centre of the stage now. He had a voice like the Last Trump, and you could hear every word he said, but somehow he didn't seem to be clicking. I suppose the fact was he was too impersonal, if that's the word I want. After Bingo's speech the audience was in the mood for something a good deal snappier than just general remarks about the Cause. They had started to heckle the poor blighter pretty freely, when he stopped in the middle of a sentence, and I saw that he was staring at old Bittlesham.

The crowd thought he had dried up.

'Suck a lozenge,' shouted someone.

Comrade Butt pulled himself together with a jerk, and even from where I stood I could see the nasty gleam in his eye.

'Ah,' he yelled, 'you may mock, comrades; you may jeer and sneer; and you may scoff; but let me tell you that the movement is spreading every day and every hour. Yes, even amongst the so called upper classes it's spreading. Perhaps you'll believe me when I tell you that here, today, on this very spot, we have in our little band one of our most earnest workers, the nephew of that very Lord Bittlesham whose name you were hooting but a moment ago.'

And before old Bingo had a notion of what was up, he had reached out a hand and grabbed the beard. It came off all in one piece, and, well as Bingo's speech had gone, it was simply nothing compared with the hit made by this bit of business. I heard old Bittlesham give one short, sharp snort of amazement at my side, and then any remarks he may have made were drowned in thunders of applause.

I'm bound to say that in this crisis young Bingo acted with a good deal of decision and character. To grab Comrade Butt by the neck and try to twist his head off was with him the work of a moment. But before he could get any results the sad policeman, brightening up like magic, had charged in, and the next minute he was shoving his way back through the crowd, with Bingo in his right hand and Comrade Butt in his left.

'Let me pass, sir, please,' he said, civilly, as he came up against old Bittlesham, who was blocking the gangway.

'Eh?' said old Bittlesham, still dazed.

At the sound of his voice young Bingo looked up quickly from under the shadow of the policeman's right hand, and as he did so all the stuffing seemed to go out of him with a rush. For an instant he drooped like a bally lily, and then shuffled brokenly on. His air was the air of a man who has got it in the neck properly.

Sometimes when Jeeves has brought in my morning tea and shoved it on the table beside my bed, he drifts silently from the room and leaves me to go to it: at other times he sort of shimmies respectfully in the middle of the carpet, and then I know that he wants a word or two. On the day after I had got back from Goodwood I was lying on my back, staring at the ceiling, when I noticed that he was still in my midst.

'Oh, hallo,' I said. 'Yes?'

'Mr Little called earlier in the morning, sir.'

'Oh, by Jove, what? Did he tell you about what happened?'

'Yes, sir. It was in connection with that that he wished to see you. He proposes to retire to the country and remain there for some little while.'

'Dashed sensible.'

'That was my opinion, also, sir. There was, however, a slight financial difficulty to be overcome. I took the liberty of advancing him ten pounds on your behalf to meet current expenses. I trust that meets with your approval, sir?'

'Oh, of course. Take a tenner off the dressing-table.'

'Very good, sir.'

'Jeeves,' I said.

'Sir?'

'What beats me is how the dickens the thing happened. I mean, how did the chappie Butt ever get to know who he was?'

Jeeves coughed.

'There, sir, I fear I may have been somewhat to blame.'

'You? How?'

'I fear I may carelessly have disclosed Mr Little's identity to Mr Butt on the occasion when I had that conversation with him.'

I sat up.

'What?'

'Indeed, now that I recall the incident, sir, I distinctly remember saying that Mr Little's work for the Cause really seemed to me to deserve something in the nature of public recognition. I greatly regret having been the means of bringing about a temporary estrangement between Mr Little and his lordship. And I am afraid there is another aspect to the matter. I am also responsible for the breaking off of relations between Mr Little and the young lady who came to tea here.'

I sat up again. It's a rummy thing, but the silver lining had absolutely escaped my notice till then.

'Do you mean to say it's off?'

'Completely, sir. I gathered from Mr Little's remarks that his hopes in the direction may now be looked on as definitely quenched. If there were no other obstacle, the young lady's father, I am informed by Mr Little, now regards him as a spy and a deceiver.'

'Well, I'm dashed!'

'I appear inadvertently to have caused much trouble, sir.'

'Jeeves!' I said.

'Sir?'

'How much money is there on the dressing-table?'

'In addition to the ten-pound note which you instructed me to take, sir, there are two five-pound notes, three one-pounds, a ten-shillings, two half-crowns, a florin, four shillings, a sixpence, and a halfpenny, sir.'

'Collar it all,' I said. 'You've earned it.'

CHAPTER THIRTEEN
The Great Sermon Handicap

fter Goodwood's over, I generally find that I get a bit restless. I'm not much of a lad for the birds and the trees and the great open spaces as a rule, but there's no doubt that London's not at its best in August, and rather tends to give me the pip and make me think of popping down into the country till things have bucked up a trifle. London, about a couple of weeks after that spectacular finish of young Bingo's which I've just been telling you about, was empty and smelled of burning asphalt. All my pals were away, most of the theatres were shut, and they were taking up Piccadilly in large spadefuls.

It was most infernally hot. As I sat in the old flat one night trying to muster up energy enough to go to bed, I felt I couldn't stand it much longer: and when Jeeves came in with the tissue-restorers on a tray I put the thing to him squarely.

'Jeeves,' I said, wiping the brow and gasping like a stranded goldfish, 'it's beastly hot.'

'The weather is oppressive, sir.'

'Not all the soda, Jeeves.'

'No, sir.'

'I think we've had about enough of the metrop. for the time being, and require a change. Shift-ho, I think, Jeeves, what?'

'Just as you say, sir. There is a letter on the tray, sir.'

'By Jove, Jeeves, that was practically poetry. Rhymed, did you notice?' I opened the letter. 'I say, this is rather extraordinary.'

'Sir?'

'You know Twing Hall?'

'Yes, sir.'

'Well, Mr Little is there.'

'Indeed, sir?'

'Absolutely in the flesh. He's had to take another of those tutoring jobs.'

After that fearful mix-up at Goodwood, when young Bingo Little, a broken man, had touched me for a tenner and whizzed silently off into the unknown, I had been all over the place, asking mutual friends if they had heard anything of him, but nobody had. And all the time he had been at Twing Hall. Rummy. And I'll tell you why it was rummy. Twing Hall belongs to old Lord Wickhammersley, a great pal of my guv'nor's when he was alive, and I have a standing invitation to pop down there when I like. I generally put in a week or two some time in the summer, and I was thinking of going there before I read the letter.

'And, what's more, Jeeves, my cousin Claude, and my cousin Eustace – you remember them?'

'Very vividly, sir.'

'Well, they're down there, too, reading for some exam or other with the vicar. I used to read with him myself at one time. He's known far and wide as a pretty hot coach for those of fairly feeble intellect. Well, when I tell you he got me through Smalls, you'll gather that he's a bit of a hummer. I call this most extraordinary.'

I read the letter again. It was from Eustace. Claude and Eustace are twins, and more or less generally admitted to be the curse of the human race.

DEAR BERTIE – Do you want to make a bit of money? I hear you had a bad Goodwood, so you probably do. Well, come down here quick and get in on the biggest sporting event of the season. I'll explain when I see you, but you can take it from me it's all right.

Claude and I are with a reading-party at old Heppenstall's. There are nine of us, not counting your pal Bingo Little, who is tutoring the kid up at the Hall.

Don't miss this golden opportunity, which may never occur again. Come and join us.

I handed this to Jeeves. He studied it thoughtfully.

'What do you make of it? A rummy communication, what?'

'Very high-spirited young gentlemen, sir, Mr Claude and

Mr Eustace. Up to some game, I should be disposed to imagine.'

'Yes. But what game, do you think?'

'It is impossible to say, sir. Did you observe that the letter continues over the page?'

'Eh, what?' I grabbed the thing. This was what was on the other side of the last page:

SERMON HANDICAP

RUNNERS AND BETTING

PROBABLE STARTERS

Rev. Joseph Tucker (Badgwick), scratch.

Rev. Leonard Starkie (Stapleton), scratch.

Rev. Alexander Jones (Upper Bingley), receives three minutes.

Rev. W. Dix (Little Clickton-in-the-Wold), receives five minutes.

Rev. Francis Heppenstall (Twing), receives eight minutes.

Rev. Cuthbert Dibble (Boustead Parva), receives nine minutes.

Rev. Orlo Hough (Boustead Magna), receives nine minutes.

Rev. J. J. Roberts (Fale-by-the-Water), receives ten minutes.

Rev. G. Hayward (Lower Bingley), receives twelve minutes.

Rev. James Bates (Gandle-by-the-Hill), receives fifteen minutes.

(The above have arrived.)

Prices. – 5-2, Tucker, Starkie; 3-1, Jones; 9-2, Dix; 6-1,

Heppenstall, Dibble, Hough; 100-8 any other.

It baffled me.

'Do you understand it, Jeeves?'

'No, sir.'

'Well, I think we ought to have a look into it, anyway, what?'

'Undoubtedly, sir.'

'Right-oh, then. Pack our spare dickey and a toothbrush in a neat brown-paper parcel, send a wire to Lord Wickhammersley to say we're coming, and buy two tickets on the five-ten at Paddington tomorrow.'

The five-ten was late as usual, and everybody was dressing for dinner when I arrived at the Hall. It was only by getting into my evening things in record time and taking the stairs to the dining-room in a couple of bounds that I managed to dead-heat with the soup. I slid into the vacant chair, and found that I was sitting next to old Wickhammersley's youngest daughter, Cynthia.

'Oh, hallo, old thing,' I said.

Great pals we've always been. In fact, there was a time when I had an idea I was in love with Cynthia. However, it blew over. A dashed pretty and lively and attractive girl, mind you, but full of ideals and all that. I may be wronging her, but I have an idea that she's the sort of girl who would want a fellow to carve out a career and what not. I know I've heard her speak favourably of Napoleon. So what with one thing and another the jolly old frenzy sort of petered out, and now we're just pals. I think she's a topper, and she thinks me next door to a looney, so everything's nice and matey.

'Well, Bertie, so you've arrived?'

'Oh, yes, I've arrived. Yes, here I am. I say, I seem to have plunged into the middle of quite a young dinner-party. Who are all these coves?'

'Oh, just people from round about. You know most of them. You remember Colonel Willis, and the Spencers—'

'Of course, yes. And there's old Heppenstall. Who's the other clergyman next to Mrs Spencer?'

'Mr Hayward, from Lower Bingley.'

'What an amazing lot of clergymen there are round here. Why, there's another, next to Mrs Willis.'

'That's Mr Bates, Mr Heppenstall's nephew. He's an assistant-master at Eton. He's down here during the summer holidays, acting as locum tenens for Mr Spettigue, the rector of Gandleby-the-Hill.'

'I thought I knew his face. He was in his fourth year at Oxford when I was a fresher. Rather a blood. Got his rowing-blue and all that.' I took another look round the table, and spotted young Bingo. 'Ah, there he is,' I said. 'There's the old egg.'

'There's who?'

'Young Bingo Little. Great pal of mine. He's tutoring your brother, you know.'

'Good gracious! Is he a friend of yours?'

'Rather! Known him all my life.'

'Then tell me, Bertie, is he at all weak in the head?'

'Weak in the head?'

'I don't mean simply because he's a friend of yours. But he's so strange in his manner.'

'How do you mean?'

'Well, he keeps looking at me so oddly.'

'Oddly? How? Give me an imitation.'

'I can't in front of all these people.'

'Yes, you can. I'll hold my napkin up.'

'All right, then. Quick. There!'

Considering that she had only about a second and a half to do it in, I must say it was a jolly fine exhibition. She opened her mouth and eyes pretty wide and let her jaw drop sideways, and managed to look so like a dyspeptic calf that I recognized the symptoms immediately.

'Oh, that's all right,' I said. 'No need to be alarmed. He's simply in love with you.'

'In love with me. Don't be absurd.'

'My dear old thing, you don't know young Bingo. He can fall in love with anybody.'

'Thank you!'

'Oh, I didn't mean it that way, you know. I don't wonder at his taking to you. Why, I was in love with you myself once.'

'Once? Ah! And all that remains now are the cold ashes? This isn't one of your tactful evenings, Bertie.'

'Well, my dear sweet thing, dash it all, considering that you gave me the bird and nearly laughed yourself into a permanent state of hiccoughs when I asked you—'

'Oh, I'm not reproaching you. No doubt there were faults on both sides. He's very good-looking, isn't he?'

'Good-looking? Bingo? Bingo good-looking? No, I say, come now, really!'

'I mean, compared with some people,' said Cynthia.

Some time after this, Lady Wickhammersley gave the signal for the females of the species to leg it, and they duly stampeded. I didn't get a chance of talking to young Bingo when they'd gone, and later, in the drawing-room, he didn't show up. I found him eventually in his room, lying on the bed with his feet on the rail, smoking a toofah. There was a note-book on the counterpane beside him.

'Hallo, old scream,' I said.

'Hallo, Bertie,' he replied, in what seemed to me rather a moody, distrait sort of manner.

'Rummy finding you down here. I take it your uncle cut off your allowance after that Goodwood binge and you had to take this tutoring job to keep the wolf from the door?'

'Correct,' said young Bingo tersely.

'Well, you might have let your pals know where you were.'
He frowned darkly.

'I didn't want them to know where I was. I wanted to creep away and hide myself. I've been through a bad time, Bertie, these last weeks. The sun ceased to shine—'

'That's curious. We've had gorgeous weather in London.'

'The birds ceased to sing—'

'What birds?'

'What the devil does it matter what birds?' said young Bingo, with some asperity. 'Any birds. The birds round about here. You don't expect me to specify them by their pet names, do you? I tell you, Bertie, it hit me hard at first, very hard.'

'What hit you?' I simply couldn't follow the blighter.

'Charlotte's calculated callousness.'

'Oh, ah!' I've seen poor old Bingo through so many unsuccessful love-affairs that I'd almost forgotten there was a girl mixed up with that Goodwood business. Of course! Charlotte Corday Rowbotham. And she had given him the raspberry, I remembered, and gone off with Comrade Butt.

'I went through torments. Recently, however, I've – er – bucked up a bit. Tell me, Bertie, what are you doing down here? I didn't know you knew these people.'

'Me? Why, I've known them since I was a kid.'

Young Bingo put his feet down with a thud.

'Do you mean to say you've known Lady Cynthia all that time?'

'Rather! She can't have been seven when I met her first.'

'Good Lord!' said young Bingo. He looked at me for the first time as though I amounted to something, and swallowed a mouthful of smoke the wrong way. 'I love that girl, Bertie,' he went on, when he'd finished coughing.

'Yes. Nice girl, of course.'

He eyed me with pretty deep loathing.

'Don't speak of her in that horrible casual way. She's an angel. An angel! Was she talking about me at all at dinner, Bertie?'

'Oh, yes.'

'What did she say?'

'I remember one thing. She said she thought you good-looking.'

Young Bingo closed his eyes in a sort of ecstasy. Then he picked up the note-book.

'Pop off now, old man, there's a good chap,' he said, in a hushed, far-away voice. 'I've got a bit of writing to do.'

'Writing?'

'Poetry, if you must know. I wish the dickens,' said young Bingo, not without some bitterness, 'she had been christened something except Cynthia. There isn't a dam' word in the language it rhymes with. Ye gods, how I could have spread myself if she had only been called Jane!'

Bright and early next morning, as I lay in bed blinking at the sunlight on the dressing-table and wondering when Jeeves was going to show up with a cup of tea, a heavy weight descended on my toes, and the voice of young Bingo polluted the air. The blighter had apparently risen with the lark.

'Leave me,' I said, 'I would be alone. I can't see anybody till I've had my tea.'

'When Cynthia smiles,' said young Bingo, 'the skies are blue; the world takes on a roseate hue; birds in the garden trill and sing, and Joy is king of everything, when Cynthia smiles.' He coughed, changing gears. 'When Cynthia frowns—'

'What the devil are you talking about?'

'I'm reading you my poem. The one I wrote to Cynthia last night. I'll go on, shall I?'

'No!'

'No?'

'No. I haven't had my tea.'

At this moment Jeeves came in with the good old beverage, and I sprang on it with a glad cry. After a couple of sips things looked a bit brighter. Even young Bingo didn't offend the eye to quite such an extent. By the time I'd finished the first cup I was a new man, so much so that I not only permitted but encouraged the poor fish to read the rest of the bally thing, and even went so far as to criticize the scansion of the fourth line of the fifth verse. We were still arguing the point when the door burst open and in blew Claude and Eustace. One of the things which discourages me about rural life is the frightful earliness with which events begin to break loose. I've stayed at places in the country where they've jerked me out of the dreamless at about six-thirty to go for a jolly swim in the lake. At Twing, thank heaven, they know me, and let me breakfast in bed.

The twins seemed pleased to see me.

'Good old Bertie!' said Claude.

'Stout fellow!' said Eustace. 'The Rev. told us you had arrived. I thought that letter of mine would fetch you.'

'You can always bank on Bertie,' said Claude. 'A sportsman to the finger-tips. Well, has Bingo told you about it?'

'Not a word. He's been—'

'We've been talking,' said Bingo hastily, 'of other matters.'

Claude pinched the last slice of thin bread-and-butter, and Eustace poured himself out a cup of tea.

'It's like this, Bertie,' said Eustace, settling down cosily. 'As I told you in my letter, there are nine of us marooned in this desert spot, reading with old Heppenstall. Well, of course, nothing is jollier than sweating up the Classics when it's a hundred in the shade, but there does come a time when you begin to feel the need of a little relaxation; and, by Jove, there are absolutely no facilities for relaxation in this place whatever. And then Steggles got this idea. Steggles is one of our reading-party, and, between ourselves, rather a worm as a general thing. Still, you have to give him credit for getting this idea.'

'What idea?'

'Well, you know how many parsons there are round about here. There are about a dozen hamlets within a radius of six miles, and each hamlet has a church and each church has a parson and each parson preaches a sermon every Sunday. Tomorrow week – Sunday the twenty-third – we're running off the great Sermon Handicap. Steggles is making the book. Each parson is to be clocked by a reliable steward of the course, and the one that preaches the longest sermon wins. Did you study the race-card I sent you?'

'I couldn't understand what it was all about.'

'Why, you chump, it gives the handicaps and the current odds on each starter. I've got another one here, in case you've lost yours. Take a careful look at it. It gives you the thing in a nutshell. Jeeves, old son, do you want a sporting flutter?'

'Sir?' said Jeeves, who had just meandered in with my breakfast.

Claude explained the scheme. Amazing the way Jeeves grasped it right off. But he merely smiled in a paternal sort of way.

'Thank you, sir, I think not.'

'Well, you're with us, Bertie, aren't you?' said Claude, sneaking a roll and a slice of bacon. 'Have you studied that card? Well, tell me, does anything strike you about it?'

Of course it did. It had struck me the moment I looked at it.

'Why, it's a sitter for old Heppenstall,' I said. 'He's got the event sewed up in a parcel. There isn't a parson in the land who could give him eight minutes. Your pal Steggles must be an ass, giving him a handicap like that. Why, in the days when I was with him, old Heppenstall never used to preach under half an hour, and there was one sermon of his on Brotherly Love which lasted forty-five minutes if it lasted a second. Has he lost his vim lately, or what is it?'

'Not a bit of it,' said Eustace. 'Tell him what happened,

Claude.'

'Why,' said Claude, 'the first Sunday we were here, we all went to Twing church, and old Heppenstall preached a sermon that was well under twenty minutes. This is what happened. Steggles didn't notice it, and the Rev. didn't notice it himself, but Eustace and I both spotted that he had dropped a chunk of at least half a dozen pages out of his sermon-case as he was walking up to the pulpit. He sort of flickered when he got to the gap in the manuscript, but carried on all right, and Steggles went away with the impression that twenty minutes or a bit under was his usual form. The next Sunday we heard Tucker and Starkie, and they both went well over the thirty-five minutes, so Steggles arranged the handicapping as you see on the card. You must come into this, Bertie. You see, the trouble is that I haven't a bean, and Eustace hasn't a bean, and Bingo Little hasn't a bean, so you'll have to finance the syndicate. Don't weaken! It's just putting money in all our pockets. Well, we'll have to be getting back now. Think the thing over, and phone me later in the day. And, if you let us down, Bertie, may a cousin's curse— Come on, Claude, old thing.'

The more I studied the scheme, the better it looked.

'How about it, Jeeves?' I said.

Jeeves smiled gently, and drifted out.

'Jeeves has no sporting blood,' said Bingo.

'Well, I have. I'm coming into this. Claude's quite right. It's like finding money by the wayside.'

'Good man!' said Bingo. 'Now I can see daylight. Say I

have a tenner on Heppenstall, and cop; that'll give me a bit in hand to back Pink Pill with in the two o'clock at Gatwick the week after next: cop on that, put the pile on Musk-Rat for the one-thirty at Lewes, and there I am with a nice little sum to take to Alexandra Park on September the tenth, when I've got a tip straight from the stable.'

It sounded like a bit out of Smiles's Self-Help.

'And then,' said young Bingo, 'I'll be in a position to go to my uncle and beard him in his lair somewhat. He's quite a bit of a snob, you know, and when he hears that I'm going to marry the daughter of an earl—'

'I say, old man,' I couldn't help saying, 'aren't you looking ahead rather far?'

'Oh, that's all right. It's true nothing's actually settled yet, but she practically told me the other day she was fond of me.'

'What!'

'Well, she said that the sort of man she liked was the self-reliant, manly man with strength, good looks, character, ambition, and initiative.'

'Leave me, laddie,' I said. 'Leave me to my fried egg.'

Directly I'd got up I went to the phone, snatched Eustace away from his morning's work, and instructed him to put a tenner on the Twing flier at current odds for each of the syndicate; and after lunch Eustace rang me up to say that he had done business at a snappy seven-to-one, the odds having lengthened owing to a rumour in knowledgeable circles that the Rev. was subject to hay fever, and was taking big chances strolling in the paddock behind the Vicarage in the early mornings. And it was dashed lucky, I thought next day, that we had managed to get the money on in time, for on the Sunday morning old Heppenstall fairly took the bit between his teeth, and gave us thirty-six solid minutes on Certain Popular Superstitions. I was sitting next to Steggles in the pew, and I saw him blench visibly. He was a little rat-faced fellow, with shifty eyes and a suspicious nature. The first thing he did when we emerged into the open air was to announce, formally, that anyone who fancied the Rev. could now be accommodated at fifteen-to-eight on, and he added, in a rather nasty manner, that if he had his way, this sort of in-and-out running would be brought to the attention of the Jockey Club, but that he supposed that there was nothing to be done about it. This ruinous price checked the punters at once, and there was little money in sight. And so matters stood till just after lunch on Tuesday afternoon, when, as I was strolling up and down in front of the house with a cigarette, Claude and Eustace came bursting up the drive on bicycles, dripping with momentous news.

'Bertie,' said Claude, deeply agitated, 'unless we take immediate action and do a bit of quick thinking, we're in the cart.'

'What's the matter?'

'G. Hayward's the matter,' said Eustace morosely. 'The Lower Bingley starter.'

'We never even considered him,' said Claude. 'Somehow or other, he got overlooked. It's always the way. Steggles overlooked him. We all overlooked him. But Eustace and I happened by the merest fluke to be riding through Lower Bingley this morning, and there was a wedding on at the church, and it suddenly struck us that it wouldn't be a bad move to get a line on G. Hayward's form, in case he might be a dark horse.'

'And it was jolly lucky we did,' said Eustace. 'He delivered an address of twenty-six minutes by Claude's stop-watch. At a village wedding, mark you! What'll he do when he really extends himself!'

'There's only one thing to be done, Bertie,' said Claude. 'You must spring some more funds, so that we can hedge on Hayward and save ourselves.'

'But—'

'Well, it's the only way out.'

'But I say, you know, I hate the idea of all that money we put on Heppenstall being chucked away.'

'What else can you suggest? You don't suppose the Rev. can give this absolute marvel a handicap and win, do you?'

'I've got it!' I said.

'What?'

'I see a way by which we can make it safe for our nominee. I'll pop over this afternoon, and ask him as a personal favour to preach that sermon of his on Brotherly Love on Sunday.'

Claude and Eustace looked at each other, like those

P.G. Wodehouse

chappies in the poem, with a wild surmise.

'It's a scheme,' said Claude.

'A jolly brainy scheme,' said Eustace. 'I didn't think you had it in you, Bertie.'

'But even so,' said Claude, 'fizzer as that sermon no doubt is, will it be good enough in the face of a four-minute handicap?'

'Rather!' I said. 'When I told you it lasted forty-five minutes, I was probably understating it. I should call it – from my recollection of the thing – nearer fifty.'

'Then carry on,' said Claude.

I toddled over in the evening and fixed the thing up. Old Heppenstall was most decent about the whole affair. He seemed pleased and touched that I should have remembered the sermon all these years, and said he had once or twice had an idea of preaching it again, only it had seemed to him, on reflection, that it was perhaps a trifle long for a rustic congregation.

'And in these restless times, my dear Wooster,' he said, 'I fear that brevity in the pulpit is becoming more and more desiderated by even the bucolic churchgoer, who one might have supposed would be less afflicted with the spirit of hurry and impatience than his metropolitan brother. I have had many arguments on the subject with my nephew, young Bates, who is taking my old friend Spettigue's cure over at Gandle-by-the-Hill. His view is that a sermon nowadays should be a bright, brisk, straight-from-the shoulder address, never lasting more than ten or twelve minutes.'

'Long?' I said. 'Why, my goodness! you don't call that Brotherly Love sermon of yours long, do you?'

'It takes fully fifty minutes to deliver.'

'Surely not?'

'Your incredulity, my dear Wooster, is extremely flattering – far more flattering, of course, than I deserve. Nevertheless, the facts are as I have stated. You are sure that I would not be well advised to make certain excisions and eliminations? You do not think it would be a good thing to cut, to prune? I might, for example, delete the rather exhaustive excursus into the family life of the early Assyrians?'

'Don't touch a word of it, or you'll spoil the whole thing,' I said earnestly.

'I am delighted to hear you say so, and I shall preach the sermon without fail next Sunday morning.'

What I have always said, and what I always shall say, is, that this ante-post betting is a mistake, an error, and a mug's game. You never can tell what's going to happen. If fellows would only stick to the good old S.P. there would be fewer young men go wrong. I'd hardly finished my breakfast on the Saturday morning, when Jeeves came to my bedside to say that Eustace wanted me on the telephone.

'Good Lord, Jeeves, what's the matter, do you think?'

I'm bound to say I was beginning to get a bit jumpy by this time.

'Mr Eustace did not confide in me, sir.'

'Has he got the wind up?'

'Somewhat vertically, sir, to judge by his voice.'

'Do you know what I think, Jeeves? Something's gone wrong with the favourite.'

'Which is the favourite, sir?'

'Mr Heppenstall. He's gone to odds on. He was intending to preach a sermon on Brotherly Love which would have brought him home by lengths. I wonder if anything's happened to him.'

'You could ascertain, sir, by speaking to Mr Eustace on the telephone. He is holding the wire.'

'By Jove, yes!'

I shoved on a dressing-gown, and flew downstairs like a mighty, rushing wind. The moment I heard Eustace's voice I knew we were for it. It had a croak of agony in it.

'Bertie?'

'Here I am.'

'Deuce of a time you've been. Bertie, we're sunk. The favourite's blown up.'

'No!'

'Yes. Coughing in his stable all last night.'

'What!'

'Absolutely! Hay-fever.'

'Oh, my sainted aunt!'

'The doctor is with him now, and it's only a question of minutes before he's officially scratched. That means the curate will show up at the post instead, and he's no good at all. He is being offered at a hundred-to-six, but no takers. What shall we do?'

I had to grapple with the thing for a moment in silence.

'Eustace.'

'Hallo?'

'What can you get on G. Hayward?'

'Only four to one now. I think there's been a leak, and Steggles has heard something. The odds shortened late last night in a significant manner.'

'Well, four to one will clear us. Put another fiver all round on G. Hayward for the syndicate. That'll bring us out on the right side of the ledger.'

'If he wins.'

'What do you mean? I thought you considered him a cert, bar Heppenstall.'

'I'm beginning to wonder,' said Eustace gloomily, 'if there's such a thing as a cert. in this world. I'm told the Rev. Joseph Tucker did an extraordinarily fine trial gallop at a mothers' meeting over at Badgwick yesterday. However, it seems our only chance. So-long.'

Not being one of the official stewards, I had my choice of churches next morning, and naturally I didn't hesitate. The only drawback to going to Lower Bingley was that it was ten miles away, which meant an early start, but I borrowed a bicycle from one of the grooms and tooled off. I had only Eustace's word for it that G. Hayward was such a stayer, and it might have been that he had showed too flattering form at that wedding where the twins had heard him preach; but any misgivings I may have had disappeared the moment he got into the pulpit. Eustace had been right. The man was a trier. He was a tall, rangy-looking greybeard, and he went off from the start with a nice, easy action, pausing and clearing his throat at the end of each sentence, and it wasn't five minutes before I realized that here was the winner. His habit of stopping dead and looking round the church at intervals was worth minutes to us, and in the home stretch we gained no little advantage owing to his dropping his pince-nez and having to grope for them. At the twenty-minute mark he had merely settled down. Twenty-five minutes saw him going strong. And when he finally finished with a good burst, the clock showed thirty-five minutes fourteen seconds. With the handicap which he had been given, this seemed to me to make the event easy for him, and it was with much bonhomie and goodwill to all men that I hopped on to the old bike and started back to the Hall for lunch.

Bingo was talking on the phone when I arrived.

'Fine! Splendid! Topping!' he was saying. 'Eh? Oh, we needn't worry about him. Right-o, I'll tell Bertie.' He hung up the receiver and caught sight of me. 'Oh, hallo, Bertie; I was just talking to Eustace. It's all right, old man. The report from Lower Bingley has just got in. G. Hayward romps home.'

'I knew he would. I've just come from there.'

'Oh, were you there? I went to Badgwick. Tucker ran

a splendid race, but the handicap was too much for him. Starkie had a sore throat and was nowhere. Roberts, of Faleby-the-Water, ran third. Good old G. Hayward!' said Bingo affectionately, and we strolled out on to the terrace.

'Are all the returns in, then?' I asked.

'All except Gandle-by-the-Hill. But we needn't worry about Bates. He never had a chance. By the way, poor old Jeeves loses his tenner. Silly ass!'

'Jeeves? How do you mean?'

'He came to me this morning, just after you had left, and asked me to put a tenner on Bates for him. I told him he was a chump, and begged him not to throw his money away, but he would do it.'

'I beg your pardon, sir. This note arrived for you just after you had left the house this morning.'

Jeeves had materialized from nowhere, and was standing at my elbow.

'Eh? What? Note?'

'The Reverend Mr Heppenstall's butler brought it over from the Vicarage, sir. It came too late to be delivered to you at the moment.'

Young Bingo was talking to Jeeves like a father on the subject of betting against the form-book. The yell I gave made him bite his tongue in the middle of a sentence.

'What the dickens is the matter?' he asked, not a little peeved.

'We're dished! Listen to this!'

I read him the note:

The Vicarage,
Twing, Glos.

MY DEAR WOOSTER – As you may have heard, circumstances over which I have no control will prevent my preaching the sermon on Brotherly Love for which you made such a flattering request. I am unwilling, however, that you shall be disappointed, so, if you will attend divine service at Gandleby-the-Hill this morning, you will hear my sermon preached by young Bates, my nephew. I have lent him the manuscript at his urgent desire, for, between ourselves, there are wheels within wheels. My nephew is one of the candidates for the headmastership of a well-known public school, and the choice has narrowed down between him and one rival.

Late yesterday evening James received private information that the head of the Board of Governors of the school proposed to sit under him this Sunday in order to judge of the merits of his preaching, a most important item in swaying the Board's choice. I acceded to his plea that I lend him my sermon on Brotherly Love, of which, like you, he apparently retains a vivid recollection. It would have been too late for him to compose a sermon of suitable length in place of the brief address which – mistakenly, in my opinion – he had designed to deliver to his rustic flock, and I wished to help the boy.

Trusting that his preaching of the sermon will supply you with as pleasant memories as you say you have of mine, I remain,

Cordially yours,
F. HEPPENSTALL.

P.S. – The hay-fever has rendered my eyes unpleasantly weak for the time being, so I am dictating this letter to my butler, Brookfield, who will convey it to you.

I don't know when I've experienced a more massive silence than the one that followed my reading of this cheery epistle. Young Bingo gulped once or twice, and practically every known emotion came and went on his face. Jeeves coughed one soft, low, gentle cough like a sheep with a blade of grass stuck in its throat, and then stood gazing serenely at the landscape. Finally young Bingo spoke.

'Great Scott!' he whispered hoarsely. 'An S.P. job!'

'I believe that is the technical term, sir,' said Jeeves.

'So you had inside information, dash it!' said young Bingo.

'Why, yes, sir,' said Jeeves. 'Brookfield happened to mention the contents of the note to me when he brought it. We are old friends.'

Bingo registered grief, anguish, rage, despair and resentment.

'Well, all I can say,' he cried, 'is that it's a bit thick! Preaching another man's sermon! Do you call that honest? Do you call that playing the game?'

'Well, my dear old thing,' I said, 'be fair. It's quite within the rules. Clergymen do it all the time. They aren't expected always to make up the sermons they preach.'

Jeeves coughed again, and fixed me with an expressionless eye.

'And in the present case, sir, if I may be permitted to take the liberty of making the observation, I think we should make allowances. We should remember that the securing of this headmastership meant everything to the young couple.'

'Young couple? What young couple?'

'The Reverend James Bates, sir, and Lady Cynthia. I am informed by her ladyship's maid that they have been engaged to be married for some weeks – provisionally, so to speak; and his lordship made his consent conditional on Mr Bates securing a really important and remunerative position.'

Young Bingo turned a light green.

'Engaged to be married!'

'Yes, sir.'

There was a silence.

'I think I'll go for a walk,' said Bingo.

'But, my dear old thing,' I said, 'it's just lunch-time. The gong will be going any minute now.'

'I don't want any lunch!' said Bingo.

CHAPTER FOURTEEN
The Purity of the Turf

After that, life at Twing jogged along pretty peacefully for a bit. Twing is one of those places where there isn't a frightful lot to do nor any very hectic excitement to look forward to. In fact, the only event of any importance on the horizon, as far as I could ascertain, was the annual village school treat. One simply filled in the time by loafing about the grounds, playing a bit of tennis, and avoiding young Bingo as far as was humanly possible.

This last was a very necessary move if you wanted a happy life, for the Cynthia affair had jarred the unfortunate mutt to such an extent that he was always waylaying one and decanting his anguished soul. And when, one morning, he blew into my bedroom while I was toying with a bit of breakfast, I decided to take a firm line from the start. I could stand having him moaning all over me after dinner, and even after lunch; but at breakfast, no. We Woosters are amiability itself, but there is a limit.

'Now look here, old friend,' I said. 'I know your bally heart is broken and all that, and at some future time I shall be delighted to hear all about it, but—'

'I didn't come to talk about that.'

'No? Good egg!'

'The past,' said young Bingo, 'is dead. Let us say no more about it.'

'Right-o!'

'I have been wounded to the very depths of my soul, but don't speak about it.'

'I won't.'

'Ignore it. Forget it.'

'Absolutely!'

I hadn't seen him so dashed reasonable for days.

'What I came to see you about this morning, Bertie,' he said, fishing a sheet of paper out of his pocket, 'was to ask if you would care to come in on another little flutter.'

If there is one thing we Woosters are simply dripping with, it is sporting blood. I bolted the rest of my sausage, and sat up and took notice.

'Proceed,' I said. 'You interest me strangely, old bird.'

Bingo laid the paper on the bed.

'On Monday week,' he said, 'you may or may not know, the annual village school treat takes place. Lord Wickhammersley lends the Hall grounds for the purpose. There will be games, and a conjurer, and coco-nut shies, and tea in a tent. And also sports.'

'I know. Cynthia was telling me.'

Young Bingo winced.

'Would you mind not mentioning that name? I am not made of marble.'

'Sorry!'

'Well, as I was saying, this jamboree is slated for Monday week. The question is, Are we on?'

'How do you mean, "Are we on?"?'

'I am referring to the sports. Steggles did so well out of the Sermon Handicap that he has decided to make a book on these sports. Punters can be accommodated at ante-post odds or starting price, according to their preference. I think we ought to look into it,' said young Bingo.

I pressed the bell.

'I'll consult Jeeves. I don't touch any sporting proposition without his advice. Jeeves,' I said, as he drifted in, 'rally round.'

'Sir?'

'Stand by. We want your advice.'

'Very good, sir.'

'State your case, Bingo.'

Bingo stated his case.

'What about it, Jeeves?' I said. 'Do we go in?'

Jeeves pondered to some extent.

'I am inclined to favour the idea, sir.'

That was good enough for me. 'Right,' I said. 'Then we will form a syndicate and bust the Ring. I supply the money, you supply the brains, and Bingo – what do you supply, Bingo?'

'If you will carry me, and let me settle up later,' said young Bingo, 'I think I can put you in the way of winning a parcel on the Mothers' Sack Race.'

'All right. We will put you down as Inside Information. Now, what are the events?

Bingo reached for his paper and consulted it.

'Girls' Under Fourteen Fifty-Yard Dash seems to open the proceedings.'

'Anything to say about that, Jeeves?'

'No, sir. I have no information.'

'What's the next?'

'Boys' and Girls' Mixed Animal Potato Race, All Ages.'

This was a new one to me. I had never heard of it at any of the big meetings.

'What's that?'

'Rather sporting,' said young Bingo. 'The competitors enter in couples, each couple being assigned an animal cry and a potato. For instance, let's suppose that you and Jeeves entered. Jeeves would stand at a fixed point holding a potato. You would have your head in a sack, and you would grope about trying to find Jeeves and making a noise like a cat; Jeeves also making a noise like a cat. Other competitors would be making noises like cows and pigs and dogs, and so on; and groping about for their potato-holders, who would also be making noises like cows and pigs and dogs and so on—'

I stopped the poor fish.

'Jolly if you're fond of animals,' I said, 'but on the whole—'

'Precisely, sir,' said Jeeves. 'I wouldn't touch it.'

'Too open, what?'

'Exactly, sir. Very hard to estimate form.'

'Carry on, Bingo. Where do we go from there?'

'Mothers' Sack Race.'

'Ah! that's better. This is where you know something.'

'A gift for Mrs Penworthy, the tobacconist's wife,' said Bingo confidently. 'I was in at her shop yesterday, buying cigarettes, and she told me she had won three times at fairs in Worcestershire. She only moved to these parts a short time ago, so nobody knows about her. She promised me she would keep herself dark, and I think we could get a good price.'

'Risk a tenner each way, Jeeves, what?'

'I think so, sir.'

'Girls' Open Egg and Spoon Race,' read Bingo.

'How about that?'

'I doubt if it would be worth while to invest, sir,' said Jeeves. 'I am told it is a certainty for last year's winner, Sarah Mills, who will doubtless start an odds-on favourite.'

'Good, is she?'

'They tell me in the village that she carries a beautiful egg, sir.'

'Then there's the Obstacle Race,' said Bingo. 'Risky, in my opinion. Like betting on the Grand National. Fathers' Hat-Trimming Contest – another speculative event. That's all, except for the Choir-Boys' Hundred Yards Handicap, for a pewter mug presented by the vicar – open to all whose voices have not broken before the second Sunday in Epiphany. Willie Chambers won last year, in a canter, receiving fifteen yards. This time he will probably be handicapped out of the race. I don't know what to advise.'

'If I might make a suggestion, sir.'

I eyed Jeeves with interest. I don't know that I'd ever seen him look so nearly excited.

'You've got something up your sleeve?'

'I have, sir.'

'Red-hot?'

'That precisely describes it, sir. I think I may confidently assert that we have the winner of the Choir-Boys' Handicap under this very roof, sir. Harold, the page-boy.'

'Page-boy? Do you mean the tubby little chap in buttons one sees bobbing about here and there? Why, dash it, Jeeves, nobody has a greater respect for your knowledge of form than I have, but I'm hanged if I can see Harold catching the judge's eye. He's practically circular, and every time I've seen him he's been leaning up against something, half asleep.'

'He receives thirty yards, sir, and could win from scratch. The boy is a flier.'

'How do you know?'

Jeeves coughed, and there was a dreamy look in his eye.

'I was as much astonished as yourself, sir, when I first became aware of the lad's capabilities. I happened to pursue him one morning with the intention of fetching him a clip on the side of the head—'

'Great Scott, Jeeves! You?'

'Yes, sir. The boy is of an outspoken disposition, and had made an opprobrious remark respecting my personal appearance.'

'What did he say about your appearance?'

'I have forgotten, sir,' said Jeeves, with a touch of austerity. 'But it was opprobrious. I endeavoured to correct him, but he outdistanced me by yards and made good his escape.'

'But, I say, Jeeves, this is sensational. And yet – if he's such a sprinter, why hasn't anybody in the village found it out? Surely he plays with the other boys?'

'No, sir. As his lordship's page-boy, Harold does not mix with the village lads.'

'Bit of a snob, what?'

'He is somewhat acutely alive to the existence of class distinctions, sir.'

'You're absolutely certain he's such a wonder?' said Bingo. 'I mean, it wouldn't do to plunge unless you're sure.'

'If you desire to ascertain the boy's form by personal inspection, sir, it will be a simple matter to arrange a secret trial.'

'I'm bound to say I should feel easier in my mind,' I said.

'Then if I may take a shilling from the money on your dressing-table—'

'What for?'

'I propose to bribe the lad to speak slightingly of the second footman's squint, sir. Charles is somewhat sensitive on the point, and should undoubtedly make the lad extend himself. If you will be at the first-floor passage-window, overlooking the back door, in half an hour's time—'

I don't know when I've dressed in such a hurry. As a rule, I'm what you might call a slow and careful dresser: I like to linger over the tie and see that the trousers are just so; but this morning I was all worked up. I just shoved on my things anyhow, and joined Bingo at the window with a quarter of an hour to spare.

The passage-window looked down on to a broad sort of paved courtyard, which ended after about twenty yards in an archway through a high wall. Beyond this archway you got on to a strip of the drive, which curved round for another thirty yards or so, till it was lost behind a thick shrubbery. I put myself in the stripling's place and thought what steps I would take with a second footman after me. There was only one thing to do – leg it for the shrubbery and take cover; which meant that at least fifty yards would have to be covered – an excellent test. If good old Harold could fight off the second footman's challenge long enough to allow him to reach the bushes, there wasn't a choirboy in England who could give him thirty yards in the hundred. I waited, all of a twitter, for what seemed hours, and then suddenly there was a confused noise without, and something round and blue and buttony shot through the back door and buzzed for the archway like a mustang. And about two seconds later out came the second footman, going his hardest.

There was nothing to it. Absolutely nothing. The field never had a chance. Long before the footman reached the half-way mark, Harold was in the bushes, throwing stones. I came away from the window thrilled to the marrow; and when I met Jeeves on the stairs I was so moved that I nearly grasped his hand.

'Jeeves,' I said, 'no discussion! The Wooster shirt goes on this boy!'

'Very good, sir,' said Jeeves.

The worst of these country meetings is that you can't plunge as heavily as you would like when you get a good thing, because it alarms the Ring. Steggles, though pimpled, was, as I have indicated, no chump, and if I had invested all I wanted to he would have put two and two together. I managed to get a good solid bet down for the syndicate, however, though it did make him look thoughtful. I heard in the next few days that he had been making searching inquiries in the village concerning Harold; but nobody could tell him anything, and eventually he came to the conclusion, I suppose, that I must be having a long shot on the strength of that thirty-yards start. Public opinion wavered between Jimmy Goode, receiving ten yards, at seven-to-two, and Alexander Bartlett, with six yards start, at eleven-to-four. Willie Chambers, scratch, was offered to the public at two-to-one, but found no takers.

We were taking no chances on the big event, and directly

we had got our money on at a nice hundred-to-twelve, Harold was put into strict training. It was a wearing business, and I can understand now why most of the big trainers are grim, silent men, who look as though they had suffered. The kid wanted constant watching. It was no good talking to him about honour and glory and how proud his mother would be when he wrote and told her he had won a real cup – the moment blighted Harold discovered that training meant knocking off pastry, taking exercise, and keeping away from the cigarettes, he was all against it, and it was only by unceasing vigilance that we managed to keep him in any shape at all. It was the diet that was the stumbling-block. As far as exercise went, we could generally arrange for a sharp dash every morning with the assistance of the second footman. It ran into money, of course, but that couldn't be helped. Still, when a kid has simply to wait till the butler's back is turned to have the run of the pantry, and has only to nip into the smoking-room to collect a handful of the best Turkish, training becomes a rocky job. We could only hope that on the day his natural stamina would pull him through.

And then one evening young Bingo came back from the links with a disturbing story. He had been in the habit of giving Harold mild exercise in the afternoons by taking him out as a caddie.

At first he seemed to think it humorous, the poor chump! He bubbled over with merry mirth as he began his tale.

'I say, rather funny this afternoon,' he said. 'You ought to have seen Steggles's face!'

'Seen Steggles's face? What for?'

'When he saw young Harold sprint, I mean.'

I was filled with a grim foreboding of an awful doom.

'Good heavens! You didn't let Harold sprint in front of Steggles?'

Young Bingo's jaw dropped.

'I never thought of that,' he said, gloomily. 'It wasn't my fault. I was playing a round with Steggles, and after we'd finished we went into the club-house for a drink, leaving Harold with the clubs outside. In about five minutes we came out, and there was the kid on the gravel practising swings with Steggles's driver and a stone. When he saw us coming, the kid dropped the club and was over the horizon like a streak. Steggles was absolutely dumbfounded. And I must say it was a revelation to me. The kid certainly gave of his best. Of course, it's a nuisance in a way: but I don't see, on second thoughts,' said Bingo, brightening up, 'what it matters. We're in at a good price. We've nothing to lose by the kid's form becoming known. I take it he will start oddson, but that doesn't affect us.'

I looked at Jeeves. Jeeves looked at me.

'It affects us all right if he doesn't start at all.'

'Precisely, sir.'

'What do you mean?' asked Bingo.

'If you ask me,' I said, 'I think Steggles will try to nobble him before the race.'

'Good Lord! I never thought of that.' Bingo blenched. 'You

don't think he would really do it?'

'I think he would have a jolly good try. Steggles is a bad man. From now on, Jeeves, we must watch Harold like hawks.'

'Undoubtedly, sir.'

'Ceaseless vigilance, what?'

'Precisely, sir.'

'You wouldn't care to sleep in his room, Jeeves?'

'No, sir, I should not.'

'No, nor would I, if it comes to that. But dash it all,' I said, 'we're letting ourselves get rattled! We're losing our nerve. This won't do. How can Steggles possibly get at Harold, even if he wants to?'

There was no cheering young Bingo up. He's one of those birds who simply leap at the morbid view, if you give them half a chance.

'There are all sorts of ways of nobbling favourites,' he said, in a sort of death-bed voice. 'You ought to read some of these racing novels. In Pipped on the Post, Lord Jasper Mauleverer as near as a toucher outed Bonny Betsy by bribing the head lad to slip a cobra into her stable the night before the Derby!'

'What are the chances of a cobra biting Harold, Jeeves?'

'Slight, I should imagine, sir. And in such an event, knowing the boy as intimately as I do, my anxiety would be entirely for the snake.'

'Still, unceasing vigilance, Jeeves.'

'Most certainly, sir.'

I must say I got a bit fed up with young Bingo in the next few days. It's all very well for a fellow with a big winner in his stable to exercise proper care, but in my opinion Bingo overdid it. The blighter's mind appeared to be absolutely saturated with racing fiction; and in stories of that kind, as far as I could make out, no horse is ever allowed to start in a race without at least a dozen attempts to put it out of action. He stuck to Harold like a plaster. Never let the unfortunate kid out of his sight. Of course, it meant a lot to the poor old egg if he could collect on this race, because it would give him enough money to chuck his tutoring job and get back to London; but all the same, he needn't have woken me up at three in the morning twice running – once to tell me we ought to cook Harold's food ourselves to prevent doping: the other time to say that he had heard mysterious noises in the shrubbery. But he reached the limit, in my opinion, when he insisted on my going to evening service on Sunday, the day before the sports.

'Why on earth?' I said, never being much of a lad for evensong.

'Well, I can't go myself. I shan't be here. I've got to go to London today with young Egbert.' Egbert was Lord Wickhammersley's son, the one Bingo was tutoring. 'He's going for a visit down in Kent, and I've got to see him off at Charing Cross. It's an infernal nuisance. I shan't be back till Monday afternoon. In fact, I shall miss most of the sports, I expect. Everything, therefore, depends on you, Bertie.'

'But why should either of us go to evening service?'

P.G. Wodehouse

'Ass! Harold sings in the choir, doesn't he?'

'What about it? I can't stop him dislocating his neck over a high note, if that's what you're afraid of.'

'Fool! Steggles sings in the choir, too. There may be dirty work after the service.'

'What absolute rot!'

'Is it?' said young Bingo. 'Well, let me tell you that in Jenny, the Girl Jockey, the villain kidnapped the boy who was to ride the favourite the night before the big race, and he was the only one who understood and could control the horse, and if the heroine hadn't dressed up in riding things and—'

'Oh, all right, all right. But, if there's any danger, it seems to me the simplest thing would be for Harold not to turn out on Sunday evening.'

'He must turn out. You seem to think the infernal kid is a monument of rectitude, beloved by all. He's got the shakiest reputation of any kid in the village. His name is as near being mud as it can jolly well stick. He's played hookey from the choir so often that the vicar told him, if one more thing happened, he would fire him out. Nice chumps we should look if he was scratched the night before the race!'

Well, of course, that being so, there was nothing for it but to toddle along.

There's something about evening service in a country church that makes a fellow feel drowsy and peaceful. Sort of end-of-a-perfect-day feeling. Old Heppenstall was up in the

214

pulpit, and he has a kind of regular, bleating delivery that assists thought. They had left the door open, and the air was full of a mixed scent of trees and honeysuckle and mildew and villagers' Sunday clothes. As far as the eye could reach, you could see farmers propped up in restful attitudes, breathing heavily; and the children in the congregation who had fidgeted during the earlier part of the proceedings were now lying back in a surfeited sort of coma. The last rays of the setting sun shone through the stained-glass windows, birds were twittering in the trees, the women's dresses crackled gently in the stillness. Peaceful. That's what I'm driving at. I felt peaceful. Everybody felt peaceful. And that is why the explosion, when it came, sounded like the end of all things.

I call it an explosion, because that was what it seemed like when it broke loose. One moment a dreamy hush was all over the place, broken only by old Heppenstall talking about our duty to our neighbours; and then, suddenly, a sort of piercing, shrieking squeal that got you right between the eyes and ran all the way down your spine and out at the soles of your feet.

'EE-ee-ee-ee-ee! Oo-ee! Ee-ee-ee-ee!'

It sounded like about six hundred pigs having their tails twisted simultaneously, but it was simply the kid Harold, who appeared to be having some species of fit. He was jumping up and down and slapping at the back of his neck. And about every other second he would take a deep breath and give out another of the squeals.

Well, I mean, you can't do that sort of thing in the middle

of the sermon during evening service without exciting remark. The congregation came out of its trance with a jerk, and climbed on the pews to get a better view. Old Heppenstall stopped in the middle of a sentence and spun round. And a couple of vergers with great presence of mind bounded up the aisle like leopards, collected Harold, still squealing, and marched him out. They disappeared into the vestry, and I grabbed my hat and legged it round to the stage-door, full of apprehension and what not. I couldn't think what the deuce could have happened, but somewhere dimly behind the proceedings there seemed to me to lurk the hand of the blighter Steggles.

By the time I got there and managed to get someone to open the door, which was locked, the service seemed to be over. Old Heppenstall was standing in the middle of a crowd of choirboys and vergers and sextons and what not, putting the wretched Harold through it with no little vim. I had come in at the tail end of what must have been a fairly fruity oration.

'Wretched boy! How dare you—'

'I got a sensitive skin!'

'This is no time to talk about your skin—'

'Somebody put a beetle down my back!'

'Absurd!'

'I felt it wriggling—'

'Nonsense!'

'Sounds pretty thin, doesn't it?' said someone at my side.

It was Steggles, dash him. Clad in a snowy surplice or

cassock, or whatever they call it, and wearing an expression of grave concern, the blighter had the cold, cynical crust to look me in the eyeball without a blink.

'Did you put a beetle down his neck?' I cried.

'Me!' said Steggles. 'Me!'

Old Heppenstall was putting on the black cap.

'I do not credit a word of your story, wretched boy! I have warned you before, and now the time has come to act. You cease from this moment to be a member of my choir. Go, miserable child!'

Steggles plucked at my sleeve.

'In that case,' he said, 'those bets, you know – I'm afraid you lose your money, dear old boy. It's a pity you didn't put it on S.P. I always think S.P.'s the only safe way.'

I gave him one look. Not a bit of good, of course.

'And they talk about the Purity of the Turf !' I said. And I meant it to sting, by Jove!

Jeeves received the news bravely, but I think the man was a bit rattled beneath the surface.

'An ingenious young gentleman, Mr Steggles, sir.'

'A bally swindler, you mean.'

'Perhaps that would be a more exact description. However, these things will happen on the Turf, and it is useless to complain.'

'I wish I had your sunny disposition, Jeeves!'

Jeeves bowed.

'We now rely, then, it would seem, sir, almost entirely on Mrs Penworthy. Should she justify Mr Little's encomiums and show real class in the Mothers' Sack Race, our gains will just balance our losses.'

'Yes; but that's not much consolation when you've been looking forward to a big win.'

'It is just possible that we may still find ourselves on the right side of the ledger after all, sir. Before Mr Little left, I persuaded him to invest a small sum for the syndicate of which you were kind enough to make me a member, sir, on the Girls' Egg and Spoon Race.'

'On Sarah Mills?'

'No, sir. On a long-priced outsider. Little Prudence Baxter, sir, the child of his lordship's head gardener. Her father assures me she has a very steady hand. She is accustomed to bring him his mug of beer from the cottage each afternoon, and he informs me she has never spilled a drop.'

Well, that sounded as though young Prudence's control was good. But how about speed? With seasoned performers like Sarah Mills entered, the thing practically amounted to a classic race, and in these big events you must have speed.

'I am aware that it is what is termed a long shot, sir. Still, I thought it judicious.'

'You backed her for a place, too, of course?'

'Yes, sir. Each way.'

'Well, I suppose it's all right. I've never known you make a bloomer yet.'

'Thank you very much, sir.'

I'm bound to say that, as a general rule, my idea of a large afternoon would be to keep as far away from a village school treat as possible. A sticky business. But with such grave issues toward, if you know what I mean, I sank my prejudices on this occasion and rolled up. I found the proceedings about as scaly as I had expected. It was a warm day, and the hall grounds were a dense, practically liquid mass of peasantry. Kids seethed to and fro. One of them, a small girl of sorts, grabbed my hand and hung on to it as I clove my way through the jam to where the Mothers' Sack Race was to finish. We hadn't been introduced, but she seemed to think I would do as well as anyone else to talk to about the rag-doll she had won in the Lucky Dip, and she rather spread herself on the topic.

'I'm going to call it Gertrude,' she said. 'And I shall undress it every night and put it to bed, and wake it up in the morning and dress it, and put it to bed at night, and wake it up next morning and dress it—'

'I say, old thing,' I said, 'I don't want to hurry you and all that, but you couldn't condense it a bit, could you? I'm rather anxious to see the finish of this race. The Wooster fortunes are by way of hanging on it.'

'I'm going to run in a race soon,' she said, shelving the doll for the nonce and descending to ordinary chit-chat.

'Yes?' I said. Distrait, if you know what I mean, and trying to peer through the chinks in the crowd. 'What race is that?'

'Egg 'n' Spoon.

'No really? Are you Sarah Mills?'

'Na-ow!' Registering scorn. 'I'm Prudence Baxter.'

Naturally this put our relations on a different footing. I gazed at her with considerable interest. One of the stable. I must say she didn't look much of a flier. She was short and round. Bit out of condition, I thought.

'I say,' I said, 'that being so, you mustn't dash about in the hot sun and take the edge off yourself. You must conserve your energies, old friend. Sit down here in the shade.'

'Don't want to sit down.'

'Well, take it easy, anyhow.'

The kid flitted to another topic like a butterfly hovering from flower to flower.

'I'm a good girl,' she said.

'I bet you are. I hope you're a good egg-and-spoon racer, too.'

'Harold's a bad boy. Harold squealed in church and isn't allowed to come to the treat. I'm glad,' continued this ornament of her sex, wrinkling her nose virtuously, 'because he's a bad boy. He pulled my hair Friday. Harold isn't coming to the treat! Harold isn't coming to the treat! Harold isn't coming to the treat!' she chanted, making a regular song of it.

'Don't rub it in, my dear old gardener's daughter,' I pleaded. 'You don't know it, but you've hit on a rather painful subject.'

'Ah Wooster, my dear fellow! So you have made friends with this little lady?'

It was old Heppenstall, beaming pretty profusely. Life and soul of the party.

'I am delighted, my dear Wooster,' he went on, 'quite delighted at the way you young men are throwing yourselves into the spirit of this little festivity of ours.'

'Oh, yes?' I said.

'Oh, yes! Even Rupert Steggles. I must confess that my opinion of Rupert Steggles has materially altered for the better this afternoon.'

Mine hadn't. But I didn't say so.

'I have always considered Rupert Steggles, between ourselves, a rather self-centred youth, by no means the kind who would put himself out to further the enjoyment of his fellows. And yet twice within the last half-hour I have observed him escorting Mrs Penworthy, our worthy tobacconist's wife, to the refreshment tent.'

I left him standing. I shook off the clutching hand of the Baxter kid and hared it rapidly to the spot where the Mothers' Sack Race was just finishing. I had a horrid presentiment that there had been more dirty work at the cross-roads. The first person I ran into was young Bingo. I grabbed him by the arm.

'Who won?'

'I don't know. I didn't notice.' There was bitterness in the chappie's voice. 'It wasn't Mrs Penworthy, dash her! Bertie, that hound Steggles is nothing more nor less than one of our leading snakes. I don't know how he heard about her, but he must have got on to it that she was dangerous. Do you know what he did? He lured that miserable woman into the refreshment-tent five minutes before the race, and brought her out so weighed down with cake and tea that she blew up in the first twenty yards. Just rolled over and lay there! Well, thank goodness, we still have Harold!'

I gaped at the poor chump.

'Harold! Haven't you heard?'

'Heard?' Bingo turned a delicate green. 'Heard what? I haven't heard anything. I only arrived five minutes ago. Came here straight from the station. What has happened? Tell me!'

I slipped him the information. He stared at me for a moment in a ghastly sort of way, then with a hollow groan tottered away and was lost in the crowd. A nasty knock, poor chap. I didn't blame him for being upset.

They were clearing the decks now for the Egg and Spoon Race, and I thought I might as well stay where I was and watch the finish. Not that I had much hope. Young Prudence was a good conversationalist, but she didn't seem to me to be the build for a winner.

As far as I could see through the mob, they got off to a good start. A short, red-haired child was making the running with a freckled blonde second, and Sarah Mills lying up an easy third. Our nominee was straggling along with the field, well behind the leaders. It was not hard even as early as this to spot the winner. There was a grace, a practised precision, in the way Sarah Mills held her spoon that told its own story. She was cutting out a good pace, but her egg didn't even wobble. A natural egg-and-spooner, if ever there was one.

Class will tell. Thirty yards from the tape, the red-haired kid tripped over her feet and shot her egg on to the turf. The freckled blonde fought gamely, but she had run herself out half-way down the straight, and Sarah Mills came past and home on a tight rein by several lengths, a popular winner. The blonde was second. A sniffing female in blue gingham beat a pie-faced kid in pink for the place-money, and Prudence Baxter, Jeeves's long shot, was either fifth or sixth, I couldn't see which.

And then I was carried along with the crowd to where old Heppenstall was going to present the prizes. I found myself standing next to the man Steggles.

'Hallo, old chap!' he said, very bright and cheery. 'You've had a bad day, I'm afraid.'

I looked at him with silent scorn. Lost on the blighter, of course.

'It's not been a good meeting for any of the big punters,' he went on. 'Poor old Bingo Little went down badly over that Egg and Spoon Race.'

I hadn't been meaning to chat with the fellow, but I was startled.

'How do you mean badly?' I said. 'We – he only had a small bet on.'

'I don't know what you call small. He had thirty quid each

way on the Baxter kid.'

The landscape reeled before me.

'What!'

'Thirty quid at ten to one. I thought he must have heard something, but apparently not. The race went by the form-book all right.'

I was trying to do sums in my head. I was just in the middle of working out the syndicate's losses, when old Heppenstall's voice came sort of faintly to me out of the distance. He had been pretty fatherly and debonair when ladling out the prizes for the other events, but now he had suddenly grown all pained and grieved. He peered sorrowfully at the multitude.

'With regard to the Girls' Egg and Spoon Race, which has just concluded,' he said, 'I have a painful duty to perform. Circumstances have arisen which it is impossible to ignore. It is not too much to say that I am stunned.'

He gave the populace about five seconds to wonder why he was stunned, then went on.

'Three years ago, as you are aware, I was compelled to expunge from the list of events at this annual festival the Fathers' Quarter-Mile, owing to reports coming to my ears of wagers taken and given on the result at the village inn and a strong suspicion that on at least one occasion the race had actually been sold by the speediest runner. That unfortunate occurrence shook my faith in human nature, I admit – but still there was one event at least which I confidently expected to remain untainted by the miasma of professionalism. I allude to the Girls' Egg and Spoon Race. It seems, alas, that I was too sanguine.'

He stopped again, and wrestled with his feelings.

'I will not weary you with the unpleasant details. I will merely say that before the race was run a stranger in our midst, the manservant of one of the guests at the Hall – I will not specify with more particularity – approached several of the competitors and presented each of them with five shillings on condition that they – er – finished. A belated sense of remorse has led him to confess to me what he did, but it is too late. The evil is accomplished, and retribution must take its course. It is no time for half-measures. I must be firm. I rule that Sarah Mills, Jane Parker, Bessie Clay, and Rosie Jukes, the first four to pass the winning-post, have forfeited their amateur status and are disqualified, and this handsome work-bag, presented by Lord Wickhammersley, goes, in consequence, to Prudence Baxter. Prudence, step forward!'

CHAPTER FIFTEEN
The Metropolitan Touch

Nobody is more alive than I am to the fact that young Bingo Little is in many respects a sound old egg. In one way and another he has made life pretty interesting for me at intervals ever since we were at school. As a companion for a cheery hour I think I would choose him before anybody. On the other hand, I'm bound to say that there are things about him that could be improved. His habit of falling in love with every second girl he sees is one of them; and another is his way of letting the world in on the secrets of his heart. If you want shrinking reticence, don't go to Bingo, because he's got about as much of it as a soap advertisement.

I mean to say – well, here's the telegram I got from him one evening in November, about a month after I'd got back to town from my visit to Twing Hall:

I say Bertie old man I am in love at last. She is the most wonderful girl Bertie old man. This is the real thing at last Bertie. Come here at once and bring Jeeves. Oh I say you know that tobacco shop in Bond Street on the left side as you go up. Will you get me a hundred of their special cigarettes and send them to me here. I have run out. I know when you see her you will think she is the most wonderful girl. Mind you bring Jeeves. Don't forget the cigarettes. – Bingo.

It had been handed in at Twing Post Office. In other words, he had submitted that frightful rot to the goggling eye of a village post-mistress who was probably the mainspring of local gossip and would have the place ringing with the news before nightfall. He couldn't have given himself away more completely if he had hired the town crier. When I was a kid, I used to read stories about knights and vikings and that species of chappie who would get up without a blush in the middle of a crowded banquet and loose off a song about how perfectly priceless they thought their best girl. I've often felt that those days would have suited young Bingo down to the ground.

Jeeves had brought the thing in with the evening drink, and I slung it over to him.

'It's about due, of course,' I said. 'Young Bingo hasn't been in love for at least a couple of months. I wonder who it is this time?'

'Miss Mary Burgess, sir,' said Jeeves, 'the niece of the Reverend Mr Heppenstall. She is staying at Twing Vicarage.'

'Great Scott!' I knew that Jeeves knew practically everything in the world, but this sounded like second-sight. 'How do you know that?'

'When we were visiting Twing Hall in the summer, sir, I

formed a somewhat close friendship with Mr Heppenstall's butler. He is good enough to keep me abreast of the local news from time to time. From his account, sir, the young lady appears to be a very estimable young lady. Of a somewhat serious nature, I understand. Mr Little is very épris, sir. Brookfield, my correspondent, writes that last week he observed him in the moonlight at an advanced hour gazing up at his window.'

'Whose window! Brookfield's?'

'Yes, sir. Presumably under the impression that it was the young lady's.'

'But what the deuce is he doing at Twing at all?'

'Mr Little was compelled to resume his old position as tutor to Lord Wickhammersley's son at Twing Hall, sir. Owing to having been unsuccessful in some speculations at Hurst Park at the end of October.'

'Good Lord, Jeeves! Is there anything you don't know?'

'I couldn't say, sir.'

I picked up the telegram.

'I suppose he wants us to go down and help him out a bit?'

'That would appear to be his motive in dispatching the message, sir.'

'Well, what shall we do? Go?'

'I would advocate it, sir. If I may say so, I think that Mr Little should be encouraged in this particular matter.'

'You think he's picked a winner this time?'

'I hear nothing but excellent reports of the young lady, sir. I think it is beyond question that she would be an admirable influence for Mr Little, should the affair come to a happy conclusion. Such a union would also, I fancy, go far to restore Mr Little to the good graces of his uncle, the young lady being well connected and possessing private means. In short, sir, I think that if there is anything that we can do we should do it.'

'Well, with you behind him,' I said, 'I don't see how he can fail to click.'

'You are very good, sir,' said Jeeves. 'The tribute is much appreciated.'

Bingo met us at Twing station next day, and insisted on my sending Jeeves on in the car with the bags while he and I walked. He started in about the female the moment we had begun to hoof it.

'She is very wonderful, Bertie. She is not one of these flippant, shallow-minded modern girls. She is sweetly grave and beautifully earnest. She reminds me of – what is the name I want?'

'Marie Lloyd?'

'Saint Cecilia,' said young Bingo, eyeing me with a good deal of loathing. 'She reminds me of Saint Cecilia. She makes me yearn to be a better, nobler, deeper, broader man.'

'What beats me,' I said, following up a train of thought, 'is what principle you pick them on. The girls you fall in love with, I mean. I mean to say, what's your system? As far as I can see, no two of them are alike. First it was Mabel the waitress, then Honoria Glossop, then that fearful blister Charlotte Corday Rowbotham—'

I own that Bingo had the decency to shudder. Thinking of Charlotte always made me shudder, too.

'You don't seriously mean, Bertie, that you are intending to compare the feeling I have for Mary Burgess, the holy devotion, the spiritual—'

'Oh, all right, let it go,' I said. 'I say, old lad, aren't we going rather a long way round?'

Considering that we were supposed to be heading for Twing Hall, it seemed to me that we were making a longish job of it. The Hall is about two miles from the station by the main road, and we had cut off down a lane, gone across country for a bit, climbed a stile or two, and were now working our way across a field that ended in another lane.

'She sometimes takes her little brother for a walk round this way,' explained Bingo. 'I thought we would meet her and bow, and you could see her, you know, and then we would walk on.'

'Of course,' I said, 'that's enough excitement for anyone, and undoubtedly a corking reward for tramping three miles out of one's way over ploughed fields with tight boots, but don't we do anything else? Don't we tack on to the girl and buzz along with her?'

'Good Lord!' said Bingo, honestly amazed. 'You don't suppose I've got nerve enough for that, do you? I just look at her from afar off and all that sort of thing. Quick! Here she comes! No, I'm wrong!'

It was like that song of Harry Lauder's where he's waiting

for the girl and says 'This is her-r-r. No, it's a rabbut.' Young Bingo made me stand there in the teeth of a nor'-east half-gale for ten minutes, keeping me on my toes with a series of false alarms, and I was just thinking of suggesting that we should lay off and give the rest of the proceedings a miss, when round the corner there came a fox-terrier, and Bingo quivered like an aspen. Then there hove in sight a small boy, and he shook like a jelly. Finally, like a star whose entrance has been worked up by the personnel of the ensemble, a girl appeared, and his emotion was painful to witness. His face got so red that, what with his white collar and the fact that the wind had turned his nose blue, he looked more like a French flag than anything else. He sagged from the waist upwards, as if he had been filleted.

He was just raising his fingers limply to his cap when he suddenly saw that the girl wasn't alone. A chappie in clerical costume was also among those present, and the sight of him didn't seem to do Bingo a bit of good. His face got redder and his nose bluer, and it wasn't till they had nearly passed that he managed to get hold of his cap.

The girl bowed, the curate said, 'Ah, Little. Rough weather,' the dog barked, and then they toddled on and the entertainment was over.

The curate was a new factor in the situation to me. I reported his movements to Jeeves when I got to the Hall. Of course, Jeeves knew all about it already.

'That is the Reverend Mr Wingham, Mr Heppenstall's new

curate, sir. I gathered from Brookfield that he is Mr Little's rival, and at the moment the young lady appears to favour him. Mr Wingham has the advantage of being on the premises. He and the young lady play duets after dinner, which acts as a bond. Mr Little on these occasions, I understand, prowls about in the road, chafing visibly.'

'That seems to be all the poor fish is able to do, dash it. He can chafe all right, but there he stops. He's lost his pep. He's got no dash. Why, when we met her just now, he hadn't even the common manly courage to say "Good evening"!'

'I gather that Mr Little's affection is not unmingled with awe, sir.'

'Well, how are we to help a man when he's such a rabbit as that? Have you anything to suggest? I shall be seeing him after dinner, and he's sure to ask first thing what you advise.'

'In my opinion, sir, the most judicious course for Mr Little to pursue would be to concentrate on the young gentleman.'

'The small brother? How do you mean?'

'Make a friend of him, sir – take him for walks and so forth.'

'It doesn't sound one of your red-hottest ideas. I must say I expected something fruitier than that.'

'It would be a beginning, sir, and might lead to better things.'

'Well, I'll tell him. I liked the look of her, Jeeves.'

'A thoroughly estimable young lady, sir.'

I slipped Bingo the tip from the stable that night, and was

glad to observe that it seemed to cheer him up.

'Jeeves is always right,' he said. 'I ought to have thought of it myself. I'll start in tomorrow.'

It was amazing how the chappie bucked up. Long before I left for town it had become a mere commonplace for him to speak to the girl. I mean he didn't simply look stuffed when they met. The brother was forming a bond that was a dashed sight stronger than the curate's duets. She and Bingo used to take him for walks together. I asked Bingo what they talked about on these occasions, and he said Wilfred's future. The girl hoped that Wilfred would one day become a curate, but Bingo said no, there was something about curates he didn't quite like.

The day we left, Bingo came to see us off with Wilfred frisking about him like an old college chum. The last I saw of them, Bingo was standing him chocolates out of the slot-machine. A scene of peace and cheery good-will. Dashed promising, I thought.

Which made it all the more of a jar, about a fortnight later, when his telegram arrived. As follows:

Bertie old man I say Bertie could you possibly come down here at once. Everything gone wrong hang it all. Dash it Bertie you simply must come. I am in a state of absolute despair and heart-broken. Would you mind sending another hundred of those cigarettes. Bring Jeeves when you come Bertie. You simply must come Bertie. I rely on you. Don't forget to bring Jeeves. Bingo.

For a chap who's perpetually hard-up, I must say that young Bingo is the most wasteful telegraphist I ever struck. He's got no notion of condensing. The silly ass simply pours out his wounded soul at twopence a word, or whatever it is, without a thought.

'How about it, Jeeves?' I said. 'I'm getting a bit fed. I can't go chucking all my engagements every second week in order to biff down to Twing and rally round young Bingo. Send him a wire telling him to end it all in the village pond.'

'If you could spare me for the night, sir, I should be glad to run down and investigate.'

'Oh, dash it! Well, I suppose there's nothing else to be done. After all, you're the fellow he wants. All right, carry on.'

Jeeves got back late the next day.

'Well?' I said.

Jeeves appeared perturbed. He allowed his left eyebrow to flicker upwards in a concerned sort of manner.

'I have done what I could, sir,' he said, 'but I fear Mr Little's chances do not appear bright. Since our last visit, sir, there has been a decidedly sinister and disquieting development.'

'Oh, what's that?'

'You may remember Mr Steggles, sir – the young gentleman who was studying for an examination with Mr Heppenstall at the Vicarage?'

'What's Steggles got to do with it?' I asked.

'I gather from Brookfield, sir, who chanced to overhear a conversation, that Mr Steggles is interesting himself in the affair.'

'Good Lord! What, making a book on it?'

'I understand that he is accepting wagers from those in his immediate circle, sir. Against Mr Little, whose chances he does not seem to fancy.'

'I don't like that, Jeeves.'

'No, sir. It is sinister.'

'From what I know of Steggles there will be dirty work.'

'It has already occurred, sir.'

'Already?'

'Yes, sir. It seems that, in pursuance of the policy which he had been good enough to allow me to suggest to him, Mr Little escorted Master Burgess to the church bazaar, and there met Mr Steggles, who was in the company of young Master Heppenstall, the Reverend Mr Heppenstall's second son, who is home from Rugby just now, having recently recovered from an attack of mumps. The encounter took place in the refreshment-room, where Mr Steggles was at that moment entertaining Master Heppenstall. To cut a long story short, sir, the two gentlemen became extremely interested in the hearty manner in which the lads were fortifying themselves; and Mr Steggles offered to back his nominee in a weight-for-age eating contest against Master Burgess for a pound a side. Mr Little admitted to me that he was conscious of a certain hesitation as to what the upshot might be, should Miss Burgess get to hear of the matter, but his sporting blood was too much for him and he agreed to the contest. This was duly carried out, both lads exhibiting the utmost willingness and enthusiasm, and eventually Master Burgess justified Mr Little's confidence by winning, but only after a bitter struggle. Next day both contestants were in considerable pain; inquiries were made and confessions extorted, and Mr Little – I learn from Brookfield, who happened to be near the door of the drawing-room at the moment – had an extremely unpleasant interview with the young lady, which ended in her desiring him never to speak to her again.'

There's no getting away from the fact that, if ever a man required watching, it's Steggles. Machiavelli could have taken his correspondence course.

'It was a put-up job, Jeeves!' I said. 'I mean, Steggles worked the whole thing on purpose. It's his old nobbling game.'

'There would seem to be no doubt about that, sir.'

'Well, he seems to have dished poor old Bingo all right.'

'That is the prevalent opinion, sir. Brookfield tells me that down in the village at the Cow and Horses seven to one is being freely offered on Mr Wingham and finding no takers.'

'Good Lord! Are they betting about it down in the village, too?'

'Yes, sir. And in adjoining hamlets also. The affair has caused widespread interest. I am told that there is a certain sporting reaction in even so distant a spot as Lower Bingley.'

'Well, I don't see what there is to do. If Bingo is such a chump—'

'One is fighting a losing battle, I fear, sir, but I did venture to indicate to Mr Little a course of action which might prove of advantage. I recommended him to busy himself with good works.'

'Good works?'

'About the village, sir. Reading to the bedridden – chatting with the sick – that sort of thing, sir. We can but trust that good results will ensue.'

'Yes, I suppose so,' I said doubtfully. 'But, by gosh, if I was a sick man I'd hate to have a looney like young Bingo coming and gibbering at my bedside.'

'There is that aspect of the matter, sir,' said Jeeves.

I didn't hear a word from Bingo for a couple of weeks, and I took it after a while that he had found the going too hard and had chucked in the towel. And then, one night not long before Christmas, I came back to the flat pretty latish, having been out dancing at the Embassy. I was fairly tired, having swung a practically non-stop shoe from shortly after dinner till two a.m., and bed seemed to be indicated. Judge of my chagrin and all that sort of thing, therefore, when, tottering to my room and switching on the light, I observed the foul features of young Bingo all over the pillow. The blighter had appeared from nowhere and was in my bed, sleeping like an infant with a sort of happy, dreamy smile on his map.

A bit thick I mean to say! We Woosters are all for the good old medieval hosp. and all that, but when it comes to finding chappies collaring your bed, the thing becomes a trifle too mouldy. I hove a shoe, and Bingo sat up, gurgling.

''s matter? 's matter?' said young Bingo.

'What the deuce are you doing in my bed?' I said.

'Oh, hallo, Bertie! So there you are!'

'Yes, here I am. What are you doing in my bed?'

'I came up to town for the night on business.'

'Yes, but what are you doing in my bed?'

'Dash it all, Bertie,' said young Bingo querulously, 'don't keep harping on your beastly bed. There's another made up in the spare room. I saw Jeeves make it with my own eyes. I believe he meant it for me, but I knew what a perfect host you were, so I just turned in here. I say, Bertie, old man,' said Bingo, apparently fed up with the discussion about sleeping-quarters, 'I see daylight.'

'Well, it's getting on for three in the morning.'

'I was speaking figuratively, you ass. I meant that hope has begun to dawn. About Mary Burgess, you know. Sit down and I'll tell you all about it.'

'I won't. I'm going to sleep.'

'To begin with,' said young Bingo, settling himself comfortably against the pillows and helping himself to a cigarette from my private box, 'I must once again pay a marked tribute to good old Jeeves. A modern Solomon. I was badly up against it when I came to him for advice, but he rolled up with a tip which has put me – I use the term advisedly and in a conservative spirit – on velvet. He may have told you that he recommended me to win back the lost ground by busying myself with good works? Bertie, old man,' said young Bingo earnestly, 'for the last two weeks I've been comforting the sick to such an extent that, if I had a brother and you brought him to me on a sick-bed at this moment, by Jove, old man, I'd heave a brick at him. However, though it took it out of me like the deuce, the scheme worked splendidly. She softened visibly before I'd been at it a week. Started to bow again when we met in the street, and so forth. About a couple of days ago she distinctly smiled – in a sort of faint, saint-like kind of way, you know – when I ran into her outside the Vicarage. And yesterday – I say, you remember that curate chap, Wingham? Fellow with a long nose.'

'Of course I remember him. Your rival.'

'Rival?' Bingo raised his eyebrows. 'Oh, well, I suppose you could have called him that at one time. Though it sounds a little far-fetched.'

'Does it?' I said, stung by the sickening complacency of the chump's manner. 'Well, let me tell you that the last I heard was that at the Cow and Horses in Twing village and all over the place as far as Lower Bingley they were offering seven to one on the curate and finding no takers.'

Bingo started violently and sprayed cigarette-ash all over my bed.

'Betting!' he gargled. 'Betting! You don't mean that they're betting on this holy, sacred— Oh, I say, dash it all! Haven't people any sense of decency and reverence? Is nothing safe from their beastly, sordid graspingness? I wonder,' said young

Bingo thoughtfully, 'if there's a chance of my getting any of that seven-to-one money? Seven to one! What a price! Who's offering it, do you know? Oh, well, I suppose it wouldn't do. No, I suppose it wouldn't be quite the thing.'

'You seem dashed confident,' I said. 'I'd always thought that Wingham—'

'Oh, I'm not worried about him,' said Bingo. 'I was just going to tell you. Wingham's got the mumps, and won't be out and about for weeks. And, jolly as that is in itself, it's not all. You see, he was producing the Village School Christmas Entertainment, and now I've taken over the job. I went to old Heppenstall last night and clinched the contract. Well, you see what that means. It means that I shall be absolutely the centre of the village life and thought for three solid weeks, with a terrific triumph to wind up with. Everybody looking up to me and fawning on me, don't you see, and all that. It's bound to have a powerful effect on Mary's mind. It will show her that I am capable of serious effort; that there is a solid foundation of worth in me; that, mere butterfly as she may once have thought me, I am in reality—'

'Oh, all right, let it go!'

'It's a big thing, you know, this Christmas Entertainment. Old Heppenstall is very much wrapped up in it. Nibs from all over the countryside rolling up. The Squire present, with family. A big chance for me, Bertie, my boy, and I mean to make the most of it. Of course, I'm handicapped a bit by not having been in on the thing from the start. Will you credit it that that uninspired doughnut of a curate wanted to give the public some rotten little fairy play out of a book for children published about fifty years ago without one good laugh or the semblance of a gag in it? It's too late to alter the thing entirely, but at least I can jazz it up. I'm going to write them in something zippy to brighten the thing up a bit.'

'You can't write.'

'Well, when I say write, I mean pinch. That's why I've popped up to town. I've been to see that revue, Cuddle Up! at the Palladium, tonight. Full of good stuff. Of course, it's rather hard to get anything in the nature of a big spectacular effect in the Twing Village Hall, with no scenery to speak of and a chorus of practically imbecile kids of ages ranging from nine to fourteen, but I think I see my way. Have you seen Cuddle Up!?'

'Yes. Twice.'

'Well, there's some good stuff in the first act, and I can lift practically all the numbers. Then there's that show at the Palace. I can see the matinée of that tomorrow before I leave. There's sure to be some decent bits in that. Don't you worry about my not being able to write a hit. Leave it to me, laddie, leave it to me. And now, my dear old chap,' said young Bingo, snuggling down cosily, 'you mustn't keep me up talking all night. It's all right for you fellows who have nothing to do, but I'm a busy man. Good night, old thing. Close the door quietly after you and switch out the light. Breakfast about ten tomorrow, I suppose, what? Right-o. Good night.'

For the next three weeks I didn't see Bingo. He became a sort of Voice Heard Off, developing a habit of ringing me up on long-distance and consulting me on various points arising at rehearsal, until the day when he got me out of bed at eight in the morning to ask whether I thought Merry Christmas!was a good title. I told him then that this nuisance must now cease, and after that he cheesed it, and practically passed out of my life, till one afternoon when I got back to the flat to dress for dinner and found Jeeves inspecting a whacking big poster sort of thing which he had draped over the back of an arm-chair.

'Good Lord, Jeeves!' I said. I was feeling rather weak that day, and the thing shook me. 'What on earth's that?'

'Mr Little sent it to me, sir, and desired me to bring it to your notice.'

'Well, you've certainly done it!'

I took another look at the object. There was no doubt about it, it caught the eye. It was about seven feet long, and most of the lettering in about as bright red ink as I ever struck.

This was how it ran:

TWING VILLAGE HALL,
Friday, December 23rd,
RICHARD LITTLE
presents
A New and Original Revue
Entitled
WHAT HO, TWING!!

Book by
RICHARD LITTLE
Lyrics by
RICHARD LITTLE
Music by
RICHARD LITTLE
With the Full Twing Juvenile
Company and Chorus.
Scenic Effects by
RICHARD LITTLE
Produced by
RICHARD LITTLE.

'What do you make of it, Jeeves?' I said.

'I confess I am a little doubtful, sir. I think Mr Little would have done better to follow my advice and confine himself to good works about the village.'

'You think the thing will be a frost?'

'I could not hazard a conjecture, sir. But my experience has been that what pleases the London public is not always so acceptable to the rural mind. The metropolitan touch sometimes proves a trifle too exotic for the provinces.'

'I suppose I ought to go down and see the dashed thing?'

'I think Mr Little would be wounded were you not present, sir.'

The Village Hall at Twing is a smallish building, smelling

of apples. It was full when I turned up on the evening of the twenty-third, for I had purposely timed myself to arrive not long before the kick-off. I had had experience of one or two of these binges, and didn't want to run any risk of coming early and finding myself shoved into a seat in one of the front rows where I wouldn't be able to execute a quiet sneak into the open air halfway through the proceedings, if the occasion seemed to demand it. I secured a nice strategic position near the door at the back of the hall.

From where I stood I had a good view of the audience. As always on these occasions, the first few rows were occupied by the Nibs – consisting of the Squire, a fairly mauve old sportsman with white whiskers, his family, a platoon of local parsons and perhaps a couple of dozen of prominent pew-holders. Then came a dense squash of what you might call the lower middle classes. And at the back, where I was, we came down with a jerk in the social scale, this end of the hall being given up almost entirely to a collection of frankly Tough Eggs, who had rolled up not so much for any love of the drama as because there was a free tea after the show. Take it for all in all, a representative gathering of Twing life and thought. The Nibs were whispering in a pleased manner to each other, the Lower Middles were sitting up very straight, as if they'd been bleached, and the Tough Eggs whiled away the time by cracking nuts and exchanging low rustic wheezes. The girl, Mary Burgess, was at the piano playing a waltz. Beside her stood the curate, Wingham, apparently recovered. The temperature, I should think, was about a hundred and twenty-seven.

Somebody jabbed me heartily in the lower ribs, and I perceived the man Steggles.

'Hallo!' he said. 'I didn't know you were coming down.'

I didn't like the chap, but we Woosters can wear the mask. I beamed a bit.

'Oh, yes,' I said. 'Bingo wanted me to roll up and see his show.'

'I hear he's giving us something pretty ambitious,' said the man Steggles. 'Big effects and all that sort of thing.'

'I believe so.'

'Of course, it means a lot to him, doesn't it? He's told you about the girl, of course?'

'Yes. And I hear you're laying seven to one against him,' I said, eyeing the blighter a trifle austerely.

He didn't even quiver.

'Just a little flutter to relieve the monotony of country life,' he said. 'But you've got the facts a bit wrong. It's down in the village that they're laying seven to one. I can do you better than that, if you feel in a speculative mood. How about a tenner at a hundred to eight?'

'Good Lord! Are you giving that?'

'Yes. Somehow,' said Steggles meditatively, 'I have a sort of feeling, a kind of premonition that something's going to go wrong tonight. You know what Little is. A bungler, if ever there was one. Something tells me that this show of his is going to be a frost. And if it is, of course, I should think it would prejudice the girl against him pretty badly. His standing always was rather shaky.'

'Are you going to try and smash up the show?' I said sternly.

'Me!' said Steggles. 'Why, what could I do? Half a minute, I want to go and speak to a man.'

He buzzed off, leaving me distinctly disturbed. I could see from the fellow's eye that he was meditating some of his customary rough stuff, and I thought Bingo ought to be warned. But there wasn't time and I couldn't get at him. Almost immediately after Steggles had left me the curtain went up.

Except as a prompter, Bingo wasn't much in evidence in the early part of the performance. The thing at the outset was merely one of those weird dramas which you dig out of books published around Christmas time and entitled Twelve Little Plays for the Tots, or something like that. The kids drooled on in the usual manner, the booming voice of Bingo ringing out from time to time behind the scenes when the fatheads forgot their lines; and the audience was settling down into the sort of torpor usual on these occasions, when the first of Bingo's interpolated bits occurred. It was that number which What's-her-name sings in that revue at the Palace – you would recognize the tune if I hummed it, but I can never get hold of the dashed thing. It always got three encores at the Palace, and it went well now, even with a squeaky-voiced child jumping on and off the key like a chamois of the Alps leaping from crag

P.G. Wodehouse

to crag. Even the Tough Eggs liked it. At the end of the second refrain the entire house was shouting for an encore, and the kid with the voice like a slate-pencil took a deep breath and started to let it go once more.

At this point all the lights went out.

I don't know when I've had anything so sudden and devastating happen to me before. They didn't flicker. They just went out. The hall was in complete darkness.

Well, of course, that sort of broke the spell, as you might put it. People started to shout directions, and the Tough Eggs stamped their feet and settled down for a pleasant time. And, of course, young Bingo had to make an ass of himself. His voice suddenly shot at us out of the darkness.

'Ladies and gentlemen, something has gone wrong with the lights—'

The Tough Eggs were tickled by this bit of information straight from the stable. They took it up as a sort of battle-cry. Then, after about five minutes, the lights went up again, and the show was resumed.

It took ten minutes after that to get the audience back into its state of coma, but eventually they began to settle down, and everything was going nicely when a small boy with a face like a turbot edged out in front of the curtain, which had been lowered after a pretty painful scene about a wishing-ring or a fairy's curse or something of that sort, and started to sing that song of George Thingummy's out of Cuddle Up!. You know the one I mean. 'Always Listen to Mother, Girls!' it's called, and he gets the audience to join in and sing the refrain. Quite a ripeish ballad, and one which I myself have frequently sung in my bath with not a little vim; but by no means – as anyone but a perfect sapheaded prune like young Bingo would have known – by no means the sort of thing for a children's Christmas entertainment in the old village hall. Right from the start of the first refrain the bulk of the audience had begun to stiffen in their seats and fan themselves, and the Burgess girl at the piano was accompanying in a stunned, mechanical sort of way, while the curate at her side averted his gaze in a pained manner. The Tough Eggs, however, were all for it.

At the end of the second refrain the kid stopped and began to sidle towards the wings. Upon which the following brief duologue took place:

Young Bingo (Voice heard off, ringing against the rafters): 'Go on!'

THE KID (coyly): 'I don't like to.'

YOUNG BINGO (still louder): 'Go on, you little blighter, or I'll slay you!'

I suppose the kid thought it over swiftly and realized that Bingo, being in a position to get at him, had better be conciliated, whatever the harvest might be; for he shuffled down to the front and, having shut his eyes and giggled hysterically, said: 'Ladies and gentlemen, I will now call upon Squire Tressidder to oblige by singing the refrain!'

You know, with the most charitable feelings towards him, there are moments when you can't help thinking that young

Bingo ought to be in some sort of a home. I suppose, poor fish, he had pictured this as the big punch of the evening. He had imagined, I take it, that the Squire would spring jovially to his feet, rip the song off his chest, and all would be gaiety and mirth. Well, what happened was simply that old Tressidder – and, mark you, I'm not blaming him – just sat where he was, swelling and turning a brighter purple every second. The lower middle classes remained in frozen silence, waiting for the roof to fall. The only section of the audience that really seemed to enjoy the idea was the Tough Eggs, who yelled with enthusiasm. It was jam for the Tough Eggs.

And then the lights went out again.

When they went up, some minutes later, they disclosed the Squire marching stiffly out at the head of his family, fed up to the eyebrows; the Burgess girl at the piano with a pale, set look; and the curate gazing at her with something in his expression that seemed to suggest that, although all this was no doubt deplorable, he had spotted the silver lining.

The show went on once more. There were great chunks of Plays-for-the-Tots dialogue, and then the girl at the piano struck up the prelude to that Orange-Girl number that's the big hit of the Palace revue. I took it that this was to be Bingo's smashing act one finale. The entire company was on the stage, and a clutching hand had appeared round the edge of the curtain, ready to pull at the right moment. It looked like the finale all right. It wasn't long before I realized that it was something more. It was the finish.

I take it you know that Orange number at the Palace? It goes:

Oh, won't you something something oranges,
My something oranges, My something oranges;
Oh, won't you something something something I forget,
Something something something tumty tumty yet:
Oh—

or words to that effect. It's a dashed clever lyric, and the tune's good, too; but the thing that made the number was the business where the girls take oranges out of their baskets, you know, and toss them lightly to the audience. I don't know if you've ever noticed it, but it always seems to tickle an audience to bits when they get things thrown at them from the stage. Every time I've been to the Palace the customers have simply gone wild over this number.

But at the Palace, of course, the oranges are made of yellow wool, and the girls don't so much chuck them as drop them limply into the first and second rows. I began to gather that the business was going to be treated rather differently tonight when a dashed great chunk of pips and mildew sailed past my ear and burst on the wall behind me. Another landed with a squelch on the neck of one of the Nibs in the third row. And then a third took me right on the tip of the nose, and I kind of lost interest in the proceedings for a while.

When I had scrubbed my face and got my eye to stop

watering for a moment, I saw that the evening's entertainment had begun to resemble one of Belfast's livelier nights. The air was thick with shrieks and fruit. The kids on the stage, with Bingo buzzing distractedly to and fro in their midst, were having the time of their lives. I suppose they realized that this couldn't go on for ever, and were making the most of their chances. The Tough Eggs had begun to pick up all the oranges that hadn't burst and were shooting them back, so that the audience got it both coming and going. In fact, take it all round, there was a certain amount of confusion; and, just as things had begun really to hot up, out went the lights again.

It seemed to me about my time for leaving, so I slid for the door. I was hardly outside when the audience began to stream out. They surged about me in twos and threes, and I've never seen a public body so dashed unanimous on any point. To a man – and to a woman – they were cursing poor old Bingo; and there was a large and rapidly growing school of thought which held that the best thing to do would be to waylay him as he emerged and splash him about in the village pond a bit.

There were such a dickens of a lot of these enthusiasts and they looked so jolly determined that it seemed to me that the only matey thing to do was to go behind and warn young Bingo to turn his coat-collar up and breeze off snakily by some side exit. I went behind, and found him sitting on a box in the wings, perspiring pretty freely and looking more or less like the spot marked with a cross where the accident happened. His hair was standing up and his ears were hanging down, and one harsh word would undoubtedly have made him burst into tears.

'Bertie,' he said hollowly, as he saw me, 'it was that blighter Steggles! I caught one of the kids before he could get away and got it all out of him. Steggles substituted real oranges for the balls of wool which with infinite sweat and at a cost of nearly a quid I had specially prepared. Well, I will now proceed to tear him limb from limb. It'll be something to do.'

I hated to spoil his day-dreams, but it had to be.

'Good heavens, man,' I said, 'you haven't time for frivolous amusements now. You've got to get out. And quick!'

'Bertie,' said Bingo in a dull voice, 'she was here just now. She said it was all my fault and that she would never speak to me again. She said she had always suspected me of being a heartless practical joker, and now she knew. She said— Oh, well, she ticked me off properly.'

'That's the least of your troubles,' I said. It seemed impossible to rouse the poor zib to a sense of his position. 'Do you realize that about two hundred of Twing's heftiest are waiting for you outside to chuck you into the pond?'

'No!'

'Absolutely!'

For a moment the poor chap seemed crushed. But only for a moment. There has always been something of the good old English bulldog breed about Bingo. A strange, sweet smile flickered for an instant over his face.

'It's all right,' he said. 'I can sneak out through the cellar and climb over the wall at the back. They can't intimidate me!'

It couldn't have been more than a week later when Jeeves, after he had brought me my tea, gently steered me away from the sporting page of the Morning Post and directed my attention to an announcement in the engagements and marriages column.

It was a brief statement that a marriage had been arranged and would shortly take place between the Hon. and Rev. Hubert Wingham, third son of the Right Hon. the Earl of Sturridge, and Mary, only daughter of the late Matthew Burgess, of Weatherly Court, Hants.

'Of course,' I said, after I had given it the east-to-west, 'I expected this, Jeeves.'

'Yes, sir.'

'She would never forgive him what happened that night.'

'No, sir.'

'Well,' I said, as I took a sip of the fragrant and steaming, 'I don't suppose it will take old Bingo long to get over it. It's about the hundred and eleventh time this sort of thing has happened to him. You're the man I'm sorry for.'

'Me, sir?'

'Well, dash it all, you can't have forgotten what a deuce of a lot of trouble you took to bring the thing off for Bingo. It's too bad that all your work should have been wasted.'

'Not entirely wasted, sir.'

'Eh?'

'It is true that my efforts to bring about the match between Mr Little and the young lady were not successful, but I still look back upon the matter with a certain satisfaction.'

'Because you did your best, you mean?'

'Not entirely, sir, though of course that thought also gives me pleasure. I was alluding more particularly to the fact that I found the affair financially remunerative.'

'Financially remunerative? What do you mean?'

'When I learned that Mr Steggles had interested himself in the contest, sir, I went shares with my friend Brookfield and bought the book which had been made on the issue by the landlord of the Cow and Horses. It has proved a highly profitable investment. Your breakfast will be ready almost immediately, sir. Kidneys on toast and mushrooms. I will bring it when you ring.'

CHAPTER SIXTEEN
The Delayed Exit of Claude and Eustace

The feeling I had when Aunt Agatha trapped me in my lair that morning and spilled the bad news was that my luck had broken at last. As a rule, you see, I'm not lugged into Family Rows. On the occasions when Aunt is calling to Aunt like mastodons bellowing across primeval swamps and Uncle James's letter about Cousin Mabel's peculiar behaviour is being shot round the family circle ('Please read this carefully and send it on to Jane'), the clan has a tendency to ignore me. It's one of the advantages I get from being a bachelor – and, according to my nearest and dearest, practically a half-witted bachelor at that. 'It's no good trying to get Bertie to take the slightest interest' is more or less the slogan, and I'm bound to say I'm all for it. A quiet life is what I like. And that's why I felt that the Curse had come upon me, so to speak, when Aunt Agatha sailed into my sitting-room while I was having a placid cigarette and started to tell me about Claude and Eustace.

'Thank goodness,' said Aunt Agatha, 'arrangements have

at last been made about Eustace and Claude.'

'Arrangements?' I said, not having the foggiest.

'They sail on Friday for South Africa. Mr Van Alstyne, a friend of poor Emily's, has given them berths in his firm at Johannesburg, and we are hoping that they will settle down there and do well.'

I didn't get the thing at all.

'Friday? The day after tomorrow, do you mean?'

'Yes.'

'For South Africa?'

'Yes. They leave on the Edinburgh Castle.'

'But what's the idea? I mean, aren't they in the middle of their term at Oxford?'

Aunt Agatha looked at me coldly.

'Do you positively mean to tell me, Bertie, that you take so little interest in the affairs of your nearest relatives that you are not aware that Claude and Eustace were expelled from Oxford over a fortnight ago?'

'No, really?'

'You are hopeless, Bertie. I should have thought that even you—'

'Why were they sent down?'

'They poured lemonade on the Junior Dean of their college. . . . I see nothing amusing in the outrage, Bertie.'

'No, no, rather not,' I said hurriedly. 'I wasn't laughing. Choking. Got something stuck in my throat, you know.'

'Poor Emily,' went on Aunt Agatha, 'being one of those

doting mothers who are the ruin of their children, wished to keep the boys in London. She suggested that they might cram for the Army. But I was firm. The Colonies are the only place for wild youths like Eustace and Claude. So they sail on Friday. They have been staying for the last two weeks with your Uncle Clive in Worcestershire. They will spend tomorrow night in London and catch the boat-train on Friday morning.'

'Bit risky, isn't it? I mean, aren't they apt to cut loose a bit tomorrow night if they're left all alone in London?'

'They will not be left alone. They will be in your charge.'

'Mine!'

'Yes. I wish you to put them up in your flat for the night, and see that they do not miss the train in the morning.'

'Oh, I say, no!'

'Bertie!'

'Well, I mean, quite jolly coves both of them, but I don't know. They're rather nuts, you know— Always glad to see them, of course, but when it comes to putting them up for the night—'

'Bertie, if you are so sunk in callous self-indulgence that you cannot even put yourself to this trifling inconvenience for the sake of—'

'Oh, all right,' I said. 'All right.'

It was no good arguing, of course. Aunt Agatha always makes me feel as if I had gelatine where my spine ought to be. She's one of those forceful females. I should think Queen Elizabeth I must have been something like her. When she holds me with her glittering eye and says, 'Jump to it, my lad', or words to that effect, I make it so without further discussion.

When she had gone, I rang for Jeeves to break the news to him.

'Oh, Jeeves,' I said, 'Mr Claude and Mr Eustace will be staying here tomorrow night.'

'Very good, sir.'

'I'm glad you think so. To me the outlook seems black and scaly. You know what those two lads are!'

'Very high-spirited young gentlemen, sir.'

'Blisters, Jeeves. Undeniable blisters. It's a bit thick!'

'Would there be anything further, sir?'

At that, I'm bound to say, I drew myself up a trifle haughtily. We Woosters freeze like the dickens when we seek sympathy and meet with cold reserve. I knew what was up, of course. For the last day or so there had been a certain amount of coolness in the home over a pair of jazz spats which I had dug up while exploring in the Burlington Arcade. Some dashed brainy cove, probably the chap who invented those coloured cigarette-cases, had recently had the rather topping idea of putting out a line of spats on the same system. I mean to say, instead of the ordinary grey and white, you can now get them in your regimental or school colours. And, believe me, it would have taken a chappie of stronger fibre than I am to resist the pair of Old Etonian spats which had smiled up at me from inside the window. I was inside the shop, opening negotiations, before it had even occurred to me that Jeeves might not approve.

And I must say he had taken the thing a bit hardly. The fact of the matter is, Jeeves, though in many ways the best valet in London, is too conservative. Hidebound, if you know what I mean, and an enemy to Progress.

'Nothing further, Jeeves,' I said, with quiet dignity.

'Very good, sir.'

He gave one frosty look at the spats and biffed off. Dash him!

Anything merrier and brighter than the Twins, when they curvetted into the old flat while I was dressing for dinner the next night, I have never struck in my whole puff. I'm only about half a dozen years older than Claude and Eustace, but in some rummy manner they always make me feel as if I were well on in the grandfather class and just waiting for the end. Almost before I realized they were in the place, they had collared the best chairs, pinched a couple of my special cigarettes, poured themselves out a whisky-and-soda apiece, and started to prattle with the gaiety and abandon of two birds who had achieved their life's ambition instead of having come a most frightful purler and being under sentence of exile.

'Hallo, Bertie, old thing,' said Claude. 'Jolly decent of you to put us up.'

'Oh, no,' I said. 'Only wish you were staying a good long time.'

'Hear that, Eustace? He wishes we were staying a good long time.'

'I expect it will seem a good long time,' said Eustace,

philosophically.

'You heard about the binge, Bertie? Our little bit of trouble, I mean?'

'Oh, yes. Aunt Agatha was telling me.'

'We leave our country for our country's good,' said Eustace.

'And let there be no moaning at the bar,' said Claude, 'when I put out to sea. What did Aunt Agatha tell you?'

'She said you poured lemonade on the Junior Dean.'

'I wish the deuce,' said Claude, annoyed, 'that people would get these things right. It wasn't the Junior Dean. It was the Senior Tutor.'

'And it wasn't lemonade,' said Eustace. 'It was soda-water. The dear old thing happened to be standing just under our window while I was leaning out with a siphon in my hand. He looked up, and – well, it would have been chucking away the opportunity of a life-time if I hadn't let him have it in the eyeball.'

'Simply chucking it away,' agreed Claude.

'Might never have occurred again,' said Eustace.

'Hundred to one against it,' said Claude.

'Now, what,' said Eustace, 'do you propose to do, Bertie, in the way of entertaining the handsome guests tonight?'

'My idea was to have a bite of dinner in the flat,' I said. 'Jeeves is getting it ready now.'

'And afterwards?'

'Well, I thought we might chat of this and that, and then it struck me that you would probably like to turn in early, as your train goes about ten or something, doesn't it?'

The twins looked at each other in a pitying sort of way.

'Bertie,' said Eustace, 'you've got the programme nearly right, but not quite. I envisage the evening's events thus: We will toddle along to Ciro's after dinner. It's an extension night, isn't it? Well, that will see us through till about two-thirty or three.'

'After which, no doubt,' said Claude, 'the Lord will provide.'

'But I thought you would want to get a good night's rest.'

'Good night's rest!' said Eustace. 'My dear old chap, you don't for a moment imagine that we are dreaming of going to bed tonight, do you?'

I suppose the fact of the matter is, I'm not the man I was. I mean, those all-night vigils don't seem to fascinate me as they used to a few years ago. I can remember the time, when I was up at Oxford, when a Covent Garden ball till six in the morning, with breakfast at the Hammams and probably a free fight with a few selected costermongers to follow, seemed to me what the doctor ordered. But nowadays two o'clock is about my limit; and by two o'clock the twins were just settling down and beginning to go nicely.

As far as I can remember, we went on from Ciro's to play chemmy with some fellows I don't recall having met before, and it must have been about nine in the morning when we fetched up again at the flat. By which time, I'm bound to admit, as far as I was concerned the first careless freshness was beginning to wear off a bit. In fact, I'd just got enough strength to say good-bye to the twins, wish them a pleasant voyage and a happy and successful career in South Africa, and stagger into bed. The last I remember was hearing the blighters chanting like larks under the cold shower, breaking off from time to time to shout to Jeeves to rush along the eggs and bacon.

It must have been about one in the afternoon when I woke. I was feeling more or less like something the Pure Food Committee had rejected, but there was one bright thought which cheered me up, and that was that about now the twins would be leaning on the rail of the liner, taking their last glimpse of the dear old homeland. Which made it all the more of a shock when the door opened and Claude walked in.

'Hallo, Bertie!' said Claude. 'Had a nice refreshing sleep? Now, what about a good old bite of lunch?'

I'd been having so many distorted nightmares since I had dropped off to sleep that for half a minute I thought this was simply one more of them, and the worst of the lot. It was only when Claude sat down on my feet that I got on to the fact that this was stern reality.

'Great Scott! What on earth are you doing here?' I gurgled.

Claude looked at me reproachfully.

'Hardly the tone I like to hear in a host, Bertie,' he said reprovingly. 'Why, it was only last night that you were saying you wished I was stopping a good long time. Your dream has come true. I am.'

'But why aren't you on your way to South Africa?'

'Now that,' said Claude, 'is a point I rather thought you would want to have explained. It's like this, old man. You remember that girl you introduced me to at Ciro's last night?'

'Which girl?'

'There was only one,' said Claude coldly. 'Only one that counted, that is to say. Her name was Marion Wardour. I danced with her a good deal, if you remember.'

I began to recollect in a hazy sort of way. Marion Wardour has been a pal of mine for some time. A very good sort. She's playing in that show at the Apollo at the moment. I remembered now that she had been at Ciro's with a party the night before, and the twins had insisted on being introduced.

'We are soul-mates, Bertie,' said Claude. 'I found it out quite early in the p.m., and the more thought I've given to the matter the more convinced I've become. It happens like that now and then, you know. Two hearts that beat as one, I mean, and all that sort of thing. So the long and the short of it is that I gave old Eustace the slip at Waterloo and slid back here. The idea of going to South Africa and leaving a girl like that in England doesn't appeal to me a bit. I'm for all thinking imperially and giving the Colonies a leg-up and all that sort of thing; but it can't be done. After all,' said Claude reasonably, 'South Africa has got along all right without me up till now, so why shouldn't it stick it?'

'But what about Van Alstyne, or whatever his name is? He'll be expecting you to turn up.'

'Oh, he'll have Eustace. That'll satisfy him. Very sound fellow, Eustace. Probably end up by being a magnate of some kind. I shall watch his future progress with considerable interest. And now you must excuse me for a moment, Bertie. I want to go and hunt up Jeeves and get him to mix me one of those pick-me-ups of his. For some reason which I can't explain, I've got a slight headache this morning.'

And, believe me or believe me not, the door had hardly closed behind him when in blew Eustace with a shining morning face that made me ill to look at.

'Oh, my aunt!' I said.

Eustace started to giggle pretty freely.

'Smooth work, Bertie, smooth work!' he said. 'I'm sorry for poor old Claude, but there was no alternative. I eluded his vigilance at Waterloo and snaked off in a taxi. I suppose the poor old ass is wondering where the deuce I've got to. But it couldn't be helped. If you really seriously expected me to go slogging off to South Africa, you shouldn't have introduced me to Miss Wardour last night. I want to tell you all about that, Bertie. I'm not a man,' said Eustace, sitting down on the bed, 'who falls in love with every girl he sees. I suppose "strong, silent", would be the best description you could find for me. But when I do meet my affinity I don't waste time. I—'

'Oh, heaven! Are you in love with Marion Wardour, too?'

'Too? What do you mean, "too"?'

I was going to tell him about Claude, when the blighter came in in person, looking like a giant refreshed. There's no doubt that Jeeves's pick-me-ups will produce immediate results in anything short of an Egyptian mummy. It's something he puts in them – the Worcester sauce or something. Claude had revived like a watered flower, but he nearly had a relapse when he saw his bally brother goggling at him over the bed-rail.

'What on earth are you doing here?' he said.

'What on earth are you doing here?' said Eustace.

'Have you come back to inflict your beastly society upon Miss Wardour?'

'Is that why you've come back?'

They thrashed the subject out a bit further.

'Well,' said Claude at last. 'I suppose it can't be helped. If you're here, you're here. May the best man win!'

'Yes, but dash it all!' I managed to put in at this point. 'What's the idea? Where do you think you're going to stay if you stick on in London?'

'Why, here,' said Eustace, surprised.

'Where else?' said Claude, raising his eyebrows.

'You won't object to putting us up, Bertie?' said Eustace.

'Not a sportsman like you,' said Claude.

'But, you silly asses, suppose Aunt Agatha finds out that I'm hiding you when you ought to be in South Africa? Where do I get off?'

'Where does he get off?' Claude asked Eustace.

'Oh, I expect he'll manage somehow,' said Eustace to Claude.

'Of course,' said Claude, quite cheered up. 'He'll manage.'

'Rather!' said Eustace. 'A resourceful chap like Bertie! Of course he will.'

'And now,' said Claude, shelving the subject, 'what about that bite of lunch we were discussing a moment ago, Bertie? That stuff good old Jeeves slipped into me just now has given me what you might call an appetite. Something in the nature of six chops and a batter pudding would about meet the case, I think.'

I suppose every chappie in the world has black periods in his life to which he can't look back without the smouldering eye and the silent shudder. Some coves, if you can judge by the novels you read nowadays, have them practically all the time; but, what with enjoying a sizeable private income and a topping digestion, I'm bound to say it isn't very often I find my own existence getting a flat tyre. That's why this particular epoch is one that I don't think about more often than I can help. For the days that followed the unexpected resurrection of the blighted twins were so absolutely foul that the old nerves began to stick out of my body a foot long and curling at the ends. All of a twitter, believe me. I imagine the fact of the matter is that we Woosters are so frightfully honest and open and all that, that it gives us the pip to have to deceive.

All was quiet along the Potomac for about twenty-four hours, and then Aunt Agatha trickled in to have a chat. Twenty minutes earlier and she would have found the twins gaily shoving themselves outside a couple of rashers and an egg. She sank into a chair, and I could see that she was not in her usual sunny spirits.

'Bertie,' she said, 'I am uneasy.'

So was I. I didn't know how long she intended to stop, or when the twins were coming back.

'I wonder,' she said, 'if I took too harsh a view towards Claude and Eustace.'

'You couldn't.'

'What do you mean?'

'I – er – mean it would be so unlike you to be harsh to anybody, Aunt Agatha.' And not bad, either. I mean, quick – like that – without thinking. It pleased the old relative, and she looked at me with slightly less loathing than she usually does.

'It is nice of you to say that, Bertie, but what I was thinking was, are they safe?'

'Are they what?'

It seemed such a rummy adjective to apply to the twins, they being about as innocuous as a couple of sprightly young tarantulas.

'Do you think all is well with them?'

'How do you mean?'

Aunt Agatha eyed me almost wistfully.

'Has it ever occurred to you, Bertie,' she said, 'that your Uncle George may be psychic?'

She seemed to me to be changing the subject.

'Psychic?'

'Do you think it is possible that he could see things not visible to the normal eye?'

I thought it dashed possible, if not probable. I don't know if you've ever met my Uncle George. He's a festive old egg who wanders from club to club continually having a couple with other festive old eggs. When he heaves in sight, waiters brace themselves up and the wine-steward toys with his corkscrew. It was my Uncle George who discovered that alcohol was a food well in advance of modern medical thought.

'Your Uncle George was dining with me last night, and he was quite shaken. He declares that, while on his way from the Devonshire Club to Boodle's he suddenly saw the phantasm of Eustace.'

'The what of Eustace?'

'The phantasm. The wraith. It was so clear that he thought for an instant that it was Eustace himself. The figure vanished round a corner, and when Uncle George got there nothing was to be seen. It is all very queer and disturbing. It had a marked effect on poor George. All through dinner he touched nothing but barley-water, and his manner was quite disturbed. You do think those poor, dear boys are safe, Bertie? They have not met with some horrible accident?'

It made my mouth water to think of it, but I said no, I didn't think they had met with any horrible accident. I thought Eustace was a horrible accident, and Claude about the same, but I didn't say so. And presently she biffed off, still worried.

When the twins came in, I put it squarely to the blighters. Jolly as it was to give Uncle George shocks, they must not wander at large about the metrop.

'But, my dear old soul,' said Claude. 'Be reasonable. We can't have our movements hampered.'

'Out of the question,' said Eustace.

'The whole essence of the thing, if you understand me,' said Claude, 'is that we should be at liberty to flit hither and thither.'

'Exactly,' said Eustace. 'Now hither, now thither.'

'But, damn it—'

'Bertie!' said Eustace reprovingly. 'Not before the boy!'

'Of course, in a way I see his point,' said Claude. 'I suppose the solution of the problem would be to buy a couple of disguises.'

'My dear old chap!' said Eustace, looking at him with admiration. 'The brightest idea on record. Not your own, surely?'

'Well, as a matter of fact, it was Bertie who put it into my head.'

'Me!'

'You were telling me the other day about old Bingo Little and the beard he bought when he didn't want his uncle to recognize him.'

'If you think I'm going to have you two excrescences popping in and out of my flat in beards—'

'Something in that,' agreed Eustace. 'We'll make it

whiskers, then.'

'And false noses,' said Claude.

'And, as you say, false noses. Right-o, then, Bertie, old chap, that's a load off your mind. We don't want to be any trouble to you while we're paying you this little visit.'

And, when I went buzzing round to Jeeves for consolation, all he would say was something about Young Blood. No sympathy.

'Very good, Jeeves,' I said. 'I shall go for a walk in the Park. Kindly put me out the Old Etonion spats.'

'Very good, sir.'

It must have been a couple of days after that that Marion Wardour rolled in at about the hour of tea. She looked warily round the room before sitting down.

'Your cousins not at home, Bertie?' she said.

'No, thank goodness!'

'Then I'll tell you where they are. They're in my sitting-room, glaring at each other from opposite corners, waiting for me to come in. Bertie, this has got to stop.'

'You're seeing a good deal of them, are you?'

Jeeves came in with the tea, but the poor girl was so worked up that she didn't wait for him to pop off before going on with her complaint. She had an absolutely hunted air, poor thing.

'I can't move a step without tripping over one or both of them,' she said. 'Generally both. They've taken to calling together, and they just settle down grimly and try to sit each other out. It's wearing me to a shadow.'

'I know,' I said sympathetically. 'I know.'

'Well, what's to be done?'

'It beats me. Couldn't you tell your maid to say you are not at home?'

She shuddered slightly.

'I tried that once. They camped on the stairs, and I couldn't get out all the afternoon. And I had a lot of particularly important engagements. I wish you would persuade them to go to South Africa, where they seem to be wanted.'

'You must have made the dickens of an impression on them.'

'I should say I have. They've started giving me presents now. At least Claude has. He insisted on my accepting this cigarette-case last night. Came round to the theatre and wouldn't go away till I took it. It's not a bad one, I must say.'

It wasn't. It was a distinctly fruity concern in gold with a diamond stuck in the middle. And the rummy thing was that I had a notion I'd seen something very like it before somewhere. How the deuce Claude had been able to dig up the cash to buy a thing like that was more than I could imagine.

Next day was a Wednesday, and as the object of their devotion had a matinée, the twins were, so to speak, off duty. Claude had gone with his whiskers on to Hurst Park, and Eustace and I were in the flat, talking. At least, he was talking and I was wishing he would go.

'The love of a good woman, Bertie,' he was saying, 'must be a wonderful thing. Sometimes—Good Lord! what's that?'

The front door had opened, and from out in the hall there came the sound of Aunt Agatha's voice asking if I was in. Aunt Agatha has one of those high, penetrating voices, but this was the first time I'd ever been thankful for it. There was just about two seconds to clear the way for her, but it was long enough for Eustace to dive under the sofa. His last shoe had just disappeared when she came in.

She had a worried look. It seemed to me about this time that everybody had.

'Bertie,' she said, 'what are your immediate plans?'

'How do you mean? I'm dining tonight with—'

'No, no, I don't mean tonight. Are you busy for the next few days? But, of course you are not,' she went on, not waiting for me to answer. 'You never have anything to do. Your whole life is spent in idle – but we can go into that later. What I came for this afternoon was to tell you that I wish you to go with your poor Uncle George to Harrogate for a few weeks. The sooner you can start, the better.'

This appeared to me to approximate so closely to the frozen limit that I uttered a yelp of protest. Uncle George is all right, but he won't do. I was trying to say as much when she waved me down.

'If you are not entirely heartless, Bertie, you will do as I ask you. Your poor Uncle George has had a severe shock.'

'What, another?'

'He feels that only complete rest and careful medical attendance can restore his nervous system to its normal poise. It seems that in the past he has derived benefit from taking the waters at Harrogate, and he wishes to go there now. We do not think he ought to be alone, so I wish you to accompany him.'

'But, I say!'

'Bertie!'

There was a lull in the conversation.

'What shock has he had?' I asked.

'Between ourselves,' said Aunt Agatha, lowering her voice in an impressive manner, 'I incline to think that the whole affair was the outcome of an over-excited imagination. You are one of the family, Bertie, and I can speak freely to you. You know as well as I do that your poor Uncle George has for many years not been a – he has – er – developed a habit of – how shall I put it?'

'Shifting it a bit?'

'I beg your pardon?'

'Mopping up the stuff to some extent?'

'I dislike your way of putting it exceedingly, but I must confess that he has not been, perhaps, as temperate as he should. He is highly-strung, and— Well, the fact is, that he has had a shock.'

'Yes, but what?'

'That is what it is so hard to induce him to explain with any precision. With all his good points, your poor Uncle George is apt to become incoherent when strongly moved. As far as I could gather, he appears to have been the victim of a burglary.'

'Burglary!'

'He says that a strange man with whiskers and a peculiar nose entered his rooms in Jermyn Street during his absence and stole some of his property. He says that he came back and found the man in his sitting-room. He immediately rushed out of the room and disappeared.'

'Uncle George?'

'No, the man. And, according to your Uncle George, he had stolen a valuable cigarette-case. But, as I say, I am inclined to think that the whole thing was imagination. He has not been himself since the day when he fancied that he saw Eustace in the street. So I should like you, Bertie, to be prepared to start for Harrogate with him not later than Saturday.'

She popped off, and Eustace crawled out from under the sofa. The blighter was strongly moved. So was I, for the matter of that. The idea of several weeks with Uncle George at Harrogate seemed to make everything go black.

'So that's where he got that cigarette-case, dash him!' said Eustace bitterly. 'Of all the dirty tricks! Robbing his own flesh and blood! The fellow ought to be in chokey.'

'He ought to be in South Africa,' I said. 'And so ought you.'

And with an eloquence which rather surprised me, I hauled up my slacks for perhaps ten minutes on the subject of his duty to his family and what not. I appealed to his sense of decency. I boosted South Africa with vim. I said everything I could think of, much of it twice over. But all the blighter did was to babble about his dashed brother's baseness in putting one over on him in the matter of the cigarette-case. He seemed to think that Claude, by slinging in the handsome gift, had got right ahead of him: and there was a painful scene when the latter came back from Hurst Park. I could hear them talking half the night, long after I had tottered off to bed. I don't know when I've met fellows who could do with less sleep than those two.

After this, things became a bit strained at the flat owing to Claude and Eustace not being on speaking terms. I'm all for a certain chumminess in the home, and it was wearing to have to live with two fellows who wouldn't admit that the other one was on the map at all.

One felt the thing couldn't go on like that for long, and, by Jove, it didn't. But, if anyone had come to me the day before and told me what was going to happen, I should simply have smiled wanly. I mean, I'd got so accustomed to thinking that nothing short of a dynamite explosion could ever dislodge those two nestlers from my midst that, when Claude sidled up to me on the Friday morning and told me his bit of news, I could hardly believe I was hearing right.

'Bertie,' he said, 'I've been thinking it over.'

'What over?' I said.

'The whole thing. This business of staying in London when

I ought to be in South Africa. It isn't fair,' said Claude warmly. 'It isn't right. And the long and the short of it is, Bertie, old man, I'm leaving tomorrow.'

I reeled in my tracks.

'You are?' I gasped.

'Yes. If,' said Claude, 'you won't mind sending old Jeeves out to buy a ticket for me. I'm afraid I'll have to stick you for the passage money, old man. You don't mind?'

'Mind!' I said, clutching his hand fervently.

'That's all right, then. Oh, I say, you won't say a word to Eustace about this, will you?'

'But isn't he going, too?'

Claude shuddered.

'No, thank heaven! The idea of being cooped up on board a ship with that blighter gives me the pip just to think of it. No, not a word to Eustace. I say, I suppose you can get me a berth all right at such short notice?'

'Rather!' I said. Sooner than let this opportunity slip, I would have bought the bally boat.

'Jeeves,' I said, breezing into the kitchen. 'Go out on first speed to the Union-Castle offices and book a berth on tomorrow's boat for Mr Claude. He is leaving us, Jeeves.'

'Yes, sir.'

'Mr Claude does not wish any mention of this to be made to Mr Eustace.'

'No, sir. Mr Eustace made the same proviso when he desired me to obtain a berth on tomorrow's boat for himself.'

I gaped at the man.

'Is he going, too?'

'Yes, sir.'

'This is rummy.'

'Yes, sir.'

Had circumstances been other than they were, I would at this juncture have unbent considerably towards Jeeves. Frisked round him a bit and whooped to a certain extent, and what not. But those spats still formed a barrier, and I regret to say that I took the opportunity of rather rubbing it in a bit on the man. I mean, he'd been so dashed aloof and unsympathetic, though perfectly aware that the young master was in the soup and that it was up to him to rally round, that I couldn't help pointing out how the happy ending had been snaffled without any help from him.

'So that's that, Jeeves,' I said. 'The episode is concluded. I knew things would sort themselves out if one gave them time and didn't get rattled. Many chaps in my place would have got rattled, Jeeves.'

'Yes, sir.'

'Gone rushing about, I mean, asking people for help and advice and so forth.'

'Very possibly, sir.'

'But not me, Jeeves.'

'No, sir.'

I left him to brood on it.

Even the thought that I'd got to go to Harrogate with Uncle George couldn't depress me that Saturday when I gazed about the old flat and realized that Claude and Eustace weren't in it. They had slunk off stealthily and separately immediately after breakfast, Eustace to catch the boat-train at Waterloo, Claude to go round to the garage where I kept my car. I didn't want any chance of the two meeting at Waterloo and changing their minds, so I had suggested to Claude that he might find it pleasanter to drive down to Southampton.

I was lying back on the old settee, gazing peacefully up at the flies on the ceiling and feeling what a wonderful world this was, when Jeeves came in with a letter.

'A messenger-boy has brought this, sir.'

I opened the envelope, and the first thing that fell out was a five-pound note.

'Great Scott!' I said. 'What's all this?'

The letter was scribbled in pencil, and was quite brief;

DEAR BERTIE. – Will you give enclosed to your man, and tell him I wish I could make it more. He has saved my life. This is the first happy day I've had for a week.

Yours,

M.W.

Jeeves was standing holding out the fiver, which had fluttered to the floor.

'You'd better stick to it,' I said. 'It seems to be for you.'

'Sir?'

'I say that fiver is for you, apparently. Miss Wardour sent it.'

'That was extremely kind of her, sir.'

'What the dickens is she sending you fivers for? She says you saved her life.'

Jeeves smiled gently.

'She over-estimates my services, sir.'

'But what were your services, dash it?'

'It was in the matter of Mr Claude and Mr Eustace, sir. I was hoping that she would not refer to the matter, as I did not wish you to think that I had been taking a liberty.'

'What do you mean?'

'I chanced to be in the room while Miss Wardour was complaining with some warmth of the manner in which Mr Claude and Mr Eustace were thrusting their society upon her. I felt that in the circumstances it might be excusable if I suggested a slight ruse to enable her to dispense with their attentions.'

'Good Lord! You don't mean to say you were at the bottom of their popping off, after all!'

Silly ass it made me feel. I mean, after rubbing it in to him like that about having clicked without his assistance.

'It occurred to me that, were Miss Wardour to inform Mr Claude and Mr Eustace independently that she proposed sailing for South Africa to take up a theatrical engagement, the desired effect might be produced. It appears that my anticipations were correct, sir. The young gentlemen ate it, if I may use the expression.'

'Jeeves,' I said – we Woosters may make bloomers, but we are never too proud to admit it – 'you stand alone!'

'Thank you very much, sir.'

'Oh, but I say!' A ghastly thought had struck me. 'When they get on the boat and find she isn't there, won't they come buzzing back?'

'I anticipated that possibility, sir. At my suggestion, Miss Wardour informed the young gentlemen that she proposed to travel overland to Madeira and join the vessel there.'

'And where do they touch after Madeira?'

'Nowhere, sir.'

For a moment I just lay back, letting the idea of the thing soak in. There seemed to me to be only one flaw.

'The only pity is,' I said, 'that on a large boat like that they will be able to avoid each other. I mean, I should have liked to feel that Claude was having a good deal of Eustace's society and vice versa.'

'I fancy that that will be so, sir. I secured a two-berth stateroom. Mr Claude will occupy one berth, Mr Eustace the other.'

I sighed with pure ecstasy. It seemed a dashed shame that on this joyful occasion I should have to go off to Harrogate with my Uncle George.

'Have you started packing yet, Jeeves?' I asked.

'Packing, sir?'

'For Harrogate. I've got to go there today with Sir George.'

'Of course, yes, sir. I forgot to mention it. Sir George rang up on the telephone this morning while you were still asleep, and said that he had changed his plans. He does not intend to go to Harrogate.'

'Oh, I say, how absolutely topping!'

'I thought you might be pleased, sir.'

'What made him change his plans? Did he say?'

'No, sir. But I gather from his man, Stevens, that he is feeling much better and does not now require a rest-cure. I took the liberty of giving Stevens the recipe for that pick-me-up of mine, of which you have always approved so much. Stevens tells me that Sir George informed him this morning that he is feeling a new man.'

Well, there was only one thing to do, and I did it. I'm not saying it didn't hurt, but there was no alternative.

'Jeeves,' I said, 'those spats.'

'Yes, sir?'

'You really dislike them?'

'Intensely, sir.'

'You don't think time might induce you to change your views?'

'No, sir.'

'All right, then. Very well. Say no more. You may burn them.'

'Thank you very much, sir. I have already done so. Before breakfast this morning. A quiet grey is far more suitable, sir.

Thank you, sir.'

CHAPTER SEVENTEEN
Bingo and the Little Woman

I t must have been a week or so after the departure of
Claude and Eustace that I ran into young Bingo Little in
the smoking-room of the Senior Liberal Club. He was lying
back in an armchair with his mouth open and a sort of goofy
expression in his eyes, while a grey-bearded cove in the middle
distance watched him with so much dislike that I concluded
that Bingo had pinched his favourite seat. That's the worst of
being in a strange club – absolutely without intending it, you
find yourself constantly trampling upon the vested interests of
the Oldest Inhabitants.

'Hallo, face,' I said.

'Cheerio, ugly,' said young Bingo, and we settled down to
have a small one before lunch.

Once a year the committee of the Drones decides that
the old club could do with a wash and brush-up, so they shoo
us out and dump us down for a few weeks at some other
institution. This time we were roosting at the Senior Liberal,

and personally I had found the strain pretty fearful. I mean, when you've got used to a club where everything's nice and cheery, and where, if you want to attract a chappie's attention, you heave a piece of bread at him, it kind of damps you to come to a place where the youngest member is about eighty-seven and it isn't considered good form to talk to anyone unless you and he went through the Peninsular War together. It was a relief to come across Bingo. We started to talk in hushed voices.

'This club,' I said, 'is the limit.'

'It is the eel's eyebrows,' agreed young Bingo. 'I believe that old boy over by the window has been dead three days, but I don't like to mention it to anyone.'

'Have you lunched here yet?'

'No. Why?'

'They have waitresses instead of waiters.'

'Good Lord! I thought that went out with the armistice.' Bingo mused a moment, straightening his tie absently. 'Er – pretty girls?' he said.

'No.'

He seemed disappointed, but pulled round.

'Well, I've heard that the cooking's the best in London.'

'So they say. Shall we be going in?'

'All right. I expect,' said young Bingo, 'that at the end of the meal – or possibly at the beginning – the waitress will say, "Both together, sir?" Reply in the affirmative. I haven't a bean.'

'Hasn't your uncle forgiven you yet?'

'Not yet, confound him!'

I was sorry to hear the row was still on. I resolved to do the poor old thing well at the festive board, and I scanned the menu with some intentness when the girl rolled up with it.

'How would this do you, Bingo?' I said at length. 'A few plovers' eggs to weigh in with, a cup of soup, a touch of cold salmon, some cold curry, and a splash of gooseberry tart and cream with a bite of cheese to finish?'

I don't know that I had expected the man actually to scream with delight, though I had picked the items from my knowledge of his pet dishes, but I had expected him to say something. I looked up, and found that his attention was elsewhere. He was gazing at the waitress with the look of a dog that's just remembered where its bone was buried.

She was a tallish girl with sort of soft, soulful brown eyes. Nice figure and all that. Rather decent hands, too. I didn't remember having seen her about before, and I must say she raised the standard of the place quite a bit.

'How about it, laddie?' I said, being all for getting the order booked and going on to the serious knife-and-fork work.

'Eh?' said young Bingo absently.

I recited the programme once more.

'Oh, yes, fine!' said Bingo. 'Anything, anything.' The girl pushed off, and he turned to me with protruding eyes. 'I thought you said they weren't pretty, Bertie!' he said reproachfully.

'Oh, my heavens!' I said. 'You surely haven't fallen in love again – and with a girl you've only just seen?'

'There are times, Bertie,' said young Bingo, 'when a look is enough – when, passing through a crowd, we meet somebody's eye and something seems to whisper . . .'

At this point the plovers' eggs arrived, and he suspended his remarks in order to swoop on them with some vigour.

'Jeeves,' I said that night when I got home, 'stand by.'

'Sir?'

'Burnish the old brain and be alert and vigilant. I suspect that Mr Little will be calling round shortly for sympathy and assistance.'

'Is Mr Little in trouble, sir?'

'Well, you might call it that. He's in love. For about the fifty-third time. I ask you, Jeeves, as man to man, did you ever see such a chap?'

'Mr Little is certainly warm-hearted, sir.'

'Warm-hearted! I should think he has to wear asbestos vests. Well, stand by, Jeeves.'

'Very good, sir.'

And sure enough, it wasn't ten days before in rolled the old ass, bleating for volunteers to step one pace forward and come to the aid of the party.

'Bertie,' he said, 'if you are a pal of mine, now is the time to show it.'

'Proceed, old gargoyle,' I replied. 'You have our ear.'

'You remember giving me lunch at the Senior Liberal some days ago. We were waited on by a—'

'I remember. Tall, lissom female.'

He shuddered somewhat.

'I wish you wouldn't talk of her like that, dash it all. She's an angel.'

'All right. Carry on.'

'I love her.'

'Right-o! Push along.'

'For goodness sake don't bustle me. Let me tell the story in my own way. I love her, as I was saying, and I want you, Bertie, old boy, to pop round to my uncle and do a bit of diplomatic work. That allowance of mine must be restored, and dashed quick, too. What's more, it must be increased.'

'But look here,' I said, being far from keen on the bally business, 'why not wait a while?'

'Wait? What's the good of waiting?'

'Well, you know what generally happens when you fall in love. Something goes wrong with the works and you get left. Much better tackle your uncle after the whole thing's fixed and settled.'

'It is fixed and settled. She accepted me this morning.'

'Good Lord! That's quick work. You haven't known her two weeks.'

'Not in this life, no,' said young Bingo. 'But she has a sort of idea that we must have met in some previous existence. She thinks I must have been a king in Babylon when she was a Christian slave. I can't say I remember it myself, but there may be something in it.'

'Great Scott!' I said. 'Do waitresses really talk like that?'

'How should I know how waitresses talk?'

'Well, you ought to by now. The first time I ever met your uncle was when you hounded me on to ask him if he would rally round to help you marry that girl Mabel in the Piccadilly bun-shop.'

Bingo started violently. A wild gleam came into his eyes. And before I knew what he was up to he had brought down his hand with a most frightful whack on my summer trousering, causing me to leap like a young ram.

'Here!' I said.

'Sorry,' said Bingo. 'Excited. Carried away. You've given me an idea, Bertie.' He waited till I had finished massaging the limb, and resumed his remarks. 'Can you throw your mind back to that occasion, Bertie? Do you remember the frightfully subtle scheme I worked? Telling him you were what's-her-name, the woman who wrote those books, I mean?'

It wasn't likely I'd forget. The ghastly thing was absolutely seared into my memory.

'That is the line of attack,' said Bingo. 'That is the scheme. Rosie M. Banks forward once more.'

'It can't be done, old thing. Sorry, but it's out of the question. I couldn't go through all that again.'

'Not for me?'

'Not for a dozen more like you.'

'I never thought,' said Bingo sorrowfully, 'to hear those words from Bertie Wooster!'

'Well, you've heard them now,' I said. 'Paste them in your

hat.'

'Bertie, we were at school together.'

'It wasn't my fault.'

'We've been pals for fifteen years.'

'I know. It's going to take me the rest of my life to live it down.'

'Bertie, old man,' said Bingo, drawing up his chair closer and starting to knead my shoulder-blade, 'listen! Be reasonable!'

And of course, dash it, at the end of ten minutes I'd allowed the blighter to talk me round. It's always the way. Anyone can talk me round. If I were in a Trappist monastery, the first thing that would happen would be that some smooth performer would lure me into some frightful idiocy against my better judgement by means of the deaf-and-dumb language.

'Well, what do you want me to do?' I said, realizing that it was hopeless to struggle.

'Start off by sending the old boy an autographed copy of your latest effort with a flattering inscription. That will tickle him to death. Then you pop round and put it across.'

'What is my latest?'

'The Woman Who Braved All,' said young Bingo. 'I've seen it all over the place. The shop windows and bookstalls are full of nothing but it. It looks to me from the picture on the jacket the sort of book any chappie would be proud to have written. Of course, he will want to discuss it with you.'

'Ah!' I said, cheering up. 'That dishes the scheme, doesn't

it? I don't know what the bally thing is about.'

'You will have to read it, naturally.'

'Read it! No, I say. . . .'

'Bertie, we were at school together.'

'Oh, right-o! Right-o!' I said.

'I knew I could rely on you. You have a heart of gold. Jeeves,' said young Bingo, as the faithful servitor rolled in, 'Mr Wooster has a heart of gold.'

'Very good, sir,' said Jeeves.

Bar a weekly wrestle with the 'Pink 'Un' and an occasional dip into the form book I'm not much of a lad for reading, and my sufferings as I tackled The Woman (curse her!) Who Braved All were pretty fearful. But I managed to get through it, and only just in time, as it happened, for I'd hardly reached the bit where their lips met in one long, slow kiss and everything was still but for the gentle sighing of the breeze in the laburnum, when a messenger-boy brought a note from old Bittlesham asking me to trickle round to lunch.

I found the old boy in a mood you could only describe as melting. He had a copy of the book on the table beside him and kept turning the pages in the intervals of dealing with things in aspic and what not.

'Mr Wooster,' he said, swallowing a chunk of trout, 'I wish to congratulate you. I wish to thank you. You go from strength to strength. I have read All For Love: I have read Only a Factory Girl: I know Madcap Myrtle by heart. But this – this is your bravest and best. It tears the heartstrings.'

'Yes?'

'Indeed yes! I have read it three times since you most kindly sent me the volume – I wish to thank you once more for the charming inscription – and I think I may say that I am a better, sweeter, deeper man. I am full of human charity and kindliness towards my species.'

'No, really?'

'Indeed, indeed I am.'

'Towards the whole species?'

'Towards the whole species.'

'Even young Bingo?' I said, trying him pretty high.

'My nephew? Richard?' He looked a bit thoughtful, but stuck it like a man and refused to hedge. 'Yes, even towards Richard. Well ... that is to say ... perhaps ... yes, even towards Richard.'

'That's good, because I wanted to talk about him. He's pretty hard up, you know.'

'In straitened circumstances?'

'Stony. And he could use a bit of the right stuff paid every quarter, if you felt like unbelting.'

He mused a while and got through a slab of cold guinea hen before replying. He toyed with the book, and it fell open at page two hundred and fifteen. I couldn't remember what was on page two hundred and fifteen, but it must have been something tolerably zippy, for his expression changed and he gazed up at me with misty eyes, as if he'd taken a shade too much mustard with his last bite of ham.

'Very well, Mr Wooster,' he said. 'Fresh from a perusal of this noble work of yours, I cannot harden my heart. Richard shall have his allowance.'

'Stout fellow!' I said. Then it occurred to me that the expression might strike a chappie who weighed seventeen stone as a bit personal. 'Good egg, I mean. That'll take a weight off his mind. He wants to get married, you know.'

'I did not know. And I am not sure that I altogether approve. Who is the lady?'

'Well, as matter of fact, she's a waitress.'

He leaped in his seat.

'You don't say so, Mr Wooster! This is remarkable. This is most cheering. I had not given the boy credit for such tenacity of purpose. An excellent trait in him which I had not hitherto suspected. I recollect clearly that, on the occasion when I first had the pleasure of making your acquaintance, nearly eighteen months ago, Richard was desirous of marrying this same waitress.'

I had to break it to him.

'Well, not absolutely this same waitress. In fact, quite a different waitress. Still, a waitress, you know.'

The light of avuncular affection died out of the old boy's eyes.

'H'm!' he said a bit dubiously. 'I had supposed that Richard was displaying the quality of constancy which is so rare in the modern young man. I – I must think it over.'

So we left it at that, and I came away and told Bingo the position of affairs.

'Allowance O.K.,' I said. 'Uncle blessing a trifle wobbly.'

'Doesn't he seem to want the wedding bells to ring out?'

'I left him thinking it over. If I were a bookie, I should feel justified in offering a hundred to eight against.'

'You can't have approached him properly. I might have known you would muck it up,' said young Bingo. Which, considering what I had been through for his sake, struck me as a good bit sharper than a serpent's tooth.

'It's awkward,' said young Bingo. 'It's infernally awkward. I can't tell you all the details at the moment, but . . . yes, it's awkward.'

He helped himself absently to a handful of my cigars and pushed off.

I didn't see him again for three days. Early in the afternoon of the third day he blew in with a flower in his buttonhole and a look on his face as if someone had hit him behind the ear with a stuffed eel skin.

'Hallo, Bertie.'

'Hallo, old turnip. Where have you been all this while?'

'Oh, here and there. Ripping weather we're having, Bertie.'

'Not bad.'

'I see the Bank Rate is down again.'

'No, really?'

'Disturbing news from Lower Silesia, what?'

'Oh, dashed!'

He pottered about the room for a bit, babbling at intervals. The boy seemed cuckoo.

'Oh, I say, Bertie!' he said suddenly, dropping a vase which he had picked off the mantelpiece and was fiddling with. 'I know what it was I wanted to tell you. I'm married.'

CHAPTER EIGHTEEN
All's Well

I stared at him. That flower in his buttonhole . . . That dazed look . . . Yes, he had all the symptoms: and yet the thing seemed incredible. The fact is, I suppose, I'd seen so many of young Bingo's love affairs start off with a whoop and a rattle and poof themselves out half-way down the straight that I couldn't believe he had actually brought it off at last.

'Married!'

'Yes. This morning at a registrar's in Holborn. I've just come from the wedding breakfast.'

I sat up in my chair. Alert. The man of affairs. It seemed to me that this thing wanted threshing out in all its aspects.

'Let's get this straight,' I said. 'You're really married?'

'Yes.'

'The same girl you were in love with the day before yesterday?'

'What do you mean?'

'Well, you know what you're like. Tell me, what made you

commit this rash act?'

'I wish the deuce you wouldn't talk like that. I married her because I love her, dash it. The best little woman,' said young Bingo, 'in the world.'

'That's all right, and deuced creditable, I'm sure. But have you reflected what your uncle's going to say? The last I saw of him, he was by no means in a confetti-scattering mood.'

'Bertie,' said Bingo, 'I'll be frank with you. The little woman rather put it up to me, if you know what I mean. I told her how my uncle felt about it, and she said that we must part unless I loved her enough to brave the old boy's wrath and marry her right away. So I had no alternative. I bought a buttonhole and went to it.'

'And what do you propose to do now?'

'Oh, I've got it all planned out! After you've seen my uncle and broken the news . . .'

'What!'

'After you've . . .'

'You don't mean to say you think you're going to lug me into it?'

He looked at me like Lillian Gish coming out of a swoon.

'Is this Bertie Wooster talking?' he said, pained.

'Yes, it jolly well is.'

'Bertie, old man,' said Bingo, patting me gently here and there, 'reflect! We were at school—'

'Oh, all right!'

'Good man! I knew I could rely on you. She's waiting

down below in the hall. We'll pick her up and dash round to Pounceby Gardens right away.'

I had only seen the bride before in her waitress kit, and I was rather expecting that on her wedding day she would have launched out into something fairly zippy in the way of upholstery. The first gleam of hope I had felt since the start of this black business came to me when I saw that, instead of being all velvet and scent and flowery hat, she was dressed in dashed good taste. Quiet. Nothing loud. So far as looks went, she might have stepped straight out of Berkeley Square.

'This is my old pal, Bertie Wooster, darling,' said Bingo. 'We were at school together, weren't we, Bertie?'

'We were!' I said. 'How do you do? I think we – er – met at lunch the other day, didn't we?'

'Oh, yes! How do you do?'

'My uncle eats out of Bertie's hand,' explained Bingo. 'So he's coming round with us to start things off and kind of pave the way. Hi, taxi!'

We didn't talk much on the journey. Kind of tense feeling. I was glad when the cab stopped at old Bittlesham's wigwam and we all hopped out. I left Bingo and wife in the hall while I went upstairs to the drawing-room, and the butler toddled off to dig out the big chief.

While I was prowling about the room waiting for him to show up, I suddenly caught sight of that bally Woman Who Braved All lying on one of the tables. It was open at page two hundred and fifteen, and a passage heavily marked in pencil caught my eye. And directly I read it I saw that it was all to the mustard and was going to help me in my business.

This was the passage:

'What can prevail' – Millicent's eyes flashed as she faced the stern old man – 'what can prevail against a pure and all-consuming love? Neither principalities nor powers, my lord, nor all the puny prohibitions of guardians and parents. I love your son, Lord Windermere, and nothing can keep us apart. Since time first began this love of ours was fated, and who are you to pit yourself against the decrees of Fate?'

The earl looked at her keenly from beneath his bushy eyebrows.

'Humph!' he said.

Before I had time to refresh my memory as to what Millicent's come-back had been to that remark, the door opened and old Bittlesham rolled in. All over me, as usual.

'My dear Mr Wooster, this is an unexpected pleasure. Pray take a seat. What can I do for you?'

'Well, the fact is, I'm more or less in the capacity of a jolly old ambassador at the moment. Representing young Bingo, you know.'

His geniality sagged a trifle, I thought, but he didn't heave me out, so I pushed on.

'The way I always look at it,' I said, 'is that it's dashed

difficult for anything to prevail against what you might call a pure and all-consuming love. I mean, can it be done? I doubt it.'

My eyes didn't exactly flash as I faced the stern old man, but I sort of waggled my eyebrows. He puffed a bit and looked doubtful.

'We discussed this matter at our last meeting, Mr Wooster. And on that occasion . . .'

'Yes. But there have been developments, as it were, since then. The fact of the matter is,' I said, coming to the point, 'this morning young Bingo went and jumped off the dock.'

'Good heavens!' He jerked himself to his feet with his mouth open. 'Why? Where? Which dock?'

I saw that he wasn't quite on.

'I was speaking metaphorically,' I explained, 'if that's the word I want. I mean he got married.'

'Married!'

'Absolutely hitched up. I hope you aren't ratty about it, what? Young blood, you know. Two loving hearts, and all that.'

He panted in a rather overwrought way.

'I am greatly disturbed by your news. I – I consider that I have been – er – defied. Yes, defied.'

'But who are you to pit yourself against the decrees of Fate?' I said, taking a look at the prompt book out of the corner of my eye.

'Eh?'

'You see, this love of theirs was fated. Since time began, you know.'

I'm bound to admit that if he'd said 'Humph!' at this juncture, he would have had me stymied. Luckily it didn't occur to him. There was a silence, during which he appeared to brood a bit. Then his eye fell on the book and he gave a sort of start.

'Why, bless my soul, Mr Wooster, you have been quoting!'

'More or less.'

'I thought your words sounded familiar.' His whole appearance changed and he gave a sort of gurgling chuckle. 'Dear me, dear me, you know my weak spot!' He picked up the book and buried himself in it for quite a while. I began to think he had forgotten I was there. After a bit, however, he put it down again, and wiped his eyes. 'Ah, well!' he said.

I shuffled my feet and hoped for the best.

'Ah, well,' he said again. 'I must not be like Lord Windermere, must I, Mr Wooster? Tell me, did you draw that haughty old man from a living model?'

'Oh, no! Just thought of him and bunged him down, you know.'

'Genius!' murmured old Bittlesham. 'Genius! Well, Mr Wooster, you have won me over. Who, as you say, am I to pit myself against the decrees of Fate? I will write to Richard tonight and inform him of my consent to his marriage.'

'You can slip him the glad news in person,' I said. 'He's waiting downstairs, with wife complete. I'll pop down and send them up. Cheerio, and thanks very much. Bingo will be most awfully bucked.'

I shot out and went downstairs. Bingo and Mrs were sitting on a couple of chairs like patients in a dentist's waiting-room.

'Well?' said Bingo eagerly.

'All over except the hand-clasping,' I replied, slapping the old crumpet on the back. 'Charge up and get matey. Toodle-oo, old things. You know where to find me, if wanted. A thousand congratulations, and all that sort of rot.'

And I pipped, not wishing to be fawned upon.

You never can tell in this world. If ever I felt that something attempted, something done had earned a night's repose, it was when I got back to the flat and shoved my feet up on the mantelpiece and started to absorb the cup of tea which Jeeves had brought in. Used as I am to seeing Life's sitters blow up in the home stretch and finish nowhere, I couldn't see any cause for alarm in this affair of young Bingo's. All he had to do when I left him in Pounceby Gardens was to walk upstairs with the little missus and collect the blessing. I was so convinced of this that when, about half an hour later, he came galloping into my sitting-room, all I thought was that he wanted to thank me in broken accents and tell me what a good chap I had been. I merely beamed benevolently on the old creature as he entered, and was just going to offer him a cigarette when I observed that he seemed to have something on his mind. In fact, he looked as if something solid had hit him in the solar plexus.

'My dear old soul,' I said, 'what's up?'

Bingo plunged about the room.

'I will be calm!' he said, knocking over an occasional table. 'Calm, dammit!' He upset a chair.

'Surely nothing has gone wrong?'

Bingo uttered one of those hollow, mirthless yelps.

'Only every bally thing that could go wrong. What do you think happened after you left us? You know that beastly book you insisted on sending my uncle?'

It wasn't the way I should have put it myself, but I saw the poor old bean was upset for some reason or other, so I didn't correct him.

'The Woman Who Braved All?' I said. 'It came in dashed useful. It was by quoting bits out of it that I managed to talk him round.'

'Well, it didn't come in useful when we got into the room. It was lying on the table, and after we had started to chat a bit and everything was going along nicely the little woman spotted it. "Oh, have you read this, Lord Bittlesham?" she said. "Three times already," said my uncle. "I'm so glad," said the little woman. "Why, are you also an admirer of Rosie M. Banks?" asked the old boy, beaming. "I am Rosie M. Banks!" said the little woman.'

'Oh, my aunt! Not really?'

'Yes.'

'But how could she be? I mean, dash it, she was slinging the foodstuffs at the Senior Liberal Club.'

Bingo gave the settee a moody kick.

'She took the job to collect material for a book she's writing called Mervyn Keene, Clubman.'

'She might have told you.'

'It made such a hit with her when she found that I loved her for herself alone, despite her humble station, that she kept it under her hat. She meant to spring it on me later on, she said.'

'Well, what happened then?'

'There was the dickens of a painful scene. The old boy nearly got apoplexy. Called her an impostor. They both started talking at once at the top of their voices, and the thing ended with the little woman buzzing off to her publishers to collect proofs as a preliminary to getting a written apology from the old boy. What's going to happen now, I don't know. Apart from the fact that my uncle will be as mad as a wet hen when he finds out that he has been fooled, there's going to be a lot of trouble when the little woman discovers that we worked the Rosie M. Banks wheeze with a view to trying to get me married to somebody else. You see, one of the things that first attracted her to me was the fact that I had never been in love before.'

'Did you tell her that?'

'Yes.'

'Great Scott!'

'Well, I hadn't been . . . not really in love. There's all the difference in the world between . . . Well, never mind that.

What am I going to do? That's the point.'

'I don't know.'

'Thanks,' said young Bingo. 'That's a lot of help.'

Next morning he rang me up on the phone just after I'd got the bacon and eggs into my system – the one moment of the day, in short, when a chappie wishes to muse on life absolutely undisturbed.

'Bertie!'

'Hallo?'

'Things are hotting up.'

'What's happened now?'

'My uncle has given the little woman's proofs the once-over and admits her claim. I've just been having five snappy minutes with him on the telephone. He says that you and I made a fool of him, and he could hardly speak, he was so shirty. Still, he made it clear all right that my allowance has gone phut again.'

'I'm sorry.'

'Don't waste time being sorry for me,' said young Bingo grimly. 'He's coming to call on you today to demand a personal explanation.'

'Great Scott!'

'And the little woman is coming to call on you to demand a personal explanation.'

'Good Lord!'

'I shall watch your future career with some considerable

interest,' said young Bingo.

I bellowed for Jeeves.

'Jeeves!'

'Sir?'

'I'm in the soup.'

'Indeed, sir?'

I sketched out the scenario for him.

'What would you advise?'

'I think if I were you, sir, I would accept Mr Pitt-Waley's invitation immediately. If you remember, sir, he invited you to shoot with him in Norfolk this week.'

'So he did! By Jove, Jeeves, you're always right. Meet me at the station with my things the first train after lunch. I'll go and lie low at the club for the rest of the morning.'

'Would you require my company on this visit, sir?'

'Do you want to come?'

'If I might suggest it, sir, I think it would be better if I remained here and kept in touch with Mr Little. I might possibly hit upon some method of pacifying the various parties, sir.'

'Right-o! But, if you do, you're a marvel.'

I didn't enjoy myself much in Norfolk. It rained most of the time, and when it wasn't raining I was so dashed jumpy that I couldn't hit a thing. By the end of the week I couldn't stand it any longer. Too bally absurd, I mean, being marooned miles away in the country just because young Bingo's uncle and wife wanted to have a few words with me. I made up my mind that I would pop back and do the strong, manly thing by lying low in my flat and telling Jeeves to inform everybody who called that I wasn't at home.

I sent Jeeves a telegram saying I was coming, and drove straight to Bingo's place when I reached town. I wanted to find out the general posish of affairs. But apparently the man was out. I rang a couple of times but nothing happened, and I was just going to leg it when I heard the sound of footsteps inside and the door opened. It wasn't one of the cheeriest moments of my career when I found myself peering into the globular face of Lord Bittlesham.

'Oh, er, hallo!' I said. And there was a bit of a pause.

I don't quite know what I had been expecting the old boy to do if, by bad luck, we should ever meet again, but I had a sort of general idea that he would turn fairly purple and start almost immediately to let me have it in the gizzard. It struck me as somewhat rummy, therefore, when he simply smiled weakly. A sort of frozen smile it was. His eyes kind of bulged and he swallowed once or twice.

'Er . . .' he said.

I waited for him to continue, but apparently that was all there was.

'Bingo in?' I said, after a rather embarrassing pause.

He shook his head and smiled again. And then, suddenly, just as the flow of conversation had begun to slacken once more, I'm dashed if he didn't make a sort of lumbering leap back into the flat and bang the door.

I couldn't understand it. But, as it seemed that the interview, such as it was, was over, I thought I might as well be shifting. I had just started down the steps when I met young Bingo, charging up three steps at a time.

'Hallo, Bertie!' he said. 'Where did you spring from? I thought you were out of town?'

'I've just got back. I looked in on you to see how the land lay.'

'How do you mean?'

'Why, all that business, you know.'

'Oh, that!' said young Bingo airily. 'That was all settled days ago. The dove of peace is flapping its wings all over the place. Everything's as right as it can be. Jeeves fixed it all up. He's a marvel, that man, Bertie, I've always said so. Put the whole thing straight in half a minute with one of those brilliant ideas of his.'

'This is topping!'

'I knew you'd be pleased.'

'Congratulate you.'

'Thanks.'

'What did Jeeves do? I couldn't think of any solution of the bally thing myself.'

'Oh, he took the matter in hand and smoothed it all out in a second! My uncle and the little woman are tremendous pals now. They gas away by the hour together about literature and all that. He's always dropping in for a chat.'

This reminded me.

'He's in there now,' I said. 'I say, Bingo, how is your uncle these days?'

'Much as usual. How do you mean?'

'I mean he hasn't been feeling the strain of things a bit, has he? He seemed rather strange in his manner just now.'

'Why, have you met him?'

'He opened the door when I rang. And then, after he had stood goggling at me for a bit, he suddenly banged the door in my face. Puzzled me, you know. I mean, I could have understood it if he'd ticked me off and all that, but dash it, the man seemed absolutely scared.'

Young Bingo laughed a care-free laugh.

'Oh, that's all right!' he said. 'I forgot to tell you about that. Meant to write, but kept putting it off. He thinks you're a looney.'

'He – what!'

'Yes. That was Jeeves's idea, you know. It's solved the whole problem splendidly. He suggested that I should tell my uncle that I had acted in perfectly good faith in introducing you to him as Rosie M. Banks; that I had repeatedly had it from your own lips that you were, and that I didn't see any reason why you shouldn't be. The idea being that you were subject to hallucinations and generally potty. And then we got hold of Sir Roderick Glossop – you remember, the old boy whose kid you pushed into the lake that day down at Ditteredge Hall – and he rallied round with his story of how he had come to lunch with you and found your bedroom full up with cats and fish, and how you had pinched his hat while you were driving past his car in a taxi, and all that, you know. It just rounded the whole thing off nicely. I always say, and I always shall say, that you've only got to stand on Jeeves, and fate can't touch you.'

I can stand a good deal, but there are limits.

'Well, of all the dashed bits of nerve I ever ...'

Bingo looked at me astonished.

'You aren't annoyed ?' he said.

'Annoyed! At having half London going about under the impression that I'm off my chump? Dash it all ... '

'Bertie,' said Bingo, 'you amaze and wound me. If I had dreamed that you would object to doing a trifling good turn to a fellow who's been a pal of yours for fifteen years ...'

'Yes, but, look here ...'

'Have you forgotten,' said young Bingo, 'that we were at school together?'

I pushed on to the old flat, seething like the dickens. One thing I was jolly certain of, and that was that this was where Jeeves and I parted company. A topping valet, of course, none better in London, but I wasn't going to allow that to weaken me. I buzzed into the flat like an east wind ... and there was the box of cigarettes on the small table and the illustrated weekly papers on the big table and my slippers on the floor, and every dashed thing so bally right, if you know what I mean, that I started to calm down in the first two seconds. It was like one of those moments in a play where the chappie, about to steep himself in crime, suddenly hears the soft, appealing strains of the old melody he learned at his mother's knee. Softened, I mean to say. That's the word I want. I was softened.

And then through the doorway there shimmered good old Jeeves in the wake of a tray full of the necessary ingredients, and there was something about the mere look of the man. . . .

However, I steeled the old heart and had a stab at it.

'I have just met Mr Little, Jeeves,' I said.

'Indeed, sir?'

'He – er – he told me you had been helping him.'

'I did my best, sir. And I am happy to say that matters now appear to be proceeding smoothly. Whisky, sir?'

'Thanks. Er – Jeeves.'

'Sir?'

'Another time . . .'

'Sir?'

'Oh, nothing . . . Not all the soda, Jeeves.'

'Very good, sir.'

He started to drift out.

'Oh, Jeeves!'

'Sir?'

'I wish . . . that is . . . I think . . . I mean . . . Oh, nothing!'

'Very good, sir. The cigarettes are at your elbow, sir. Dinner will be ready at a quarter to eight precisely, unless you desire to dine out?'

'No. I'll dine in.'

'Yes, sir.'

'Jeeves!'

'Sir?'

'Oh, nothing!' I said.

'Very good, sir,' said Jeeves.

GLOSSARY OF TERMS

Assistant-master: A teacher not responsible for a boarding house (in a public school).

Australian crawl: A swimming stroke, also known as "the front crawl."

Bally: A less offensive euphemism for the more offensive British term bloody.

Bite the bullet: To go ahead and do something, to 'get it over with.' This phrase probably came from the wartime practice of giving wounded soldiers a bullet to bite on during a surgery.

Blood club: A "blood," slang for an ostentatiously fashionable person; a 'blood club' is a club filled with persons of that sort.

Bohea: A type of black tea.

C3 collection: Men who enlisted in the British army received a medical classification ranging from A1 to C3, according to the Military Service Act, 1916. C3 was the lowest grade; this term, then, implies someone inferior, of a lower calliber.

Charlotte Corday Rowbotham: Marie Anne Charlotte Corday d'Armont, more famously known as Charlotte Corday, was a figure in the French Revolution. She murdered Jacobin leader Jean-Paul Marat in his bath in revenge for his role in the purging the Girondist moderates. She was guillotined in 1793, and gained the posthumous nickname l'ange de l'assassinat (the angel of assassination).

Chemmy: from Chemin-de-fer, a form of baccarat (casino card game) using six packs of cards. The Inimitable Jeeves holds the first noted use of the term "chemmy."

Cokernut shies: A coconut shy is a carnival game where the aim is to knock coconuts off poles by throwing wooden balls.

Collar: Verb: to "take by the collar," capture, or take.

Costermongers: Street sellers of fruits and vegetables.

Cox of my college boat: The coxswain is the person who steers a rowing boat and instructs the the oarsmen.

Dickey: A detachable shirt-front for evening wear.

Dishing (of plans). To spoil, finish: from the idea that one completes (finishes) cooking by dishing the food up.

Down express: A train traveling away from London.

Eftsoons or right speedily: "Soon afterwards."

Epris: French, enamoured.

Extension night: On 'Extension Night,' a club had a license to stay open later than usual.

Extinguisher: A candle-snuffer.

First crack out of the box: To "have a crack" at something is to make an attempt. "First crack out of the box" means a first attempt, and this phrase may trace its origin to American-baseball. A baseball batter stands in a chalk-outlined area called the "batter's box" before cracking the ball with the bat and running the bases.

Form book: A better's guide for racehorses, containing statistics of each horse's performance.

Gizzard: The second stomach of birds.

Hammams: A Turkish bath.

Harrods: A department store in London.

Hidalgo: Spanish: a gentleman.

Homburg: A stiff wool felt hat with a curled brim and a dented crown, popularized by Edward VII in the 1890s.

I've got my chemise on it: Chemise is French for shirt, the phrase implies a large wager has been made.

Jamboree: A party, loud, boisterous revelry.

Landaulette: A vehicle, a car body style where the rear passengers are covered by a convertible top—a that folds over the rear seats.

Limado: Perhaps another way to say "limonade."

Locum tenens: (Latin: holding the place) A professional, usually a physician or clergyman, hired to replace another during an absence.

Lofted: In golf, when one hits a ball upwards to soar over an obstacle.

Mais oui, mais oui, c'est trop fort!: French: "Yes, indeed, it's too much."

Map: A slang term coined by Wodehouse, meaning face.

Mazzard: The head. Most notably used by Shakespeare in Hamlet, "Knockt about the Mazard with a Sextons Spade."

Miss-in-baulk: From the game of billiards: a deliberate miss designed to leave the cue ball in the 'safety' of the baulk area is called a miss in baulk. Conversationally, a miss-in-baulk means a deliberate avoidance of something.

Norfolk suit: A loose-fitted jacket with a waistband, worn by adults, paired with knee-breeches. A potentially silly looking, old-fashioned outfit for a boy.

Oolong: A Chinese tea that is dark in color.

Page-boy: A boy-servant to run errands and perform light household chores.

Persp: Short for 'perspiration.'

Pink 'Un: *The Sporting Times*, as it was unofficially known;

a weekly British newspaper devoted to sport and especially horse racing.

Poleaxed blanc-mange: When slaughtering an animal, one hits the animal on the head with a poleax to stun them. Someone looks like "they've been poleaxed" if they are shocked or stunned. A blanc-mange is a dessert made with gelatin that quivers and jiggles. Bertie Wooster strings both of these phrases together for a vivid and ridiculous image.

Punters: Slang, customers, someone placing a bet.

Right-and-left-hand knockers: A "knocker," is slang for a skilled boxer; also slang for a fault-finder.

Rummy: Odd or strange..

S.P.: Starting Price (in the realm of horse racing). A better could place a wager on the odds at the moment of placing the wager (A.P. or ante-post) or on the odds when the race started (S.P.).

Shindy: a row, a commotion.

Smalls: A nickname for Responsions, the first of the three examinations once required to obtain a degree from Oxford.

Snootering: A Wodehouse-coined verb meaning 'harass' or to 'snub.' Its first appearance is in The Inimitable Jeeves.

Sponge-bag trousers: Sponge-bags were cases for toiletries (toothbrush, soap, etc) used when traveling, and were at one point made from a material with a houndstooth pattern. When this pattern was used for formal trousers, it resembled toiletry cases.

Stumer: Slang for a dud or a flop.

Ten o'clock, a clear night and all's well: A city night-watchman would call out on the hour if all was safe.

The old tum: stomach.

Waukeesis: Possibly a Wodehouse-coined term, something close to the name-brand of a shoe like 'Walk Easy.'

Wedding breakfast: Wedding ceremonies had to be held in the morning, by law, so the celebratory meal (breakfast) took place afterwards.

Whack up the ginger: To gather up the courage.

Whangee: Refers to the type of bamboo used for making walking canes.